Praise for the Baby Boomer Mysteries

"Santangelo has come up with an intriguing premise, drawing on the much-publicized fact that the baby boomer generation will soon be facing retirement, and she develops it cleverly....We'll look forward to more Boomer mysteries in the years to come.... Pure fun—and don't be surprised if retired sleuths become the next big trend."

—*Booklist.com*

"*Retirement Can Be Murder* is a fun chick lit investigative tale starring Carol Andrews super sleuth supported by an eccentric bunch of BBs (baby boomers), the cop and the daughter. Carol tells the tale in an amusing frantic way that adds to the enjoyment of a fine lighthearted whodunit that affirms that 'every wife has a story.'"

—Harriet Klausner, National Book Critic

"*Moving Can Be Murder* is jam-packed with Carol's cast of best buds and signature Santangelo fun! The author has penned a magnificent cozy that will leave you panting from the excitement, laughing at the characters, and—no surprise here—begging for more."

—Terri Ann Armstrong, Author of *How to Plant a Body*

"With her Baby Boomer mystery series, Susan Santangelo documents her undeniable storytelling talents. *Class Reunions Can Be Murder* is an especially well crafted and entertaining mystery which plays fair with the reader every step of the way....An outstanding series."

—*Midwest Book Review*

"In the mood for a light mystery? Susan Santangelo's *Funerals Can Be Murder* is a fun, relaxing, read, with a great voice. Protagonist (and busybody) Carol Andrews could be your new best friend. She's funny, bright, ironic, a great listener . . . her only problem is finding too many bodies."

—Lea Wait, Author of *Shadows on a Maine Christmas*

"Susan Santangelo's latest *Baby Boomer Mystery, Second Honeymoons Can Be Murder*, keeps a smile on your lips and the pages turning one right after the other. What's not to like? An engaging mystery and laugh-out loud characters right to the very last page."
—Susan Kiernan-Lewis, Award-winning Author of the *Maggie Newberry Mystery* Series

"*Dieting Can Be Murder* is the seventh entry in Santangelo's *Baby Boomer Mystery* series and they keep right on rockin' and rollin' along. Once again Carol Andrews puts her wits to work with hilarious results—getting herself in and out of trouble while keeping up with her intriguing circle of friends. She can count me among them!"
—Carol J. Perry, Author of the *Witch City Mystery* Series

"If you're a fan of Susan Santangelo's humorous *Baby Boomer Mystery* series, *Dieting Can Be Murder*, the seventh book in the series, won't disappoint. Carol Andrews needs to lose the weight she gained on her recent second honeymoon. But where Carol goes, dead bodies follow, and such is the case when another dieter in her weight loss group is murdered. Of course, Carol can't help but start nosing around to find the killer. After all, the woman collapsed and died on top of her."
—Lois Winston, *USA Today* Bestselling Author of the Critically Acclaimed *Anastasia Pollack Crafting Mystery* Series

"Fans of this, Susan Santangelo "Every Wife Has a Story" series, will be delighted that all the regular characters are back, including Sister Rose, who's still running the thrift shop, Sally's Closet, where Carol continues to volunteer. In fact, it's odd goings on there that lead Carol to finally resolving this, her seventh murder case."
—Anne L. Holmes, APR ("Boomer in Chief"), National Association of Baby Boomer Women

Dieting
Can Be Murder:

Every Wife Has a Story

A Carol and Jim Andrews Baby Boomer
Mystery

Seventh in the Series

Susan Santangelo

SUSPENSE PUBLISHING

DIETING CAN BE MURDER
by
Susan Santangelo

PAPERBACK EDITION
* * * * *
PUBLISHED BY:
Suspense Publishing

Susan Santangelo
Copyright 2017 Susan Santangelo

PUBLISHING HISTORY:
Suspense Publishing, Paperback and Digital Copy, 2017

Cover and Book Design: Shannon Raab
Cover Artist: Elizabeth Moisan

ISBN-13: 978-1547219049
ISBN-10: 1547219041

Publisher's Note: The recipes in this book are to be followed exactly as written. The publisher and the author are not responsible for a reader's specific health or allergy needs which may require medical supervision. The publisher and the author are not responsible for any adverse reactions to the recipes contained in this book.

This one's for Oprah.

Acknowledgments

Thank you to my wonderful family—David, Mark, Sandy, Jacob and Rebecca. And especially to my husband Joe, who keeps me on my toes and inspires me every day.

A big thank you to my First Readers Club, including Marti Baker, Jenny Rush from the Clearwater FL Library, Sandy Pendergast, and Cathie LeBlanc.

Thanks to Elizabeth Moisan for once again providing terrific artwork for the front cover.

To my fellow volunteers at The Attic, the Morton Plant Hospital resale shop in Clearwater, FL, I'm grateful for your extra sharp eyes as you sort donations. You provided an important piece of this plot!

A big thank you to all my long-time friends from New England for their ongoing support and friendship, and to the new friends I've made in Clearwater, Florida, especially the members of the Clearwater Welcome Newcomers Club, St. Brendan's CCW, and the staff of the Clearwater Library.

To all my friends and cyber friends from Sisters in Crime, especially the New England, Florida, and Gulf coast chapters, thanks for sharing your expertise with me. I always learn something new, and the support is fantastic.

Boomer and Lilly send special doggy love to Lynn Pray and Courtney Lynn Cherico, Pineridge English Cockers, Rehoboth MA.

Huge thanks to Melda Pike for providing so many of the chapter headings used in this book. They made me laugh out loud!

For Marvelous Maven Mary Lynn Kiley, and the staff of the Centerville MA Library, thank you so much for the contest to choose a recipe for this book. Everyone who entered is a winner as far as I'm concerned.

To Shannon and John Raab, and everyone at Suspense Publishing, who help me in so many ways, thank you for coming with me on this incredible journey

And to everyone who's enjoyed this series—the readers I've met at countless book events, those who have e-mailed me, and especially those who've posted online reviews for the books—thanks so much! Hope you enjoy this one, too. And keep those chapter headings coming!

Terms That Readers May Find Helpful

Diet: "Restrict oneself to small amounts of special kinds of foods to lose weight." (*Oxford Dictionary*)

Diet: "A regulated selection of foods for medical reasons or cosmetic weight loss." (*The Free Dictionary*)

Dieting: "The deliberate selection of food to control body weight." (*Wikipedia*)

Denial: "The action of declaring something to be untrue." (*Oxford Dictionary*)

Denial: "A defense mechanism in which the existence of unpleasant internal or external realities is denied and kept out of conscious awareness." (*The Free Dictionary*)

De Nile: A river in Egypt.

Dieting
Can Be Murder:

Every Wife Has a Story

Susan Santangelo

Fairport, Connecticut, Early Spring

The first time I saw Pat Mathews, she was walking toward me on Fairport Beach. The last time I saw her, she fell on top of me and died right after we'd completed a motivational exercise to help us lose weight. And in between these two encounters, we'd had a nodding, "supermarket friendly" sort of acquaintance. In fact, I didn't know much about her until after she collapsed on me.

Of course, I'm getting way ahead of myself. One of my worst faults, according to my husband, Jim. And, of course, if I hadn't taken a recent trip to Florida (Jim's idea) for a second honeymoon (also Jim's idea), and gained several extra pounds (also Jim's fault—he fell in love with those "all-you-can-eat" buffets Florida is famous for and wanted to be sure we both got his money's worth), I wouldn't have started a desperate weight-loss regimen when we got home to Fairport, Connecticut. I wouldn't have started my daily walks on the beach, joined Tummy Trimmers to lose weight, and met Pat in the first place.

So, I guess you can say that this time, my getting involved in solving what turned out to be a murder was totally Jim's fault. That's my story, and I'm sticking to it.

Chapter 1

I'm not fat. I'm fluffy.

"I look like a beached whale," Jenny moaned. "Just look at my belly. It's huge!"

I eyed my darling daughter with a skeptical eye. True, her tummy had just a new hint of roundness. "You're four months pregnant," I said. "Believe me, you look wonderful." I gave her a big kiss. "And perfectly normal."

"If anyone in our family looks like a beached whale," I said, looking down at my own middle, "it's me. I'm sure I gained ten more pounds while Dad and I were in Florida. I had way too much fun."

"Fun? You must be kidding," Jenny said. "Unless you consider having your life threatened by a crazed woman 'fun.' Besides, you and Dad were in Florida on your second honeymoon. Sort of."

"I guess, when you put it that way, I'm entitled to each of these extra pounds," I said. "But I wish I hadn't brought them back to Connecticut with me." I sighed. "It's a good thing airlines only weigh luggage these days, not passengers, too."

"Why are you moaning about gaining some weight, Carol?" my clueless husband said, strolling into the kitchen and giving our daughter a hug. "Everybody knows that when women get older, they get fatter."

"Jim," I said. "I am not fat. And I am certainly not old. Mature, yes. Old, no." I tried not to notice that Jim rolled his eyes when I described myself as mature.

"Mom's not fat," Jenny said. She looked down at her belly again. "I'm the one who's fat. And I'm only going to get fatter in the next few months. I hate myself! I really do. I'm sure Mark does, too." And she dissolved into tears.

"Hormone overload," I mouthed to Jim, who clearly was out of his element with two females on the edge at the same time. He raised his eyebrows, then gestured to our two canines, Lucy and Ethel. "This might be a good time for me to give Lucy and Ethel a little exercise," he said. "Then you and Jenny can have a little 'girl' time." He clipped leashes onto the dogs and made his escape like he was an Olympic sprinter.

"Take your time, dear," I said to his retreating back. I handed Jenny a tissue and gestured her into a chair at our kitchen table.

"I don't have time for a long chat," she protested, checking her smartphone. "I have to teach a class at the college in half an hour."

"What I have to say won't take long," I assured her, plopping my tush into a chair directly across from her. "You probably won't believe me, but I bet that every woman feels like you do about herself at one time or the other while she's pregnant. I know that I did. But you will get through this, just like I did. And have a wonderful present to show for the experience when it's over, just the way I did." I beamed at her. "I had you. And you were worth every single minute of my pregnancy. Your baby will be, too. Just wait and see. I know what I'm talking about."

Jenny refused to meet my gaze. "I suppose you think I'm being stupid," she said. "And selfish. I'm sure Mark does. When I try to tell him how I'm feeling, he doesn't want to hear it. He just tells me that he loves me and that I'm always beautiful to him."

"Mark doesn't think you're being stupid or selfish," I said. "He just doesn't know what to say to you so you'll feel better about yourself. After all, despite the fact that he's wonderful, he's a guy. And guys have no clue how to deal with an emotional woman. As Exhibit A, I offer your father. Just look at how fast he scurried out of the house. And, Lord knows, he's had years of practice, dealing with me. Mark's just a beginner. Give him some time and he's bound to improve."

Jenny's eyes swam with tears. "I'm just so afraid, Mom. I wish I could talk to you about it, but I can't. I really can't."

"Sweetheart," I said, grabbing her hand and squeezing it,

"there's nothing to be afraid of. Labor may not be a walk in the park, but if I got through it, and millions of other women over the years did, you will, too. And you have a fabulous obstetrician who's delivered hundreds of babies over the years. Practice makes perfect, right?"

Jenny nodded. "I guess."

"And, by the way," I added, "there isn't a single thing in this entire world that you can't talk to me about. I mean it." And I squeezed her hand a little harder for extra emphasis.

"Mom, you don't understand," Jenny said. "I'm not afraid of the labor pains. Or the delivery, although I'm sure from what I've read that neither will be a breeze. I'm scared stiff about what happens after the baby comes. To me."

"Oh, now I get it," I said. And I really did. How well I remembered those sleepless nights, walking the floor with a colicky Jenny as she screamed her lungs out, while Jim slept blissfully on, completely unaware of her cries. "Not every baby has colic, like you did. Your brother Mike didn't have it. I don't think it's hereditary." I frowned. "At least, I don't think it is."

"That's not it either, Mom," Jenny said, looking even more miserable. "Oh, heck, there's no easy way to say this. And I don't want to hurt your feelings. Honestly, I don't. But I'm afraid of looking like you after I have the baby. Of saying goodbye to my flat belly forever, the way you did after you had me. There, I've finally said it."

Don't show Jenny how hurt you are, Carol. You know this is Jenny's hormones talking, not Jenny herself. Don't overreact, the way you usually do.

"Please don't hate me for what I said, Mom," Jenny begged. She jumped up from her chair and smothered me in a hug. "I'm so sorry. I should have kept my big mouth shut. I'm really being stupid."

"I could never hate you, sweetie," I assured her, returning her hug and trying to remain calm. "I love you, no matter what. You know that."

"I do, Mom. Thanks for understanding. You're the best." Jenny checked her smartphone again. "Yikes! I have to leave now or I'll be late for class." And she, and her hormones, were gone, leaving me alone in my kitchen, feeling very sorry for myself. It was going to be a very long pregnancy, and not just for Jenny and Mark.

Chapter 2

I was cleaning my kitchen when I suddenly realized, OMG, I'm late for Facebook!

I spent the rest of the morning doing housework.

Let me repeat that, in case you think you misread the previous sentence. I SPENT THE REST OF THE MORNING DOING HOUSEWORK.

Did you faint? Do you think I've lost my mind? Or that I'm lying to you? If you've known me for a while, any of these reactions would be totally understandable.

If you haven't met me before, let me set the record straight. My name is Carol Andrews, and I'm not ashamed to admit that I avoid most household tasks—like cleaning and, yes, even cooking—like the bubonic plague. During the good old days BJR (Before Jim's Retirement), I had a cleaning service that came in once a week to make my home sparkle. Dust bunnies, dog hair, be gone! AJR (After Jim's Retirement) there were budget cuts. Major budget cuts. The federal government could get some handy tips from my husband, believe me.

Of course, one of the first things that was cut by my new Retiree-in-Residence was my weekly cleaning service. I still remember the last time the cleaning crew came to perform their magic. When we hugged goodbye, there were many tears, and not just from me. With all the money I'd spent over the years, I'd put several of the crews' kids through college. Okay, that's a slight exaggeration. Emphasis on the word "slight."

I'd wasted too much time walking down Memory Lane. That kind of exercise doesn't burn any calories. But cleaning, that was another story. If I really worked my tush off this morning, I bet I'd be a size 6 with a washboard belly by the time lunchtime rolled around. With that as an incentive, I pulled out the vacuum cleaner and got to work.

"You really are no help at all," I told Lucy and Ethel, snoozing in a corner of the kitchen next to the heating vent. (Like me, they're having re-entry issues after spending their vacation in the Sunshine State.) "Just look at all the dog hair inside this vacuum cleaner bag before I throw it away. Yuck." I tipped the bag carefully, giving both canines a clear view of the contents.

Lucy gave me one of her famous doggy stares, the one that lasers right in on her favorite human (that would be me) and doesn't blink. For a long time. Until I got the message. Which I did, eventually.

A little gratitude would be appreciated, instead of all this criticism. We did save your life in Florida, remember?

Swear to God, that's what Lucy said.

"Okay, you've got a point," I admitted. "In case I didn't say it before, thank you for saving my life. And I haven't used the vacuum for a long time. In fact, I can't remember the last time I dragged it out of the closet and actually used it."

Lucy yawned. She knew she'd won that round. I could swear she gave me a smirk before she rolled over and went back to sleep. I could be mistaken, though.

By the end of an hour, I was completely finished. Don't misunderstand—I don't mean I'd finished cleaning the house. I was completely finished with the job of cleaning the house. Or, to be accurate (and truthful), I was finished with all I intended to do in the housecleaning department for the day. Or, maybe, even for the week. I was confident that my "once-over lightly, and I promise I'll do better next time" style had succeeded in an immediate weight loss of at least five pounds.

I looked at myself in the newly polished full-length mirror on our bathroom door, something I never do. I was thrilled to see that my face was flushed because of all the unusual exertion. In fact, I realized my whole body was sweating. And everybody who's heard of Richard Simmons and sweated to his oldies knows that sweating means weight loss. Yes! Time to weigh myself.

I already knew what my post-Florida weight was. And I'm not telling you, so don't bother asking me. It's a secret that's as closely guarded as my natural hair color, which I haven't seen in more than thirty years.

I hopped on the scale, confidence oozing from every skinny pore of my being. And squinted at the number that treacherous scale was telling me. Oh, no. How could this be possible? I had actually gained a pound from what I weighed yesterday! I checked behind me, to see if Lucy and Ethel had joined me on the scale. They follow me pretty much everywhere, so this wasn't as ridiculous as it sounds, for all of you skeptics who think I was grasping at straws. But, alas, my scale only held one body, and it was mine.

Then, I realized the scale must be wrong. Poor thing, we'd had that sucker for at least five years, and it was feeling its age and was no longer accurate. Or else the cold of a New England winter had affected its accuracy. Especially since Jim insists on keeping our house thermostat so low, to save a few bucks, that I've sometimes had to add so many layers of clothing to get warm that I can't bend my arms. And I'm not exaggerating. Time to throw out that old scale and get a new one. Which meant a retail therapy opportunity was in my immediate future. Yeah! Isn't it impressive how I can justify almost anything?

Now that I had a shopping expedition looming on my personal horizon, my mood instantly lightened. I bid the vacuum a fond farewell and shoved it back in the hall closet, promising to give it another outing before the end of the year. Splish, splash—a shower and shampoo. Then a quick trip to my closet to find some jeans (designer, of course) to wear.

That's when reality came crashing in. Because, none of them fit. Even the really old ones with the elasticized waistbands. Sheesh, how much weight did I gain in Florida, anyway? Or was it possible that my jeans were jealous that they didn't get to come on the trip, and punished me by shrinking two sizes in my darkened closet? Nah. Even my overactive imagination didn't think that was possible.

At this rate, I'd be shopping for new clothes in the maternity department along with Jenny. No way was I going to let that happen.

I finally found a pair of chinos that I could zip up without a problem. Yay me! Take that, you ungrateful jeans. My chinos still loved me. I layered on a turtleneck shirt and black wool sweater (so slimming!) to protect myself against the chilly early spring temperatures waiting to assault me once I headed outdoors. I topped off my ensemble with a down coat that Jim says makes me look like the Michelin man, and a jaunty red beret, slipped on my UGG boots (at least my feet were still the same size), and I was good to go.

"I'll be out for a while," I told Lucy and Ethel, now snoozing on our quilted bedspread. They always want to know my whereabouts, just like Jim does, and they don't have cell phones so I can't check in with them. "If you have any doggy needs, speak up now."

The dogs' response was to burrow under the quilt.

"I'll take that as a 'no,' " I said, picking up the bathroom scale and preparing to recycle it. And then I had one of my truly brilliant ideas. Instead of relegating the scale to a recycling bin, I would donate it to our local upscale thrift shop, Sally's Closet. Maybe it would be kinder to a total stranger than it had been to me.

Chapter 3

The only coordinated thing about me is my clothes.

Sally's Closet is definitely one of Connecticut's major bargain shopping opportunities. Maybe some of you wrinkle up your noses at the thought of wearing a garment that has been pre-loved by another person. My answer to that is, get over yourself. You don't know what treasures you could be missing. And, who knows? Maybe that pair of Calvin Klein black jeans, or that cool Coach purse, have been to a party at a mansion on Beachside Avenue that you'd never be invited to in a million years. Ah, if only clothing could talk, what tales they'd tell!

Sally's Closet is housed in a white Colonial-type building not far from the Fairport train station. The shop features gently loved clothing and accessories for women, men and children, small size furniture, and household items. All the proceeds from the shop support the parent organization, Sally's Place, which helps victims of domestic abuse and other traumas. So shopping at Sally's Closet is really doing a good deed.

I impress that concept on Jim every time I arrive home with still another purchase from Sally's Closet. He actually suggested we save all the cash register receipts from my shopping expeditions there and take them as tax donations, but when he pitched that idea to our accountant, the man nixed it in a hurry. He did give Jim points for creative thinking, though.

The director of Sally's Place—and the manager of the thrift shop—is my former English teacher/sometimes nemesis/frequent moral compass, Sister Rose. We had a somewhat bumpy (I'm being kind) relationship during my high school years at Mount St. Francis Academy, but since we've reconnected as adults (at least, one of us is), things have gotten a lot better. Most of the time. But old habits die hard, and nobody—not even Jim—has the ability to make me snap to attention and behave myself like Sister Rose.

Today, the street in front of Sally's Closet was even more crowded than usual, and finding on-street parking was impossible. But because I've done some volunteer work at the shop in the past, I knew there was a parking lot hidden behind the building, inside a chain link fence. I don't share that information with too many people, so mum's the word, okay?

Ignoring the sign on the shop's back door, "Donations only accepted from 10 a.m. to noon. No exceptions," I headed around the building toward the front entrance, clutching my coat closed with one hand and my treacherous scale in the other. I knew, without a doubt, that I was an exception to that sign, and I (and my generous donation of a sometimes accurate bathroom scale) would be greeted by Sister Rose with open arms, even if the time was well after noon. Of course, she was bound to lay a major guilt trip on me to come back and put in some volunteer hours at the shop, but that was something I could deal with after years of practice.

I skidded to a stop in front of the thrift shop's front window, blinded by a huge sign. "Annual Half Price Sale."

Timing is everything, Carol, and yours is perfect.

Not allowing myself to be diverted by the resort clothes attractively displayed next to the sale sign, I pasted a big smile on my face and pushed open the door. Not only could I donate my lying scale (and get the tax receipt that Jim always insists on), but I'd been given an unexpected mega shopping opportunity. Wahoo!

The thrift shop was mobbed with customers. I'd never seen it so crowded before. Two women were arguing over a red Ralph Lauren sweater that still bore the original price tag. I could have told them that the color would be terrible on either of them, but since my opinion wasn't asked for, and I abhor violence, I moved on. Quickly.

Once again, I was struck by how attractive the shop merchandise was presented, everything arranged neatly according to size and color, with my very favorite rack, labeled "Designer Duds," front and center. I had to give Sister Rose a lot of credit for keeping the shop so orderly in all the chaos, even though customers were doing their best to grab as many bargains as they could, and paying no attention whatsoever to rehanging rejected pieces.

I couldn't help but notice that the display case featuring more upscale handbags displayed a sign proclaiming "Mary Frances Purses." While these whimsical purses are not my style, I knew they retailed for around $300 a piece, so I just had to stop and give them a quick once-over. Hey, I'm only human. You (and Jim) will be glad to know I didn't succumb to their siren song, even though they were a steal (figuratively speaking).

I expected to see Sister Rose behind the cashier's desk. But instead, there was a stranger there, wrapping china for a customer, and there was an ever growing line of other customers impatient to pay for their bargains and leave. I could tell she was overwhelmed. Who wouldn't be?

"Can I help you?" I asked the cashier, a tall brunette of a "certain age" whose name badge identified her as "Gloria." "I volunteer here, too, though I'm not wearing my apron today. I'm pretty good at wrapping and bagging. I've had lots of experience."

"You're an answer to a prayer," Gloria said. "Thank you so much." I scurried behind the counter and between the two of us we managed to take care of the impatient line of customers in record time.

"Wow," Gloria said. "Is it always this busy? I was ready to break down and cry until you stepped in and helped me. And I was terrified that Sister Rose would come out from the sorting room and see how slow I was at taking care of all those people.

"By the way," she said, offering me her hand, "I'm Gloria Watkins, newbie volunteer who's ready to faint."

"I'm Carol Andrews," I said. "Sister Rose and I go back a long way. Believe it or not, she was my high school English teacher. She can be a little scary, but she's really okay once she gets to know you. No kidding."

"So you've lived in Fairport for a long time," Gloria said.

"My whole life," I admitted. "I never really wanted to live anywhere else. It's a great place to raise a family, and all my friends live here, too. It's, well, it's home."

"I envy you," Gloria said. "I'm new in town, and don't know

25

many people yet. That's one of the reasons I decided I had to start volunteering somewhere. I think it's much harder to meet new people when you don't have children. I also love to shop for bargains. The thrift shop seems to be a perfect fit for me, once I figure out how to deal with Sister Rose."

I laughed. "I'm still trying to figure out that one."

I still had the bathroom scale I'd come in to donate. I wanted to get rid of it pronto. Both my hands needed to be free to scour the racks, looking for all those bargains I felt certain were waiting there just for me. "I don't mean to desert you," I said to Gloria, "but the shop is quieter now. I think you'll be okay. If you have a problem and need help, there's a buzzer next to the cash register that you can press. I need to head to the back room and drop off my donation. And maybe we can make a date to have coffee soon."

"I'll be fine now," Gloria said. "Thanks again for helping me out. And coffee sounds great. My schedule is pretty open."

"I'll figure something out and get back to you," I said. "My life isn't that busy, either, but if I don't check my home calendar, I always end up with two commitments at the exact same time. How do I reach you?"

"I plan to volunteer here a few days a week for now," Gloria said. "Why not pop in the next time you're in the area and we'll see what we can come up with?"

"Works for me," I said. "And now I'd better drop off this donation and say hello to Sister Rose."

I expected to see a cadre of volunteers busy pricing new merchandise in the back room. But, instead, no one was there. And the shelves were overflowing with donations.

Uh, oh. Better be careful. Sister Rose will have a volunteer apron on you in record time. There goes the rest of your day. And you know volunteers aren't allowed to shop during their shift.

I found an empty spot on one of the shelves, and, just as quiet as a little mouse, I said goodbye to my scale, promising that it would have a new home soon with someone who would love it. I could hear Sister Rose's voice coming from her inner sanctum. "Of course I understand that you can't come in today, dear. Now, don't you worry about it. Just stay home and take care of yourself and your family. Maybe you can come in tomorrow afternoon, instead."

I heard the sound of the telephone being replaced in its cradle.

"Lord, you surely are testing me today," Sister Rose said. "And, after all, I'm only one person."

I tiptoed to her office door and peeked inside. Sister Rose's eyes were closed, and her lips were moving. I figured she was probably praying, and hesitated to interrupt her. Well, truthfully, I figured that, since her eyes were closed, I'd be able to make my escape without her ever knowing that I was there.

I know. I am a terrible person.

Just think of all the times she's come through for you. Stay and help her. It won't kill you.

I sighed. Then coughed, to let her know someone was there.

"Hello, Carol," Sister Rose said, opening her eyes and giving me a big smile. "I knew you were there. And I was praying that you'd come to my rescue." She narrowed her eyes and gave me The Look she used to terrorize me with while I was in high school. And which was just as effective today as it was way back then. "You *are* staying to volunteer for the afternoon, aren't you?"

"Well, of course I am," I stammered. "I came to bring in a donation, but then I saw how short-handed you were and thought maybe I could help. I just didn't want to interrupt your prayers."

"Don't kid a kidder, Carol. I bet you were planning to make a speedy exit."

I started to remind her that I did peek in her office door to say hello, but Sister Rose held up her hand. "I know you too well, Carol. And for too long. Maybe you wanted to say hello, but you had no intention of staying. You have the same guilty look on your face that you used to have when I caught you sneaking out of study hall without finishing your homework."

"When I came into the shop today, I saw right away that the cashier needed help," I said, trying not to sound defensive, "so I jumped right in. Gloria was very grateful."

"Yes, I can already tell that Gloria will be one of our most reliable volunteers," Sister Rose said. Was it my imagination, or did she put extra emphasis on "reliable," implying that I wasn't? "And the fact that she's had previous cashier experience is a blessing."

I nodded. Even though I knew how completely overwhelmed Gloria was when faced with a long line of impatient customers. Let Sister Rose figure that out for herself.

Without waiting for a thank you from Sister Rose that I knew I'd get eventually, I changed the subject. "You're usually fully staffed for sale times," I said. "Why didn't your regular volunteers show up today? Sometimes when I come in to help out, there are so many other people that I have nothing to do." *So don't blame me if you're short-handed today. It's not my fault.* Of course, you know I didn't have the nerve to say that last part out loud.

Sister Rose handed me a lavender thrift shop apron, accompanied by a lecture. "We have several young mothers on the volunteer roster, and there's some sort of intestinal virus going around the schools like wildfire. Lots of children are out sick, so the mothers stayed home to take care of them. Family always comes first."

I nodded in agreement, but Sister Rose wasn't quite finished yet. "There's always something to do around here, Carol. And, if you stuck to a regular volunteer schedule, instead of dropping in and out when you feel like it, I'd know when you were coming in advance, so there'd be no problem with work."

I could feel my face flush from anger. Or maybe, from guilt. Take your pick. Either way, I knew I was licked. Because Sister Rose was right about my casual approach to volunteering. She did need to work on her managerial skills, though. Reaming someone out who was offering, out of the goodness of her heart, to help, wasn't guaranteed to inspire loyalty. Or a regular schedule.

I swallowed the snappy comeback that flashed into my head. It was so horrible that I'm not even going to share it with you, and you know that I tell you just about everything. Instead, I flashed a bright smile. "You're right, Sister. But my life is often chaotic, so it's very hard to know when I can come in. Perhaps I should call first, to see if you need help?"

Sister Rose responded with a thin-lipped smile. "That's a good idea. And a nice compromise. You still have some of the skills I taught you when you were on the debate team at Mount Saint Francis." She gestured toward the overflowing donations. "I don't mean to appear ungrateful. And I can really use your help. Any dent you can make in pricing this merchandise would be appreciated. In fact," she pulled out a chair and sat down opposite me, "I have a few minutes before I have to relieve Gloria. Maybe if we work together, we can finish going through this bag."

Well, that certainly eliminated any chance I had to claim any treasures that might be hidden among the donations for my very own. Sister Rose frowns on that sort of thing. And don't bother asking for any discount on purchases, either. As she so often says, the women who are served by Sally's Place need all the financial support the thrift shop can provide, and that's why we're all here. Well, most of us.

I dumped the bag of donated clothes in the middle of the sorting table and got to work. Fortunately, everything was clean, although badly in need of ironing, a task I abhor. The clothes even passed the spots and sniff test. (You wouldn't believe some of the absolute garbage some people bring in, and then have the nerve to demand a donation receipt so they can claim it on their taxes.)

"So, speaking of family, how are Jenny and Mark?" Sister Rose asked. "And that rascal son of yours. Any word from him? I know how you worry."

"Oh, Sister, I have such wonderful news! Jenny and Mark are…"

My big announcement about Jenny's pregnancy was interrupted by a loud banging on the back door. Then an impatient ringing of the doorbell.

"I'll get it," Sister Rose said, her voice tinged with annoyance. "Some would-be donors have no patience. This happens all the time."

I was glad that, for once, I wasn't the object of Sister Rose's annoyance. But I was sure she'd turn on the charm for the donor. After all, you never knew what treasures could be on their way into the shop.

"Destiny!" Sister Rose said, throwing her arms around the young woman framed in the doorway. "What a lovely surprise. Come on in, dear. It's cold outside."

"I couldn't wait to tell you my news," said the girl, returning Sister Rose's hug with greater enthusiasm than I'd ever dare to do. "I got a real job. And I owe it all to you!"

Was that a blush I saw on Sister Rose's cheeks? Nah, that wasn't possible. Not the Iron Nun. Oops. I didn't mean to tell you that. But we used to call her that in high school. Not to her face, of course.

"Take off your coat and sit down, dear," Sister Rose said. "We have a lot of catching up to do. I can't wait to hear your news." She turned and caught sight of me, pretending to go through the donations but hanging on every word of this surprising conversation. Who the heck was Destiny, anyway? She was too young to have been one of Sister Rose's students at Mount Saint Francis. The school closed twenty years ago and is now an assisted living facility. Yes, that's right. No cracks about that, okay?

"Oh, Carol, you're still here."

"Yes, Sister. I'm going through these clothes, just like you asked me to do." Obedient Catholic school girl that I am.

"I've decided you'll be of more use in the shop right now than here in the back room," Sister Rose said firmly, pushing the donations to the side of the table. "These can wait a while. Just let me tell Gloria that it'll be a little while longer before I can relieve her. I'll be right back, Destiny." And she vanished into the recesses of the shop.

Clearly, Sister Rose wanted to get rid of me. Which, of course, piqued my curiosity and fired up my well-known imagination. I knew something was up, and I knew that Nancy, Claire and Mary Alice—my cadre of BFFs and fellow Mount Saint Francis alumnae—would want all the details if I decided to share this info with them. Which, of course, I fully intended to do at my earliest opportunity.

"Hi, I'm Carol Andrews," I said, offering my hand to Destiny for a quick handshake. Her grip was surprisingly strong for such a small, delicate-looking person. "I'm an old friend of Sister Rose's." A bit of a stretch, but it was for a good cause, right? "In fact," I continued, "I was one of her students many years ago at Mount Saint Francis. You're too young to have gone there. Maybe your mother did?"

"Isn't she wonderful?" Destiny gushed. "I just love her. She saved my life, and I mean that literally. I don't know what would have happened to me without her help. She's always believed in me, even when nobody else did."

"Yes, she's something, all right," I agreed. "How long have you known her?"

Before Destiny could answer, I heard Sister Rose's voice from the bric-a-brac area of the shop. "Let me find a volunteer to help you with that." She appeared in the doorway, effectively bringing my interrogation—I mean, my chat—to a grinding halt. Which I was sure was her intention. "Carol, dear, would you please help this customer carry some glasses to the checkout desk? She has too many to carry all by herself. Thank you so much."

And, in the blink of an eye, I found myself on the other side of the sorting room door. Rats. Just when things were getting interesting.

Chapter 4

The word DIET really stands for, "Did I Eat That?"

Rather than let my unbridled curiosity about Destiny and Sister Rose dominate my thoughts, when I got home I forced myself to be a good girl and concentrate on my own life. Although I admit that I did a quick online search for Destiny, and came up with no hits. Of course, I didn't have a clue what her last name was, which really hampered my investigating. But how many people named Destiny could be living in Fairport, Connecticut?

I even resisted texting my very best friend, Nancy Green, who is the top-selling Realtor in town (her words, not mine), to ask her to check out Destiny through her powerful real estate connections. If you rent or own property around here, Nancy and her cohorts can track you down. It's scary, how much information they have at their fingertips. Figuratively speaking.

One of the reasons I resisted contacting Nancy is that I'd have to tell her about my foray to Sally's Closet, which would annoy her because she hadn't been included. And if I told her about the half-price sale, and all the goodies which she had missed out on (especially those Mary Frances handbags), she probably wouldn't speak to me for at least a week. But because we've been best friends since our grammar school days, she'd eventually forgive me.

By the way, I was able to score two pairs of jeans with elastic waistbands from my shopping trip, so I finally had a few wardrobe changes to choose from while I planned my battle strategy to shed those temporary extra pounds as quickly as possible. I planned to re-donate the jeans once I had achieved my own battle of the bulge victory. And speaking of clothing donations, I was deeply regretting my most recent one, since I was positive that, with my new, steely resolve to lose weight, I would have been back in my snappy size 10 Lilly Pulitzer white jeans embroidered with pink whales in time for our first backyard barbecue, which we host on Mother's Day weekend. It's traditional (in my mind—I doubt anyone else cares) that I wear white jeans *before* Memorial Day, since I am not a person who is a slave to other people's fashion rules. And this year, the barbecue would be even more special, because we'd be celebrating Jenny's pregnancy, too.

No donor's remorse, Carol. The white jeans have probably found themselves a new home by now with someone who'll love them just as much as you have. You should have looked for them when you went to the thrift shop to donate that stupid scale. But you didn't. So get over yourself. And besides, they'll probably look better on their new owner than they did last year on you. Remember how tight they were the last time you put them on? You could hardly breathe.

I sighed. Because I'm basically an insecure person—there, I've finally admitted it!—once I make a decision, I immediately worry that I've made the wrong one. Another one of my less stellar personality traits guaranteed to drive Jim nuts. "You can't be on both sides of an issue, Carol," he's always telling me. "Just make up your mind and, once you do, stick to your decision. No waffling."

Of course, this pep talk usually follows a decision I've made to go along with whatever my husband of thirty plus years has already decided to do. Like the time Jim wanted to sell our beautiful antique house and downsize to a condominium. I had seller's remorse before the ink was even dry on the listing agreement. Maybe some of you remember that, but in case your memory is as bad as mine, I'll remind you that we didn't sell the house after all, thanks to the potential buyer turning up dead in my living room. There's nothing like a dead buyer to put the brakes on a house sale, let me tell you.

This is why you never get anything accomplished. You waste so much time thinking about ridiculous things, instead of taking action and doing something. If you care about those stupid jeans, pick up the phone and call Sister Rose to see if they've been sold. And if they have, then move on, already. But maybe she's put them away to sell for summer, because of the color. Maybe.

I hate myself when I act so bossy. But better to boss myself around than a total stranger, right? Of course, right. And if an innocent question about Destiny and her relationship to Sister Rose should just happen to escape my lips in the middle of the conversation, well, I'm not responsible. After all, I've been known to blurt things out without thinking. Sometimes. Okay, often.

Satisfied that I had come up with an attack plan that, if it succeeded, would net me my white jeans and some possible juicy information to share, I checked my phone contacts list for the thrift shop number and made the call. One ring. Two rings. Three rings. Then voicemail.

Wow, the half-price sale must be making Sister Rose crazy busy. Like me, she always picks up by the third ring.

My stomach growled, reminding me that I'd only had a single cup of coffee so far today. No cereal. No fruit. No bagel. No muffin. I suddenly felt lightheaded, like I was going to faint. But maybe, just maybe, if I weighed myself this very minute, I had already lost a pound. And if that was true, I'd reward myself by having a light lunch—maybe a little fruit or a yogurt—and by evening I would weigh even less. And then I could allow myself one teensy glass of white wine (with lots of ice) as a reward.

Oh, Carol, you are so brilliant. You don't need anybody's help to lose some weight. You can do it all on your own. Just skip a few of your favorite snacks. Easy peasy.

Just to be sure my resolve was strong, I repeated my new mantra out loud. "You do not need anyone else's help to lose some weight. You can do it all on your own." And I thrust my clenched fist into the air. "All on your own. Yesssss!"

I thought I heard a snicker from the bed where both the dogs were still snoozing. I cocked my head to see if the sound was repeated. And waited for the follow-up which I knew would come.

In less than a minute, Lucy arose from her nap (yes, she arose—that's the only verb I can think of to describe her movement), yawned, turned her back on me like I was invisible (which I frequently am unless it's snack time or meal time), and padded into the office. I, of course, followed her at a discreet distance. I didn't want to give her the satisfaction of knowing that she was leading and I was, well, following her.

Lucy planted herself in front of the computer, stretched

luxuriously, and hopped onto my desk chair. Fortunately, my
computer was already on, so she didn't have to boot it up herself.
(And I am only partly kidding.) She put both front paws on the
desk, turned around, and gave me a stare. Then she swiveled
around and stared at the computer screen, turned and stared back
at me. I swear, she must have done this five or six times.

And finally, the lightbulb dawned. In her doggy opinion, far
superior to any human's, I could not lose weight all by myself. I
needed a little help from the Internet. Cosmic guidance, so to
speak.

"Okay, Lucy. I get it," I said. "And, you're right. I bet I can find
a website with the answer to all my problems in a flash." I eyed my
desk chair. "But that means you have to move. We can't both use
the computer at the same time, and your paws aren't as flexible
as mine." I pointed toward the sofa, where Ethel was already in
residence. "Share the sofa with Ethel. She won't mind. You can
check your email later."

After a loud sigh, indicating her displeasure at having to move,
my Canine-in-Chief surrendered my chair to me. In less time than
it took me to log on, she was curled up next to Ethel and snoring
even louder than Jim, which is really saying something because he
snores like a freight train every single night. Which, of course, he
denies.

How I envied any creature who was able to fall asleep so quickly!
Another curse of advancing age, at least for me, is occasional bouts
of insomnia. If any of you have any helpful tips in that department,
I'd love it if you'd share them sometime.

I resisted the siren call of my email inbox, indicating that I
had twenty new unread messages. I told myself that most of them
were probably from people I didn't know, with information I didn't
need. And I knew that, once I started reading them, my whole
momentum would be lost.

I'm no Internet novice, so I knew that putting in the proper
search words was the first step toward my personal weight loss
plan. Dieting for Dummies? Nah. No way would I allow that to be
part of my search history. Quick Diets That Really Work? Nah. Too
general. Easy Dieting? Painless Dieting? Wonderful Weight Loss?
Miracle Weight Loss?

Hmm. I liked the sound of that last one. Miracles? I wondered
if there was a patron saint of diets. Maybe I should ask Sister Rose

about that, the next time I saw her. Except, of course, I'd probably forget by then.

No time like the present, Carol. Maybe a little divine intervention is exactly what you need. And Jim is always telling you that you can find anything you need to know on the Internet.

I was doubtful that the Internet superhighway reached all the way to heaven, but what the heck. It was worth a shot. So, I Googled "Patron Saint of Weight Loss." And I actually got a few hits.

The first link brought me to information about St. Jude, the patron saint of hopeless causes. That depressed the heck out of me. I really hoped that my desire to lose weight wasn't a hopeless cause. I could do it. I knew I could! So I said a thank you prayer to St. Jude (just to be on the safe side), and told him I'd check back in with him later if I needed him.

The next website told me that the great St. Thomas Aquinas, whose syllogisms had baffled me all through Freshman Year Logic class, had waged a battle with his weight all his life. Hmm. Maybe this was a possibility. Except that I'd never been able to understand much about St. Thomas Aquinas and his thought process when I was in school, so why did I think reaching out to him now would help me? With a sigh, I said a polite thank you and moved along.

I learned that the beloved mid-twentieth-century Pope (now Saint) John XXIII was also overweight. Now, here was someone I really admired. And someone who had actually lived during the same time as me. I felt kind of funny asking for help losing weight to a pope, though. It didn't seem respectful.

I finally happened on St. Margaret of Cortona, listed by several sources as the favored patron saint of weight loss because she overcame many temptations in her life. She's also the go-to saint of falsely accused people, penitent women, and the homeless. I've never been homeless, thank goodness, but I am frequently penitent, having been falsely accused on too many occasions to list by you-know-who. Plus, St. Margaret was a woman who lived in Italy, the home of my very favorite food in the whole world—pasta! I was sure that one of the temptations she overcame in her life was her own "battle of the bulge" from being tempted to eat too much pasta. So she was bound to understand where I was coming from more than a man would, right? Of course, right. Her annual feast day is February 22, which is around the time when Jim and I left on our Florida trip and my mega weight gain began. Although, to be honest, the pounds had been creeping on steadily for the past several years, a little at a time. I set May 22 as my own personal weight loss benchmark for a loss of, say, fifteen pounds. That seemed logical. After all, that was almost two months away, and I could certainly lose fifteen pounds by then.

Maybe I'd start every day from now on with a quick hello to St. Margaret, and ask her for help in choosing my food wisely for that day. A perfect plan. Assuming I remembered to do it, of course.

Satisfied that I was off to a positive (some might even say, heavenly) start, I returned to my Google search of the perfect diet. Something that wouldn't require any major changes in my life—like exercising, heaven forbid. I was sure St. Margaret had never put on a pair of running shoes and done a few laps around the town limits of Cortona to work off a large helping of ravioli. And if she didn't do it, I certainly wasn't going to, either.

Plus, I really didn't want to change my basic food choices. My meal choices also had to be palatable enough to satisfy Jim, and although he's usually pretty easy to please—as long as his portion is generous enough—he does have his limits. Like knockwurst, for instance. I once served that very early in our marriage. A mistake I never repeated.

There may be a few of you who are also struggling to lose weight, so in the interest of sharing knowledge and saving you some time, here are some actual diets I found online. And rejected for one reason or another. I'll leave it up to you to make your own decisions.

The first one that attracted my attention was The Five Bite Diet. Then I wondered how big a single bite was. Would half a cheeseburger or pizza be a bite? According to the rules of this diet, you're supposed to eat five bites of any food twice a day. I rejected this one because I had no way of determining what a bite meant. I certainly wasn't getting into measuring and weighing anything.

The next diet I found was The Lip Gloss Diet. According to the rules of this one, you use lip gloss constantly and draw all the nutrition you need to survive from the Hindu Life Force called Prana. I discarded this one after I found out through a little more research that people have died while on this diet. I didn't want to lose weight that badly!

I kind of liked The Sleeping Beauty Diet, where you knock yourself out for several days and when you wake up you're down a dress size. But I decided against it because, as I already told you, I don't sleep very well these days and I didn't want to take sleeping pills.

Next!

I was curious about The Chew But Don't Swallow Diet. You get all the nutrients through chewing but none of the bulk of the food because you don't swallow. I decided that sounded too weird and kept on searching. I just knew that, if I persevered, my absolutely perfect weight loss plan was just a few clicks away.

And, bingo! I found it. So totally ideal. So me! The Wearing Blue Sunglasses While Eating Diet. I bet you didn't know this, but according to researchers in Japan, blue is the least appetizing color. (I'm not talking about clothing or decorating choices here, so bear with me, okay?) The researchers found that if you look at your food through blue-tinted glasses, you'll eat less. What's not to love about this? Absolutely nothing! I have blue eyes, and I look terrific when I wear blue. Everybody says so. Not only would I be losing weight, but I'd look stylish while I was doing it. Plus, Johnny Depp, one of my very favorite actors, is known to wear blue sunglasses.

I was feeling skinnier already. Until I realized that, while I was Googling with my right hand, my left hand was busy with a bag of stale potato chips that someone (not mentioning any names but it wasn't me) had left by the computer.

This weight loss thing might be a little more challenging than I'd originally thought.

Chapter 5

I always start a new diet on the same day. Tomorrow.

It turns out that buying a pair of blue sunglasses wasn't as easy as I thought, either. I figured that I could use this retail opportunity as a way to ease myself into my weight loss regimen with a big smile on my face because, like most women, I love to shop. And I don't trust the ones who say they don't, because I know they're lying, and I don't hang out with people I can't trust to tell the truth. In case you were all wondering.

I also believe in "shopping local"—patronizing as many merchants in my fair town of Fairport as possible, as often as possible. No cyber shopping for me if I can avoid it.

When I visited my regular retail outlets the following day, (and I hope you won't think I'm bragging when I tell you that several merchants in town keep a reserved parking spot right in front of their stores for me), I did manage to score a few bargains. But, alas, no blue sunglasses. A few enterprising shopkeepers offered to see if they could special order a pair for me, but I knew Jim would have an absolute fit about that—a special order usually means a "special" price.

Of course, I didn't tell anyone why I was looking for such a unique pair of shades. I preferred to keep my unique weight loss regimen to myself. It was nobody's business but my own. And I just knew that I couldn't start to *really* lose weight until I had those sunglasses in my hot little hands.

I know. I know. You all think I'm procrastinating. And you'd be absolutely right. I really did want to lose a few pounds. I just didn't want to work hard to do it. I bet all of you have struggled with the same thing. I wanted to close my eyes one night as a size 14, and wake up the next morning as a size 8. Hmm. Maybe I should talk to St. Jude, who specializes in hopeless causes. He might have a few tips for me, after all. Even though he was a man.

After a fruitless and frustrating attempt to "shop local" for blue sunglasses, I had to admit defeat, and headed home to log onto my computer and an adventure in cyber shopping. Which was not to be. At least, not right away.

You've heard the one about the road to you-know-where being paved with good intentions, right? Well, the road to you-know-where took a detour onto my street, Old Fairport Turnpike. When I turned into my driveway, I saw my son-in-law's car was already parked there, and Mark was sitting on the front steps. He didn't look happy. I realized in a flash that there was only one possible reason why Mark looked so miserable. Something must have happened to Jenny. What if she was hurt? What if she'd lost the baby?

I slammed on my brakes just in time to avoid doing a rear-ender to Mark's car. I hope you'll give me extra points for my quick action, because my hands were shaking so much that I could barely function.

Calm, Carol. Be calm. Don't anticipate trouble.

I pasted on a fake smile as I approached my son-in-law. "This is a lovely surprise, Mark. How's my favorite Fairport detective?"

Mark sprang to his feet and gave me a quick peck on the cheek. "How am I? I wish I could give you a straight answer, Carol. I've never been more confused in my life."

I laughed, relieved. I realized that Mark was here to ask for my help in solving one of his official police cases. I don't want to brag, but I have been extremely helpful to the Fairport Police over the past few years. So much so that I heard it mentioned that the chief of police wanted to give me a special citation and make me an honorary member of the force. Because I'm modest to a fault, however, I already decided that I would refuse the honor when it came. I'm just doing my job as a concerned citizen.

"Come on in and tell me all about it," I said, leading the way toward the side door which offers direct access to my kitchen.

"Down, girls," I said to Lucy and Ethel, who greeted us with extra enthusiasm when they caught sight of one of their other favorite humans. Mark has been known to keep doggie treats in his jacket pocket, and when it comes to food, my two canines have a memory like an elephant. (I know that's a mixed metaphor, but you get what I mean, right?)

"Do you have time for a quick cup of coffee? I'm sorry that all I can offer you is left over from breakfast. It probably tastes terrible by now."

Mark laughed, pulled out a chair and made himself comfortable at the kitchen table. "Your coffee can't be any worse than the coffee at the police station," he said. "Sometimes I think a spoon could stand up in one of those cups all by itself."

I busied myself with pouring the old coffee into two mugs and nuking them in the microwave. Truth to tell, I'd gotten a little misty, seeing Mark at the same kitchen table where he and Jenny used to do their homework together all those years ago. But since Mark was here on a professional matter, I needed to be, well, professional. No time to go down memory lane, even if it is one of my favorite streets.

The microwave dinged, and I placed the two mugs on the table. "Drink this at your own risk," I said, settling my derriere in a chair. "Now, tell me what you're confused about. Confusion is one thing I'm very familiar with. At least, that's what your father-in-law says about me. What kind of a case is this, and how can I help you? Robbery? Identify theft?" I gasped as a horrible thought hit me. "Oh, my goodness. It's not a murder, is it? Oh, golly, I can see by your face that it is a murder. Is it someone I know? Oh, that's terrible." This time, my eyes did more than mist over. They filled up and spilled down my cheeks. All on their own.

"Whoa, Carol," Mark said. "You've got it all wrong. There is no murder. And there's no identity theft or robbery case, either. In fact, there's no case at all." He shook his head to clear it. Funnily enough, I've seen Jim do exactly the same thing on more than one occasion.

"Now, I'm the one who's confused," I confessed. "What's going on?"

"It's Jenny," Mark said, looking miserable. "I don't understand her at all these days. I really need your help. I don't have anybody else I can talk to about this."

Uh oh. Trouble in paradise. I was conflicted. On the one hand,

I was flattered that Mark had asked for my help. On the other hand, I knew I shouldn't get involved in the intimate details of my daughter's marriage. And as I've told all of you countless times, I *never* interfere with the lives of either of my children now that they're adults.

On the other hand, well, I only have two hands. And maybe I could be helpful, just this once. And Mark did ask me. It's not like I called him at the police station and asked him what was going on with his marriage. Right? Of course, right. Besides, my son-in-law looked absolutely miserable. How could I not help?

Then I had a sudden flash of intuition. *Maybe Mark just wants to talk. Unburden himself to someone he knows he can trust. Just sit back and listen.*

I took a sip from my coffee mug and grimaced. It was even more terrible than I'd expected. Oh, well. I swallowed and nodded my head, trying to look encouraging without actually speaking. Mark sighed and looked into his mug, like he was hoping to find the answers to his problem there. No way that was going to happen—the coffee was so sludgy that even a fortune teller couldn't read anything in it.

The seconds ticked by, and finally I couldn't stand the silence any more. I reached across the table and gave Mark's hand a squeeze. That was enough.

"I'm having some trouble figuring out what to say, Carol," Mark said. "Because I don't understand what's wrong." He shook his head. "And if I can't understand what's wrong, then how can I explain it to you?" He started to get up from his chair. "I guess I shouldn't bother you. I'm sure it'll all work out."

No way was I going to let him get away without telling me what was bothering him. "Just hold it right there," I said in my most take-charge tone of voice, the one I used on the kids when they were acting up. "Tell me what's going on." I zipped my lips. "I promise I won't interrupt."

Mark cleared his throat. "This is stupid. I know that if I could get Jenny to talk to me, we could work this out. But I never know what kind of a mood she's going to be in. They change constantly. And I always say the wrong thing and upset her. Or make her mad. She's just not my Jenny. And I don't know what to do to change it."

I smiled. What a relief. This was something I could deal with. "Jenny's pregnant, Mark," I said. "Her hormones are all out of whack. Believe me, I know what I'm talking about. After all, I've been pregnant twice myself. And I was no joy to be around some of the time."

"You can say that again," Jim said.

I jumped. "You startled me," I said. "When did you come home? And why did you sneak into the kitchen?" I pushed my mug of coffee toward him. "Here, you drink this. You made it this morning, and you get to finish it."

"I didn't sneak into the kitchen," Jim said, settling himself at the table and ignoring the coffee. Smart guy. "You just didn't hear me. Maybe I'm not the only one who's losing his hearing in this family."

Ouch. That really hurt. I'm always complaining that I have to repeat things to Jim, because he doesn't hear me the first time I say something. Jim claims I talk too fast. And often from another room in the house.

I decided to tackle the hearing issue another time. Right now, I was focused on Jenny and Mark, and their marriage. And my grandchild-in-the-making. So I just smiled sweetly at my husband and said, "You may be right about my hearing, dear. I was explaining to Mark that all women have emotional highs and lows when they're pregnant when you interrupted us. I'm surprised you remember anything about my pregnancies. They were such a long time ago."

"Some things are etched in my memory forever," Jim said, tapping his forehead for emphasis. "Nine months can be an awfully long time." He reached over and gave Mark a pat on the back. "But don't worry. It's all worth it in the end, when that beautiful baby is born. You'll see."

"It's a relief to know that Jenny doesn't really hate me," Mark said. He ran his fingers through his hair in a gesture of frustration that was remarkably similar to one Jim uses frequently. "But what do I do in the meantime? How do I get through the next few months until the baby is born and keep Jenny happy?"

My turn to put in some parental advice.

With a warning "don't interrupt me" look in the direction of my husband, I said to Mark, "Part of the problem is that when a woman is pregnant, she feels like she's unattractive. Not desirable. She worries about the weight gain, and whether she'll lose it after the baby comes. And when you couple all that with the possibility that she may not be feeling well physically because of morning sickness, plus worrying about maintaining a healthy lifestyle during pregnancy to ensure a healthy baby, that's an awful lot for a young woman like Jenny to deal with at one time.

"But, I have an idea." I beamed at Mark. "And I think you're going to love it. I'm positive Jenny will. How about the two of you going away for a romantic weekend somewhere? Maybe a bed and breakfast on Nantucket?"

Mark shook his head. "I don't think Jenny would be able to tolerate the ferry ride to the island. And you know how she is about small planes. That won't work. But I do like the idea of going away together."

"How about a weekend trip to New York?" Jim interjected. "I'm on an Internet travel site that's always offering special deals. Want me to go and check?" Without giving either me or Mark a chance to answer, Jim bounced up from his chair and headed toward his computer, whistling while he walked. There's nothing like the search for a bargain to put extra pep in that man's step.

"I'd better leave now, Carol," Mark said. "Thanks for letting me vent a little. You and Jim have been a real help. Taking Jenny away on a romantic weekend is a great idea. I'll see what I can figure out. But now, I have to get back on the job." Then, he added, grinning, "I'm sure you don't want the safety of Fairport solely in the hands of your old pal, Paul Wheeler."

"It's a good thing I wasn't swallowing any coffee when you made that crack, buster," I said. "You know that your partner thinks I'm an interfering busybody, even though I have helped the police solve quite a few crimes over the past few years." Just between you and me, "quite a few crimes" wasn't completely accurate. But since I was talking to my son-in-law, and he knew all about my foray into sleuthing AJR (After Jim's Retirement), I knew he'd forgive me for stretching the truth a little.

"Correction," Mark said, inching toward the kitchen door. "Paul thinks you're an interfering, *elderly* busybody." And he made a speedy exit before I could think of an appropriate comeback. The little stinker.

Chapter 6

Everyone is entitled to my opinion.

Jim made himself scarce after eating the turkey and cheese sandwich on light whole wheat bread that I'd made for him. I guess he'd figured out from the way I slammed the plate down in front of him (I know, maturity is not my strong suit and it's too late to change that now) that I was miffed at him for something. Of course, he was completely clueless as to the reason, but I'm betting that all of you who've been married a long time have already figured it out. For those of you who haven't, let me spell it out.

I was mad at Jim for interfering in my conversation with Mark. Not only had he interfered—he'd one-upped me. *I* was the one who suggested that Mark take Jenny away for a romantic getaway to cheer her up, and I was just starting to roll with some ideas when Jim came up with the New York City idea. Which was a great one, don't get me wrong. I just wish it'd been mine.

Why, oh why, did my husband always have to stick his two cents in when it wasn't asked for? Not that we're the least bit competitive, mind you. Don't get the wrong idea. I frequently welcome his input. When I ask for it. Which isn't very often.

"You two are so lucky," I said to Lucy and Ethel, who were parked right beside me as I rinsed the luncheon plates and loaded the dishwasher. (Which then Jim would totally rearrange.) "You have no guy to interfere with your lives every waking minute." Lucy gave me a skeptical look, one I've seen far too often. She adores Jim, and has been known to take his side in any marital spats. Probably because he sneaks her extra biscuits when I'm not looking. And Ethel, always the follower, goes along with Lucy.

I sighed, suddenly remembering how upset I was recently when it looked like Jim was going back to his public relations job in New York City. Sometimes it's hard to straddle both sides of the fence. And it's painful, too.

My stomach growled again. Traitor. I had allowed myself half a sandwich for a late lunch, but that hadn't filled me up. Not only was I used to eating at least twice that much at lunch, I'll confess that I usually followed lunch with a yummy snack about an hour later. Please note that I used the word "yummy," to describe my snack. Not healthy. Even though a handful of Cheese Doodles may contain a miniscule amount of protein somewhere among all the saturated fat, sodium and calories.

I was not cut out to be a martyr. I knew I'd never last on the Carol Andrews Unique Weight Loss Plan (once I actually began it) unless I allowed myself some flexibility. To be determined later.

First, I had to order my secret weapon. So I fired up my computer, put "Blue Sunglasses" into the all-knowing search engine, and bingo! I found a pair of beauties that were only $7.99, plus shipping. Blue frames and blue lenses. Perfect. So I ordered a pair and prepared to pay an extra $10 for one-day shipping. Jim would have a fit if he saw this on the credit card, but hopefully he wouldn't figure it out. I could hardly wait until tomorrow. And I was sure I'd be at least two pounds thinner by the end of the week. Yeah!

I'll tell you a little secret about eyeglasses and age. Maybe you've already figured this out for yourself, but after spending a certain number of years on this earth, the eyes, like all other body parts, begin to need extra help to do their job. I'm talking about prescription glasses—bifocals, even trifocals. Of course, some of you may wear contacts, but I've never quite figured out how they work. And with my luck, when I tried to insert one, I'd poke my eye and end up in the Fairport Hospital Emergency Room.

The only reason why I'm bringing this up now is to prepare you for one of my biggest disappointments ever. The blue sunglasses arrived promptly the following morning by FedEx. I couldn't wait to take them for a test run, and hoped they'd do their job. No, not just a job. I was hoping for a blue sunglasses miracle. I'd weighed myself right after I got out of bed on my brand new bathroom scale, sans pajamas (not a pretty sight), and I had *gained* half a pound from the night before, which was the last time I'd weighed myself. How was it possible for me to gain weight while I was sleeping? Had I dreamed about double hot fudge sundaes, or maybe a cheeseburger and extra fries?

No matter. I had this whole weight loss thing under control now that I had my magic glasses. Except…except that…when I put them on and tried to walk across the kitchen to the refrigerator, I couldn't see out of the darn things. In fact, they made me dizzy. I slammed into one of the dog crates (fortunately, empty) and banged my big toe so hard I thought I'd broken it. Which would teach me that I should wear real shoes in the house instead of bedroom slippers. I limped over to the nearest chair, howling in pain, still wearing the glasses. I am nothing if not stubborn. Besides, they matched the outfit I had carefully chosen for the day—a pair of Jim's blue sweatpants and a Fairport College sweatshirt. I was so frustrated—and so mad at myself—that I put my head down on the table and bawled my eyes out. Nobody can throw a pity party better than I can.

Buck up, Carol. If at first you don't succeed and all that stuff. What did you expect for only $7.99? Of course, they aren't prescription glasses. Maybe you can wear the blue sunglasses over your regular glasses. Or just wear them when you're eating. That's why you got them in the first place!

I nodded in satisfaction. Two great ideas. I just love it when I'm brilliant.

Ping!

My phone announced the arrival of a text, startling me. I ignored it, figuring it was probably Jim, wondering what was for lunch. Before you jump to criticize me for abandoning my wifely duties, let me confess that I could hear my phone, but had no idea where it was. Something that happens to me all too frequently, and gets me into serious trouble.

Ping!

Sheesh. Another text. Immediately followed by my phone's personal ringtone, the opening bars of the Nat King Cole classic, *Unforgettable.* Jim's idea—he says I am unforgettable, and I choose to take that as a compliment.

The Blue Sunglass Diet would have to wait. I had to find my phone, and fast. Two texts and a phone call meant crisis mode. I prayed it wasn't Jenny. The first few months of pregnancy can be very precarious.

I finally located the phone in a box of dog biscuits. Don't ask me how it got there; Lucy and Ethel never borrow it. Just praise me for finding it, okay? Squinting to read the texts without my bifocals, I was relieved to see they were both from Nancy.

Text 1: *Where r u? I have news!*

Text 2: *Where r u? I'm going to call you right now and you better pick up the phone!*

I double-checked and saw that the phone call was from her, too. That Nancy. Everything was fraught with drama where she was concerned. She was the same way when we were both kids at Mount Saint Francis, back in…. Never mind that part. Maybe she'd calmed down a little by this time, but I wasn't taking any chances. Best to answer by text, because when Nancy gets excited, she tends to babble and not make a lot of sense. Sort of like, well, never mind about that part, either.

Me: *What the heck is so urgent?*

Nancy: *Two words. Lori Todesco.*

Me: *Who? Was she in our class?*

Nancy: *No, silly. Don't you remember her?*

Me: *Nope. No idea. Was she a teacher?*

Nancy: *Meet me at Maria's Trattoria in an hour and I'll explain everything.*

Me: *I can't. I'm on a….* I stopped typing. Who better to meet and not eat with than my very best and thinnest friend? Nancy is the only one of my group of three closest friends who actually exercises at least four times a week, and she has more self-control over her food choices than anyone else I've ever known. Don't misunderstand. I don't mean that Nancy has a problem. She's just rather preoccupied with her looks, and wants to do whatever she can to preserve them. For as long as possible.

I carefully deleted my initial response to Nancy's invitation.

Me: *C u there.*

For all I knew, Nancy had her very own pair of blue sunglasses, and she'd been keeping them a secret from me all these years.

Chapter 7

Veni, vidi, veggie. I came, I saw, I had a salad.

It had been several months since I'd visited Maria's Trattoria. In fact, I couldn't remember the last time I'd had a meal there. Since Nancy had joined The Admiral's Table at the Fairport Yacht Club, the members-only restaurant had become our new favorite gathering place.

I felt a little guilty when I walked into Maria's, but the guilt was immediately replaced by sensory overload and I almost swooned in ecstasy. How could I watch my calories when the delightful aromas made my taste buds dance for joy?

I saw Maria Lesco, the restaurant's owner and chef extraordinaire, keeping a close eye on her staff and her customers from her vantage point in the kitchen, cleverly placed dead center in the room for that very reason. Maria was one of the few people I knew who had successfully made the transition to a productive retirement. In her younger days, she was a much-respected elementary school teacher whose no-nonsense attitude inspired a love of learning into all her students—my own two kids included. Her back-to-school parent/teacher conferences were the stuff of legends. When Maria finally decided to retire, she surprised us all by opening Maria's Trattoria. None of us ever suspected that under that starchy exterior beat the heart of a gourmet chef.

Maria and I have become friends, to our mutual surprise. She's even been an unofficial member of my sleuthing team when I find myself, through no fault of my own, in the middle of still another criminal investigation that seems to baffle the local constabulary. I gave her a jaunty wave and was rewarded by a chilly smile. Oh, dear. Guess I wouldn't be getting any complimentary espresso this time.

I fingered the blue sunglasses, tucked in my jacket pocket. *This is your official debut, so don't fail me now.* I had come up with what I thought was a plausible explanation as to why I was wearing the glasses—an eye infection. I'd decided to test my fictitious eye infection story on Nancy to see if she believed me, so I could use it on Jim later on.

I already knew I'd never make my way across the crowded restaurant toward Nancy while I was wearing the darn glasses, so I put them on when I was as close to our table as possible. Fortunately, Nancy was busy texting on her phone and barely acknowledged me when I sat down, so she didn't notice. I already knew what I'd order, so I didn't have to read the menu, thank goodness. Maria's made the best Caesar salad in town, and we always have it. But this time, being extra virtuous, I'd order low-fat dressing served on the side. My plan was to only eat a few bites, just to be sociable, and bring the rest home for dinner.

Nancy clicked off her phone and gave me her full attention for the first time. And immediately squealed, as only she can. "Sweetie, what's wrong with you? Why are you wearing those horrible sunglasses?"

"I have an eye infection," I said. "It could be allergies. The doctor isn't sure. So while I go through a series of tests, he told me to wear these glasses while I'm in a public place, to avoid making my eyes worse." Of course, that was a complete line of horse manure. But Nancy bought it, hook, line and sinker. She shrank back from me, just a little. "Is it contagious?"

I shook my head. "I promise you, what I have is definitely not contagious."

"But if the doctor isn't sure exactly what you have, how can he be sure it's not contagious?" Nancy persisted.

Sheesh. Give me a break.

"He's pretty sure it's an allergy," I repeated. "And allergies aren't contagious. Really."

Nancy still looked skeptical. "Maybe you should be seeing an allergist, Carol, instead of an eye doctor. Are your eyes red and itchy?"

"It's not pink eye, if that's what you're worried about." I whipped off the glasses and gave her a quick peek at my baby blues. "See?"

"They look absolutely normal to me," Nancy said. "Or as normal as any part of you ever looks." She giggled and patted my hand. "Sorry, Carol. I couldn't resist."

Humph. "I bet you didn't try very hard," I snapped back.

"Maybe you should ask Mary Alice to look at them when she gets here," Nancy suggested. "Even though she's a nurse, not a doctor, she may have some ideas."

Oh, dear. Although Mary Alice is one of my best friends, what I really did *not* need was someone with any medical knowledge checking me out. Well, I'd just have to do what I do best, yack away about other subjects and hope Mary Alice didn't want to take a close look at my eyes. For now, it was time to change the subject.

"You didn't mention Mary Alice would be coming when you texted me," I said. "I'll be glad to see her. Is Claire coming, too? It'd be great to have our group together again for lunch."

"Really, Carol, you need to keep up more with our friends," Nancy said. "Claire and Larry are still in Florida. They'll probably be gone until Memorial Day, when the lease on their condo expires." Nancy frowned. "Of course, if they'd let me show them some properties to buy while we were all in Florida, they wouldn't have to worry about expired leases."

I sat back in my chair and let Nancy continue venting. I was secretly glad that I didn't have to deal with Claire for a while. We've all been close friends since pre-puberty, but as we've aged, Claire's tongue has become increasingly critical, and most of her barbs were aimed at moi. At least, that's how it felt to me. And, yes, I am too sensitive for my own good. Or for anybody else's.

I could see Mary Alice heading toward us, so I whipped off the sunglasses and tucked them under my napkin.

"Carol, your eyes," Nancy said. "Shouldn't you be wearing your glasses?"

"They're not itchy right now," I said, which was perfectly true, especially since they never had been in the first place. "The doctor said I should only wear the glasses if my eyes were bothering me."

I jumped up and gave Mary Alice a big hug, deflecting Nancy's question. "How's my favorite nurse in the whole world? We sure missed you when we were in Florida, right Nancy?"

"Not as much as I missed being there, believe me," Mary Alice said, returning my hug and bending down to give Nancy a peck on the cheek. "You picked the right time to get out of Fairport. You missed at least two major snowstorms."

Mary Alice settled in her chair, took a sip of water, leaned back, then asked, "So, what's new? One at a time, please. We have lots to catch up on."

"I have a bit of news," I said, jumping in before Nancy could, no mean feat. "Jenny's pregnant. She and Mark are expecting at the end of the summer. Isn't that great?" My eyes filled up, which Nancy immediately misinterpreted. She pointed toward my glasses and said, "You should keep wearing those."

I pushed her hand away. "Never mind that now, Nancy. Mary Alice, aren't you happy at my news?"

"I'm so thrilled I'm speechless," Mary Alice said. I looked at her to be sure she wasn't kidding. If I'd said that, well, let's just say that rarely happens to me. She grabbed my hand and squeezed it tight. "This is your dream, Carol, to be a grandmother while you're still young and healthy enough to enjoy it. I just think it's wonderful. Can the rest of us be honorary grandmothers?"

I laughed. "I'll have to check with the parents, but I'm pretty sure that'll be okay with them. I'm happy to share my grandchild-to-be with you."

"How is Jenny feeling?" Mary Alice asked. "Any morning sickness?"

"She's feeling fine, thank God," I said. "Except that she's already obsessing about gaining weight while she's pregnant." I frowned. "And to tell you the truth, I'm trying hard not to get too involved and be a helicopter mom. Or grandmother-to-be, depending on your point of view. You both know I always make a concerted effort to let both the kids lead their own lives without any interference from me."

This was an outrageous lie, and both my friends knew it. Nancy bit her lip, to keep herself from making a snappy comeback, no doubt.

Mary Alice, ever the diplomat, changed the subject. "How long have you been back from Florida, Carol?" she asked. "I've talked to Nancy, but haven't heard from you. I was beginning to worry that I'd done something to offend you."

I immediately felt guilty. "I know I should have called you," I said. "But I never know when the best time is for us to talk. Since you're only doing special duty cases now, you seem to work a lot of nights. I didn't want to take a chance and wake you up if you were just coming off a night shift." I frowned, then added, "Besides, to tell you the truth, since we got back from our trip, I've been in a blue funk."

Oops. The minute the words "blue funk" flew out of my mouth, I wanted to take them back. I knew what Nancy's reaction would be. Rats!

"Carol, you should ask Mary Alice to look at your eyes," Nancy said, reaching under my napkin and grabbing the glasses. "She's having some eye problems," Nancy explained to Mary Alice, "and the doctor suggested wearing these to help. Have you ever heard of such a thing?"

Mary Alice took the glasses and examined them. "What the heck are these supposed to do? They're not even prescription strength." She leaned over and peered at my face. "Your eyes look perfectly okay to me. Of course, I'm not an eye specialist. But be careful with these, Carol. They could harm your eyes, not help them. And who's the person who prescribed them? Are you sure he's a real doctor?"

Well, what could I do? I was trapped and I knew it. "To be perfectly honest..." I stammered. I felt a hand on my shoulder. "Maria! I'm so glad to see you." I said. *If you only knew how glad.* "I waved when I came in but you were busy and didn't notice."

"I'm glad you all stopped in," Maria said with just a hint of frostiness in her voice. "It's been quite a while since I've seen you."

"I've been away," Nancy and I both said at the exact same time. "And Mary Alice has been working extra hours at the hospital."

Maria's face softened. "I figured it was something like that. I know you love the food here." I guess we were forgiven. Sort of.

"So, what can I get you for lunch? Caesar salads all around? Extra dressing and croutons for Carol and dressing on the side for Nancy and Mary Alice?"

"Perfect," Nancy said.

I held up my hand. "No extra croutons and dressing for me, and I'd like the dressing on the side, too. Low-fat, please. And I'd like a take-out box. I'll take whatever I don't eat home for Jim."

"Now I know there's something wrong with you," Nancy said after Maria headed back toward the kitchen. "What gives, Carol? First your eye problem and now a radical change in your eating choices. Are you sick? Is there something terribly wrong that you're not telling us? Oh, God, Carol, I couldn't stand it if anything happened to you. And we're at that time of life when heart attacks can happen in an instant." Her eyes filled with tears.

Holy cow. And people accuse me of being overly dramatic.

"I agree with Nancy," Mary Alice said. "Something's definitely up with you, Carol. Quit stalling and tell us what it is."

"I had a little lunch at home, so I'm not really hungry," I said. That, at least, was true, because I wasn't hungry—I was starving. Nancy and Mary Alice still looked concerned about me. And I knew it was because they cared, not because they were being nosy. So I finally said, "I'm trying to lose some weight. Since we got back from Florida, nothing fits me. I even donated my very favorite pair of Lilly Pulitzer jeans to Sally's Closet because I couldn't zip them up. I hope Sister Rose hasn't sold them yet. I want them back. To motivate me. I guess I have a bad case of donor's remorse."

"Thank goodness this is all about losing weight," Nancy said. "I thought you were dying. And what about those blue sunglasses? Is that part of your weight loss plan, too? Leave it to you to come up with something so silly."

I nodded. "I feel so stupid. I should have just told you what was going on in the first place. Wearing blue sunglasses when you eat is supposed to make your food look less appetizing, so you'll eat less. And it must be true. I found it on the Internet."

Mary Alice looked skeptical and started to respond, but Nancy beat her to it. No big surprise. "You must be kidding, Carol. You can't trust anything you find on the Internet. Except for my postings on Realtor.com, of course. My listing information is always one hundred percent accurate." Trust Nancy to always bring the conversation back to real estate.

"Losing weight is very simple," Nancy continued. Spoken like someone who's never had a weight problem in her whole life. Even when she was in her last month of pregnancy, she looked trim. And she lost her so-called baby weight about half a minute after the birth.

Mary Alice interrupted Nancy's ramblings. "Losing weight is not so simple," she corrected. "But it's really about healthy choices. Food choices, life choices, exercise. If you really want to lose weight, Carol, you have to change the way you look at food."

"Exactly!" I said triumphantly. "That's why I bought the blue sunglasses."

Mary Alice shook her head. "That's not what I mean and you know it, Carol. I'm talking about emotional eating, for example. Every time you feel stressed or upset, I bet you reach for something to snack on. And I'm not talking about an apple or a banana, either. I'm talking about things like cookies, chips, or ice cream. Foods that are loaded with sugar or saturated fats." She fixed me with a look that telegraphed, loud and clear, that I was about to be the recipient of one of her all-too-frequent lectures on how to achieve a healthy lifestyle. "You already know what you should do to lose some weight and be healthy, Carol. You should watch what you're eating and start exercising. You just refuse to do it. These blue sunglasses are another of your avoidance tactics. The next thing you'll try is installing a mirror in your kitchen, so you can watch yourself eat."

"Why would anyone want to watch themselves eat?" Nancy asked. "That's ridiculous."

"Actually, this idea makes more sense than eating with blue sunglasses on," Mary Alice said. "Some researchers did a marketing study on consumer behavior, and they discovered that watching yourself eat something unhealthy, like a slice of chocolate cake, can make you eat less. Apparently, people don't want to actually see themselves making unhealthy choices. It makes it too real."

I fantasized briefly on which wall in my kitchen would be the most effective place to hang a mirror. Directly opposite the kitchen table would be the best. Unfortunately, that wouldn't work as our table and chairs are in a corner of the kitchen that's surrounded by windows on three sides. I didn't want to rearrange the entire kitchen. Oh, well. It was a thought.

"You've been known to make some unhealthy food choices, too, Mary Alice," I shot back. "Especially ice cream with hot fudge sauce. It's been our official snack ever since we were kids."

"I know I have, Carol," Mary Alice said. "But I don't do it all the time." She eyed my midsection. "The way I suspect you do." She looked at Nancy. "Back me up here, okay? You do agree with me, don't you?"

"Not only do I agree with you, Mary Alice," Nancy said, "but I know how we can all stay trim, eat healthy, and have fun at the same time. Lori Todesco."

Chapter 8

I'm in the Fitness Protection Program. I'm hiding out from exercise.

"Who the heck is Lori Todesco?" I asked, taking a tiny bite of my Caesar salad and grimacing. It definitely needed more dressing. I added another generous splash, rationalizing that since the dressing was low-fat, it didn't really count. Unfortunately, it was also low-flavor, much too bland for my taste. Oh, well. I dumped the remainder of the dressing onto my salad and resolved to love it, even if it had no taste. No way would I bother to bring it home. "You mentioned her before but I still don't recognize the name. And how can she help me lose weight?"

"I think Lori Todesco was two years ahead of us at Mount Saint Francis," Mary Alice said. "Claire would probably remember."

Nancy shook her head. "Nope, wrong guess. She didn't go to school with us. But she was a very important person in our lives when we were in school. Let me give you a hint." She started to hum a song so off-key and so loud that I had to cover my ears. "Nancy, please stop. You're embarrassing yourself. And us. Everyone's looking at you. If your singing is supposed to help us, it's not. You know you can't carry a tune. That's why you never made the glee club. Although, if you keep singing, maybe it'll ruin my appetite, which would be another way for me to lose weight."

"You are so *not* funny, Carol," Nancy said, blushing just a little. (Unlike me, she doesn't take criticism well.) "But no matter how much you tease me, I'm still not going to tell you who Lori Todesco is. You have to guess." She frowned, then must have realized that she could be adding a wrinkle to her face and quickly stopped herself. "Eat your lunch, while I think of another clue."

There are few things in life that drive me as nuts as not knowing something that someone else knows. I hope that makes some sense to you. In other words, I'm curious. Some people have even called me nosy. I was ready to give Nancy a hard shake. Maybe that would force her to tell us who the heck she was talking about.

"You really are a meanie," I said finally, giving up on my salad—which definitely needed real dressing to make it palatable to me. "You know this is one surefire way to drive me crazy, don't you?"

"Yes, I do," Nancy said, smiling just a little and looking smug. "Okay, here's another clue. Lori was so famous that she even had her own fan club back then. And we were all members. All the girls in our class wanted to look like her. You even tried to dye your hair like hers once, Carol. But it came out terrible. Thank goodness you used a rinse that washed right out, before your mother saw it. We hung out with Lori and her cool friends every afternoon after school. Now do you know who I'm talking about?"

I was ready to throttle Nancy if she didn't stop teasing us. Of course, I was extra cranky because I was also extra hungry.

Mary Alice ignored our bickering. She's heard it too many times before, and she knew that Nancy and I would make up. Eventually. "All I remember about what we did after school was going to someone's house and doing our homework," she said. "That is, if we didn't have a club meeting, or basketball practice, sodality, or," looking directly at me, "detention. You did get in trouble quite a few times for smoking in the bathroom, Carol."

I burst out laughing. "That's because Sister Rose always caught me, while my partner-in-crime, here," I gestured at Nancy, "usually made a hasty escape and left me to take the blame."

"You're getting warmer, Mary Alice," Nancy said, ignoring my accusation because she knew it was true. "We did go to someone's house after school to do our homework together. And what else did we do? From three o'clock to four o'clock every single afternoon?"

I grinned. "We watched television. And danced."

"Bingo," said Nancy. "You win the prize, Carol."

"But I still don't get it," I said.

"Neither do I," Mary Alice said, now clearly getting impatient,

DIETING CAN BE MURDER

too.

Nancy sighed. "Okay. I guess because you remembered us watching television, I can tell you the rest. What show did we watch every day?"

"*New England Rock and Roll Dance Party!*" Mary Alice and I chorused. "I loved that show," I said, lost in my memories. "The couples on that show were so cool."

"That's right," Nancy said. "And who was the coolest couple of all? The one we all wanted to meet in person?"

"Louie and Lori!" Mary Alice squealed. "Oh, my gosh. I haven't thought of them in years. Do you mean to tell me that Lori Todesco is *that* Lori? Is that what all your teasing is about?"

"I wonder whatever happened to her," I said. Then I had a terrible thought. "There wasn't an obituary about her in the paper, was there?"

Nancy swatted me. "No, doofus. If she died, how could she help you lose weight?"

"I give up," Mary Alice said. "We both do, right Carol? No more teasing. Tell us what you're talking about right now." She yawned for effect. "I need to get home and curl up under the covers. I'm so exhausted."

I flashed a grin at Mary Alice. She had played the absolute perfect card. Nancy can't stand thinking she's responsible for anyone's discomfort. Especially her own, of course.

"I was on desk duty this morning at the office," Nancy began. "You know we all have to take turns doing that, right? Whoever has desk duty deals with any walk-ins the office gets for that day. And any walk-in automatically becomes that agent's client if the relationship progresses. Are you with me so far?"

"Nancy, puleeze. We don't need a Real Estate 101 lecture. For Pete's sake, get to the point. And people say I take too long when I tell a story." I sat back in my chair and folded my arms. "If Claire was here right now, she would have throttled you for sure. You know how impatient she is."

"Oh, all right. But you two are really spoiling my fun," Nancy said. She paused and took a tiny bite of her own Caesar salad, chewing it as slowly as possible to draw out the suspense. Then, she grinned and put her fork down. "Around ten o'clock this morning, a very stylish woman came into the office, looking for a retail rental in Fairport. I thought she looked vaguely familiar, but I couldn't place her. Of course, I brought her right into the conference room and had her fill out our basic questionnaire right away. It's a new policy the agency has instituted for potential renters and buyers. We have to be sure they're serious. Some people just like to drive around and look at properties. It wastes a lot of our time."

"Just like you're doing right now," I said, channeling Claire all the way from Florida.

"Huh?" Nancy said. "What do you mean?"

"You're wasting time. So is this woman Lori Todesco? Is that your point?"

"Yes," Nancy said. "She's chosen Fairport to launch her brand new weight-loss program and she's looking for a space to rent. That's where I can help her. Plus, I've decided to join Lori's very first group. And you, Carol, are going to join with me."

"Whoa, Nancy, not me," I said. "You know how I hate being forced to do anything. And I certainly don't want to be in a group of strangers. I like to do my own thing. I don't want to be told I have to eat seaweed to lose weight. Or some other nutty thing. No way. I'm going to lose weight all by myself, in my own way. And, by the way, since when did you become an expert in renting retail spaces? I thought you only handled residential properties."

I know. I was trying to change the subject away from forcing me into a lock-step weight loss program by diverting Nancy into talking about the real estate business again. She fell for it a little while ago, but this time, she refused to be sidetracked. "In this real estate market, everyone in our office has been ordered to diversify," she said. "All our agents now handle both residential and commercial listings. It's our new company policy. Although," she looked thoughtful, "with so many local companies relocating to Boston, we're probably going to be inundated with people who need to put their houses on the market and move to Massachusetts. Lori's timing is perfect. In another few months, I might not have the time to give her the personal attention she wants." She shook her finger at me. "And I know exactly what you're doing, Carol. You're changing the subject so you won't have to deal with my brilliant idea. I refuse to let you do that to me again. Am I right, Mary Alice? Isn't that what she's doing? Don't you agree with me that this new weight-loss program is a terrific idea?"

"Leave me out of this," Mary Alice said. "I don't want to get into another one of your squabbles, especially not without Claire here to referee. And as far as this so-called weight-loss program is concerned, I'd have to know way more about it before encouraging anyone, especially one of my best friends, to sign on."

"But this program will be fun," Nancy insisted. "And the group won't all be strangers. After all, I'll be there, too. Lori is offering special discounts to be part of the inaugural group."

"I don't think so," I said again. "It's just not my thing. I'm not into 'organized' anything."

"What about you, Mary Alice?" Nancy asked, switching gears with lightning speed. "How about if you join with me? It's such a great opportunity. Even though you really don't need to drop any pounds, the exercise will definitely be good for you. We all need some extra help tightening up the body after a certain age, right?" Spoken by the woman with the flattest tummy and tightest upper arms I'd ever seen, except for Michelle Obama. And the chances of my ever getting the opportunity to check Michelle out in person were zilch.

"You're kidding, right Nancy?" I asked. "Didn't you listen to a word Mary Alice just said?"

Nancy tossed her head in a gesture of impatience I know all too well. Which telegraphed loud and clear that she had done absolutely no research at all about Lori Todesco's weight loss program, had no idea what the actual diet was all about, and wasn't going to let this go. She'd just keep on talking until she wore us down and we agreed to join with her.

"I may not know all the program specifics," Nancy admitted. "After all, I just met Lori Todesco this morning. But she certainly sounded like she knew what she was talking about. And she's the poster child for looking terrific. She's at least four years older than we are, and looks ten years younger."

"What's the name of this new weight-loss program?" I asked. "Maybe if there's a website, we can check it out." I pulled my phone from my purse. (I bet some of you are surprised I was able to find it so quickly. Or, at all.) "Google and I are ready," I said, my fingers poised and ready to search.

"You're not going to like what it's called," Nancy said. "I didn't, either. It's called Tummy Trimmers."

"Tummy Trimmers," I said, wrinkling my nose. "That's a horrible name. For some reason, it reminds me of that 1980s movie, *Ghostbusters*." I warbled a revised version of the movie's theme song to prove my point. "Want a trimmer waistline and tighter thighs? Who ya gonna call? Tummy Trimmers!" We all doubled over with the giggles.

"Actually, that's not bad, Carol," Nancy said, tapping my lyrics into her phone. "I may suggest to Lori that she use that idea to advertise the program."

"Do I get royalties?" I asked. "After all, this was my idea."

"You're kidding, right?" Nancy said.

"Not really," I said. "Jim is always after me to figure out how to either save or earn money. Maybe I can become a lyricist in my advancing years."

"Actually, you can tell Lori about your idea, yourself. She's meeting me here in about ten minutes. And then you can both grill her all you want about the program." Nancy picked up her fork and prepared to pick at her Caesar salad, effectively bringing our "discussion" to an end.

"Why do I get the feeling that this is some kind of setup?" I asked, ignoring the basket of freshly baked rolls that was singing a siren song to me from the center of our table. Instead, I speared a bite-size morsel of lettuce and tried to convince myself that several mouthfuls of the green stuff would satisfy my hunger pangs. Don't get me wrong. I love salad. But somehow, it always tastes better when it's slathered with high-calorie dressing and loaded with garlic croutons. So, sue me. I have a very discerning palate.

I turned my attention to my smartphone, and tapped in "Tummy Trimmers." If Lori was arriving in just a few minutes, I wanted to decline any invitation to join the darn program, and knowledge is power, right? I scanned the information quickly, doing my best without rummaging for my glasses.

"Tummy Trimmers is much more than a diet program," I read aloud. "It's a new way to embrace, and live, and love your life. Diet and exercise are important components, as are yoga and meditation, Pilates, dance, and so much more. Discover the *you* that *you* were always meant to be! Dance your way to the *New You* through the music you remember from your youth. What are you waiting for? Let's rock and roll! More information coming soon. Stay tuned!" This was accompanied by a graphic of a woman wearing a pink sweater, a black felt skirt embroidered with a pink poodle, and black ballet flats. I was betting that the sweater was probably buttoned up the back, the way we used to when we were kids. I handed the phone over to Nancy so she could take a quick gander.

"If this is Tummy Trimmers, leave me out of it," I said. "I gave away my poodle skirt years ago. And besides, some of this sounds familiar." I searched my memory bank and, amazingly, came up with the answer. "This program sounds a lot like the one Claire was involved in a few years ago. I think it was called Waist Whittlers. Do you both remember that? She'd joined the program when she went to Florida, but when she came back to Fairport, she lost interest. And gained back all the weight she'd lost." I turned and signaled Maria for the check. "I'm leaving. Right now."

As I rose from my chair and prepared to vamoose, I saw a tall, red-headed woman walking toward our table. She was gorgeous, without a single wrinkle on her perfect face, and had a lithe, dancer's body, the kind most twenty-somethings would probably kill for. If this was Lori, and she could help me to look like her, well, I'll have what she's having. Or, at least, I'll think about it.

Chapter 9

I tried some Downy Wrinkle Resistant Plus the other day, but it didn't help. My body still looks the same.

"I hope it's all right that I call you Nancy," the woman said, sitting down at our table and making herself comfortable. "Or would you prefer to be called Mrs. Green? After all, this is a business relationship."

Nancy looked confused at the reference to her marital status, which she frequently forgets. Not that I'm criticizing her, mind you. I'm just explaining things for those of you who may not be part of Nancy's inner circle. True to form, however, my BFF quickly recovered. "Please, call me Nancy," she said. "I hope that you and I can become friends as well as business associates, Lori. And speaking of friends," Nancy continued, gesturing at Mary Alice and me, "I'd like you to meet two of my very dearest ones, Mary Alice Costello and Carol Andrews. We've all been big fans of yours ever since we were in grammar school. You were our idol on *New England Rock and Roll Dance Party*. We all wanted to grow up and be just like you."

Mary Alice shook her head at Nancy's reference to Lori's being older than us, then whispered to me, "I think Nancy just lost a client."

But Lori ignored Nancy's gaffe. (Perhaps she has selective hearing, like Jim.) And I had to give her credit for good manners and self-control. Either that, or she was the greatest actress to call Connecticut home since Katharine Hepburn. Nancy's reference to her age didn't seem to faze Lori in the slightest. Probably because she looked so much better—and younger—than the rest of us, even though she was several years older. "I had a feeling that coming to Connecticut was the right thing for me," Lori said. "Meeting all of you confirms that I made the right decision. Fairport is the perfect place to launch my new weight-loss program, and I'm already making new friends." She beamed a thousand-watt smile at the three of us.

Was it my imagination, or did her gaze linger on me longer than Nancy and Mary Alice? I found myself blushing, something I haven't done since Jim...never mind about the details. Let's just say that it had been a long time since I blushed.

Forget it, Lori. I have no desire to look as gorgeous as you. Well, that's not true. I have a burning desire to look exactly like you. But I'm sure I can't afford the exorbitant prices you're sure to charge. Jim would have a fit.

I allowed myself a brief fantasy. Jim saw the credit card bill and noticed a hefty (pardon the pun) charge to Tummy Trimmers on the statement. He dropped to his knees in front of me and said, sobbing, "Carol, darling, there's no need for you to lose weight. Especially at these prices. Besides, I think you're absolutely perfect the way you are. Why are you never satisfied with how you look? At your age, just settle down and be content, for heaven's sake. I'm begging you!"

Content? Like a cow? Was my dear husband comparing me to a cow? That was an insult if I ever heard one. How dare Jim insult me in my private fantasy? The nerve.

I must have completely zoned out, because, the next thing I heard was Nancy's tinkling laugh. A sure sign that she was either making fun of me, or had talked me into doing something I didn't want to do while I was temporarily visiting another stratosphere.

"I am right, aren't I, Carol?" Nancy asked. "Weren't you talking just before Lori got here about how you want to drop some pounds, but you don't want to do it the traditional way? I was just telling Lori about your blue sunglasses." And there was that darn tinkling laugh again.

My cheeks flamed with embarrassment. I was ready to give Nancy a swat for spilling the beans to Lori about my feeble (and stupid) attempt to lose weight without really trying.

To my utter amazement, Lori covered my hand (the one I was curling into a fist) and gave it a squeeze. "Nancy, shame on you," she said. "There's no reason to humiliate one of your best friends. Carol is typical of the kind of woman my program is targeted toward. Someone who wants to drop some pounds, but is too savvy to do it by traditional means. She's looking for a revolutionary new approach to weight loss, and Tummy Trimmers is it. Isn't that true, Carol? Isn't that what you're looking for?"

By this time, Lori was squeezing my hand so tight I was afraid she'd cut off the circulation. I flexed my fingers as best as I could, and Lori loosened her grasp. "I'm sorry, Carol. I hope I wasn't hurting you. Sometimes, I don't know my own strength." And there came another thousand-watt smile, but this time it was aimed solely at me. "I have just had the most brilliant idea," Lori said, turning her chair toward me and effectively cutting Nancy and Mary Alice out of the conversation. "I think we should make you the model for Tummy Trimmers. You know, we'll have a photographer take some 'before' pictures, follow you along as you progress on the program, and then…pow! Unveil the 'new you.' What do you think?"

"Me?" I repeated. "You want to make me the model for Tummy Trimmers? I don't know if I'm comfortable with this. I don't like being the center of attention."

That was a total lie, of course. But Lori had no way of knowing that. Just for good measure, I gave Nancy a little nudge under the table, reminding her to keep her big mouth shut. I knew I could count on Mary Alice's discretion. As long as I didn't look directly at her, because I was sure she was biting her lips to keep from laughing.

"You're just being modest," Lori said. "You're absolutely perfect. Just like Oprah is for Weight Watchers. Everyone will want to look like you."

"Lori," I said, "I'm flattered, of course. But I think everyone would want to look like you, not like me."

"But the public can't follow my progress on Tummy Trimmers," Lori pointed out. She spread her arms wide. "I'm already the 'after.' I need you to be the beginning and the middle, journeying toward the end. Don't you see? A role model for women everywhere."

"Well, when you put it like that…." I was beginning to weaken. I looked at Nancy and Mary Alice for help, but none was forthcoming from either of them. Then, Jim's face flashed into my consciousness, and I realized that he'd never go for my spending big bucks on a weight loss program. (See previous fantasy.)

"I don't mean to be crass," I said. "But how much is this program going to cost me? What's the fee structure? I'd have to talk it over with my husband before I agree. We're trying to watch expenses because our first grandchild is on the way."

Lori's eyes widened. "Carol, you wouldn't pay anything for the program. It would be absolutely free, but only for you. As long as you consent to let us document your participation."

I could tell from the look on Nancy's face that this conversation wasn't going the way she had expected it to. She had already cast herself in the role of Tummy Trimmers' numero uno client, and instead, the spotlight was shining on me, not her. Who knew that lugging around some extra pounds in my later years could make me a star?

"Assuming I agree to do this," I said, "I'd be much more comfortable if both Nancy and Mary Alice were part of the first group, too. In fact, before you arrived, Lori, Nancy was telling us about some sort of discount you were offering to be part of the first group. Nancy was very excited."

"You'll both definitely get a significant discount for joining," Lori said, smiling at Mary Alice and Nancy. "Absolutely."

Looking mollified, Nancy said, "You can definitely count me in. Mary Alice, what about you?"

"I'm still not at all clear on what Tummy Trimmers is all about," said Mary Alice, always the cautious one in our group. "What if I start it and realize it's not for me. Can I drop out? Are there any penalties?"

"None at all," Lori assured her. "But, I guarantee, you're going to have so much fun that you'll want to keep coming. Just the chance to work out to some of the oldies we all danced to years ago will energize you. You'll love it."

"I have to think about it," Mary Alice said. "I'll let you know if I decide to join."

"I have a few rental properties I want to show you that might work for Tummy Trimmers, Lori," Nancy said. She checked her phone. "I just got a text from one of the property owners wanting to know where we are. We had an appointment at 1:30."

"We can't leave yet, Nancy," Lori said. "Carol hasn't given me her answer. If you need a little more time to mull over my offer, that's fine. But please don't take too long. I want to launch Tummy

Trimmers as soon as possible."

I had another fantasy. This one was of me in white Lilly Pulitzer jeans (except these were two sizes smaller than the ones I had donated) walking Lucy and Ethel around Fairport. They were wearing matching pink and green bandanas—very stylish. My jeans were topped by a skinny pink and green tee-shirt emblazoned with a Tummy Trimmers logo. We were turning heads everywhere we walked. Some people even snapped pictures of us with their camera phones.

Or, even better, we were riding in a snappy red convertible as part of Fairport's annual July 4 parade. The convertible top was down, so all the parade gawkers could marvel at the new, lithe me. I responded to the cheers with a gracious wave, the way Queen Elizabeth always does, and Lucy and Ethel woofed. I heard several people comment that I looked even more svelte in person than I did in the media ads. I smiled and tried to look modest. "I owe it all to Tummy Trimmers," I said. "The program changed my life. It can change yours, too."

It could happen. Of course, it could happen. But there was no time to lose. So, for Lucy and Ethel's sake, and all those potential fans who needed a role model, I heard myself say, "All right, Lori. Count me in."

"Fabulous," Lori said. "I guarantee you, in just a few short weeks, you won't even recognize yourself."

Nancy brought me back to earth with a thud. "The first order of business is to find a place for the program. Come on, Lori. We'll take my car."

"Want me to come, too?" I asked. I thought it was a reasonable request. I mean, after all, if I was going to be the role model for Tummy Trimmers, I should have a say in where the program is housed, right? Of course, right.

I guess Nancy didn't agree, because she grabbed Lori's arm and they were out the restaurant door in a flash. But, BFF that I am, I ignored the fact that she hadn't left any money for her share of the check.

When Mary Alice suggested we split the bill evenly, I declined. "I'll pay for Nancy's lunch, too," I said, over Mary Alice's protests. I hope you're all proud of me.

Chapter 10

Does texting count as exercise?

There was an extra bounce in my step as I left Maria's Trattoria. And I'm not just talking about the weather, although I was thrilled to notice that the daffodils were finally beginning to bloom around the gazebo in the center of town. Even though I'd only been in Florida a short time, I'd become accustomed to seeing flowers blooming everywhere. When I got back home, the sudden lack of foliage was depressing. But spring was finally coming to our fair corner of the world, which meant that wearing shorts and even the dreaded bathing suit would soon follow. Yikes!

"First things first, Carol," I said, then realized that I was talking to myself out loud again. I clamped my lips shut and sprinted to the privacy of my car so I could continue my conversation. "First things first," I repeated, just in case I was tempted to veer into another conversation topic. "What's the most important next step in your new adventure?" That was a no brainer. No, not rushing home to share the news of my selection as the public persona of Tummy Trimmers with Lucy, Ethel and Jim (notice the pecking order). Not a quick phone call to Jenny, or text to son Mike, either.

I briefly considered stopping at Crimpers, my local hair salon, and sharing my good news with Deanna, my favorite hairstylist/confidante. And possibly booking her now for a regular schedule of touchups so my naturally blonde hair could remain, well, "naturally" blonde. Then, I dismissed that idea. I had a far more important task to accomplish. I needed to get to Sally's Closet right away and see if by any remote chance I could rescue my white Lilly Pulitzer jeans in case someone else hadn't nabbed them, because I was positive I'd lose enough weight in the next few weeks to fit into them. And while I was there, I might make a donation of my own. I'm sure you can figure out what. The blue sunglasses, of course!

I found a parking space right in front of Sally's Closet, which was a miracle. I said a silent prayer of thanksgiving to the patron saint of parking and considered that a very positive sign that my jeans—and Sister Rose—would be glad to see me.

The shop seemed empty when I walked in, which probably accounted for my luck in finding a parking space. And the cashier's desk, always manned by Sister Rose or one of her trusted volunteers, was vacant as well.

I checked my watch. Oh, no. It was almost time for the shop to close. I knew I'd better hurry, or I'd be in trouble with the good sister for making her stay late. And I'd been in enough trouble with her over the years to know that I didn't want to risk that happening again. But I just had to scour the racks in search of my white jeans. And while I was at it, I'd also take a quick peek at the rack marked "Today's New Arrivals." After all, I'm only human. And the half-price sale sign was still visible, so my heart soared at the possibility of scoring a great bargain. Or five.

Sadly, there was still no sign of my jeans, so I'd have to console myself with another treasure. As I began to whip through the New Arrivals rack with the speed of a pro with a black belt in shopping, I heard voices coming from another part of the shop. How annoying, when I was trying to focus. I realized that one of the voices belonged to Sister Rose, who was helping a last-minute customer. And, knowing her, she was hurrying the customer along so she could close Sally's Closet on time. I ducked behind the New Arrivals rack and continued my search. No sense in making my presence known before I absolutely had to.

"I don't have much experience with this type of clothing, dear," Sister Rose said. "But I'd say that dress would look very nice on you."

"Do you really think so, Sister? I wish Mom was here to help me pick out some clothes. I just don't think I'm ready for real maternity clothes yet. But my other clothes don't fit anymore and I have to wear something!"

I recognized the voice of the last-minute customer as my own darling daughter and mom-to-be. Although I was dying to check out the rest of the new clothing donations, there was always tomorrow, as Scarlett O'Hara famously said. Jenny and I hadn't spoken since our little tiff about her weight, and mine, and I was anxious for a reconciliation.

Just pretend there's nothing wrong between you and Jenny. After all, she just said that she wished you were here to help her pick out clothes. That's a very positive sign that she misses you as much as you miss her.

Fortified by my personal pep talk, and with a big smile on my face, I headed toward Jenny and Sister Rose. On my way, I spotted a darling cornflower blue shift dress that reminded me of one that I had when I was in college. I wore mine so often that my friends said the dress was my new version of our old high school uniform. I knew this dress would look adorable on Jenny. She has the same coloring as I do—blonde hair and blue eyes. It was a perfect dress to wear for a quick trip to the grocery store, or even when she was teaching one of her college classes. And it would fit her for the next few months.

Brandishing the dress, I rounded the corner and headed straight to my daughter. "Surprise, sweetie," I said. "You didn't think you could go shopping without me, did you?" Jenny laughed and I gave her a smooch on the cheek. What the heck. I was in a good mood so I gave Sister Rose a little hug, too. Which flustered the heck out of the good sister. Even though she gave me a quick smile, I couldn't tell if she was really glad to see me or not. So I just forged ahead.

"Look what I just found. Isn't this adorable?" I held the blue dress up against Jenny's barely noticeable tummy. "I think it's a perfect in-between dress, when some of your old clothes are a little too tight, but you're not ready to wear maternity clothes yet. What do you think? Why don't you try it on?"

A flash of annoyance crossed Sister Rose's face. But, she recovered quickly, thank goodness. I had seen that look too many times before. "I'm surprised that you're shopping so late in the day, Carol," she said. "I assumed you'd be home preparing dinner for your husband by now."

Ouch.

"I wanted to ask you if the Lilly Pulitzer white jeans I donated are still here," I said as Jenny disappeared into a fitting room, the blue dress over her arm. "I was going to call you, but when I drove by the shop and saw a parking spot right in front, I figured I could stop in." I cleared my throat and pushed forward. "I decided that, if they're still here, I want them back. But I couldn't find them. Have they been sold already? I'll be glad to pay for them," I added, when Sister Rose didn't respond. I guess she'd never heard of donor's remorse. The look of annoyance was back on her face, and this time, she didn't try to hide it.

"Carol, *dear*, don't you remember that Sally's Closet closes promptly at four o'clock?" Sister Rose checked her watch. "It's already ten after four, and I still have to tally up the day's receipts. Plus, I have a meeting with a potential contributor and I simply cannot keep her waiting. I have no time to check to see if we still have your jeans. I can't keep track of every single donation. You can always come back in the morning and continue your search. And while you're here, you could volunteer for a few hours. We can really use your help."

Yikes. Another bullseye. I felt like I'd been called to the principal's office and reprimanded for my bad behavior, a feeling I should have gotten over after all these years, but which rears its head much too often in my so-called adult life.

"I'm sorry, Sister," I said, figuratively tugging on my forelock. "Let me peek in the fitting room and hurry Jenny along. I'll come back tomorrow." *Mea culpa. Mea culpa.*

Jenny poked her head out of the fitting room. "Mom, could you come here a minute, please? I want to show you something."

I flashed Sister Rose an apologetic smile. "Daughters always want their mothers' approval on clothing purchases. I'll be quick."

I think I heard a tsk from Sister Rose. But since my back was to her, I can't swear to it.

"Coming, sweetie," I called. "If you're not sure about the dress, let me buy it for you, anyway. Sister Rose wants to close the shop, and we can always re-donate it if you change your mind."

I peeked around the fitting room curtain. "Are you decent?" Jenny was still wearing the dress, and it looked adorable on her. "That's so cute on you, Jenny. I'll definitely buy it. And it has pockets, too. Perfect! You know I'm a big fan of pockets."

"I'm glad you like the dress, Mom. But that's not why I called you. Look what I found in one of the pockets." Jenny held out a thick roll of twenty-dollar bills secured by an elastic band. "I counted it. There's a thousand dollars here."

"What? You're kidding," I said, taking the money and looking at it closely. "Who would leave all that cash in a dress and then donate it to a thrift shop? That's just crazy. Sister Rose needs to know about this right away." And I was betting she wouldn't be in such a hurry for us to leave once I told her what Jenny had found.

The sister in question had already turned off the music in the thrift shop and flipped the front door sign to "Closed." And just in case we didn't get the message, most of the store lights were shut off. She brightened when she saw us heading her way. "Ready to check out? I'm surprised you're still wearing the dress, Jenny. You must really love it. Why don't you tell me what the price ticket says and I'll ring up the sale while you get your other clothes?" *And hurry up.* Sister Rose didn't really say that, of course. But it was crystal clear that she was thinking it.

"Sister, before you ring up the sale, you'd better take a look at what Jenny found in one of the dress pockets." I held out the cash. "Maybe it's an anonymous donation."

Sister Rose took the money from me, then sat down in her chair with a thud. I'd never seen her react that way before, and as I told Nancy later, it was pretty scary. I was afraid the poor woman was going to faint. Or worse, have a heart attack, right there in front of Jenny and me.

"You're telling me you found all this money in a dress pocket?" Sister Rose asked.

Jenny nodded. "I counted it. There's a thousand dollars here."

"My heavens," Sister said, staring at the roll of bills in her hand. "The good we could do for the domestic violence program with this. It's like a miracle." Carefully, she put the money down on the counter. "But we can't keep it. We have to find the person who left the money in the pocket, and give it back to them. For now, I'm locking it in the office filing cabinet. I'll deal with this tomorrow."

I knew she was right. Keeping the money, even for such a worthy cause, was plain wrong. Darn it.

"I'll grab my other clothes," Jenny said. "I can just throw my coat on over this dress. I hope Mark likes it."

"Before you leave, Jenny, let me take a quick picture of the dress," Sister Rose said, taking a cell phone out of the cash register. "I want to show the dress to all the volunteers, to see if anyone remembers who donated it. And what's the price of the dress? The tag should be on the hem of the right sleeve."

"Nope," I said, giving the dress a closer look before Jenny headed toward the fitting room again. "There's no tag. Maybe it fell off."

No mistaking the *tsk* that came from Sister Rose this time. "I hate to accuse any of our customers, but that's happening more and more. Sometimes I think people pull them off because they're hoping to get a cheaper price. Let's say six dollars for the dress, okay?" As she took the money from me, she added, "And I'll see you here bright and early tomorrow, Carol, right? You can search for your jeans while you mark some donations. And until I can determine the source of the money, I insist that you not say anything about this to anyone else. Promise me."

"Don't worry, Sister," I said, trying not to take offense at the obvious implication that I can't be trusted to keep a secret. "You can rely on me. And Jenny won't say anything, either. Not even to Mark. But if you decide that you need a little assistance from the police in this situation, be sure to let us know. With Mark being a police detective, I'm sure he'd be glad to help." And I gave her a sweet smile.

Sister Rose isn't the only person in the world who insists on having the last word.

Chapter 11

I just did a week's worth of cardio exercise in
five minutes. I walked into a spider's web.

Jenny and I parted company on the sidewalk in front of Sally's
Closet, but not before I told her about joining Tummy Trimmers,
and how Lori Todesco had chosen me to be the official face (and
body) of her new weight-loss program.

"That's so cool, Mom. Congratulations," Jenny said. "You'll be
famous!"

I laughed. "I don't know if I should be congratulated, Jenny," I
said. "After all, Lori chose me because I need to lose weight. Maybe
Tummy Trimmers will help me lose my pot belly, too. Although
somehow, I think I'm stuck with that forever."

"What's the first step, Mom? I mean, when does the program
start?"

"I don't know the official opening date," I confessed. "Nancy
was showing Lori some rental properties this afternoon. I haven't
heard whether Lori found one she thought would work. I've finally
decided I need to lose weight and make healthier food choices.
But I'm afraid that, if Tummy Trimmers doesn't start right away,
I'll change my mind and chicken out. And I know I have to start
exercising. You know I've avoided that for years."

"I have an idea, Mom," Jenny said, her hand poised on the door
handle of her car. "My obstetrician suggested that I start a daily
thirty-minute walking routine. It's safe exercise, and now that I'm

past my first trimester and all is well, I'm raring to go. Why don't you walk with me? We can meet every morning at the beach around eight o'clock and walk for half an hour. It's an easy way to drop a little weight. We could start tomorrow. What do you say?"

"What a great idea," I said. "I love it. And I love you for suggesting it. I'll see you at Fairport Beach tomorrow morning at eight sharp." A sudden thought occurred to me, and my eyes misted over. I tried not to let Jenny see, but being my daughter, not much got past her.

"What's the matter, Mom? If you don't want to do this, it's okay. I'm not trying to force you."

"I do want to do it," I said. "But it just occurred to me that there'll be three of us on this walk."

Jenny looked confused. "Dad? Mark? Oh, wait. I get it. You want to bring Lucy. I noticed she's put on a little weight, too. But I'm not sure if dogs are allowed on the beach now."

I laughed. "No, Jenny. Not Lucy. You, me and Baby makes three. This'll give me a chance to get to know my grandchild-to-be."

The next morning dawned far too early for me. When the alarm on my phone went off, I rolled over, grabbed the darn thing, and groaned when I saw it was only 7:30. One of the (few) benefits of having Jim retired is that he doesn't have to leave the house before the sun's up to catch a train to New York. I enjoy having some extra snooze time, particularly since I don't sleep well at all these days. I know getting up often in the middle of the night is all part of the aging process for most women, and I do try to make the best of it. Especially considering what the alternative is. Whine, whine, whine.

I searched my fuzzy brain cells to come up with a valid reason why I'd set my alarm for such an early hour. Yesterday's events fought for a place in my consciousness. Tummy Trimmers. Lori. Sally's Closet. White Lilly jeans. Mysterious money in dress pocket. Walking on beach with Jenny.

That was it! I had a date with my daughter. I bolted out of bed, startling Jim and the dogs, all of whom had rolled over for another snooze.

I had no time for a shower, even a quick one. Usually I hate leaving the house before I'm shampooed, shower fresh, with makeup deftly applied. *Suck it up, Carol. You'll be outside in fresh air, so if you're even the least bit "offensive," nobody'll notice. Or care. Jenny certainly won't. You can shower when you get home.*

Praying I wouldn't see anyone I knew while I was "au naturel," so to speak, I slipped on baggy sweatpants and a pullover shirt, laced up my sneakers (bending down to accomplish that simple task counted as exercise for me, too), grabbed a bottle of water from the fridge and the car keys. Day 1 of the No-Kidding-Around, This-Time-I'm-Really-Going-To-Do-It, Carol Andrews Weight-Loss Program had begun.

"Slow down, Jenny," I said, pausing to catch my breath. "We're not training for a marathon, you know."

"Sorry, Mom," Jenny said, bouncing a little in place so as not to lose her momentum. "I forgot that this is your first time doing this."

"It's not my first time *walking*," I clarified with a grin. "I've been doing that for a long time. It's just that I'm not used to walking quite so fast. I'm really feeling my age."

"Age is just a number," Jenny said in the authoritative voice of a young person. She gestured toward a tall woman speed-walking toward us wearing huge sunglasses, yoga pants and a red tee shirt, her white hair flying around her shoulders. "That woman looks like she won't see seventy again. Look at her go."

"Hush, she'll hear you," I cautioned. I gave the woman a friendly wave and cheery good morning as she passed us, which she ignored.

"No way she heard you, Mom," Jenny said. "Didn't you notice she was wearing ear buds? She's listening to something on her phone. Probably music. Mark says that's very dangerous, because if anyone's being stalked by a potential attacker, the victim can't hear the stalker approaching."

At my alarmed expression, Jenny clarified. "That doesn't happen very often, Mom, so don't freak. Especially in Fairport. And Mark's a policeman, so he's always extra cautious, especially about me." She patted her tummy. "I guess I should say, 'us.' I've got to start thinking for two now."

"How is my grandchild this morning?" I asked.

Jenny grinned. "All is well. I think I'm finally getting over the morning sickness stage. And, by the way, we'd better get moving. I have to get home, shower, and get to school, remember? I think I'll wear that cute dress you bought me yesterday at Sally's Closet."

"I should give Sister Rose a quick call this morning and find out what she decided to do about the money you found in the pocket," I said, conveniently forgetting the fact that I had been strong-armed by the good sister into volunteering at the shop today. "In all the years I've known her, I never saw her react to any situation that way. She doesn't like surprises. Maybe, if you're a nun, you don't have too many of those."

"This sure was a giant one," Jenny agreed. "And quit stalling. I have fifteen more minutes tops to walk, and then I have to leave."

"Lead on," I said, trying to appear enthusiastic. "And you're right. That woman who passed us before is years older than me. If she can do it, I can do it. But she did look right at me and didn't answer me. I still think that was rude."

"There may be a protocol among walkers the same way there is for people working out at a gym," Jenny said, pulling on my arm to get me going again. "It's considered impolite to speak to someone while they're working out. You can nod, but not speak. Disturbing someone when they're in their 'zone' is strictly forbidden."

"That explains why I don't go to the gym," I said, puffing heavily as I struggled to keep up with Jenny's faster pace. "According to your father, I can't keep quiet for more than a single minute. Even if I have laryngitis."

"That reminds me, Mom," Jenny said, slowing down a bit to let me catch up, "what did Dad say when you told him last night about Tummy Trimmers? I'll bet he was surprised. Mark was, when I shared your news with him."

"You told Mark?" I repeated stupidly. "Already?"

"We're married, Mom," Jenny reminded me. "I didn't tell him about finding the money, because Sister Rose asked us not to. But Mark and I don't keep secrets from each other."

Neither did I, until I'd been married for a while. I didn't really say that, of course.

"You don't mind that I told him about Tummy Trimmers, do you, Mom? He thought it sounded great. But I'm sure he won't tell anybody else about it." Jenny looked upset, which made me feel guilty, a feeling I'm all too familiar with.

"It's okay, sweetie. I'm sure Mark has other things to think about than his mother-in-law joining a new weight-loss program. Tummy Trimmers is just something I don't want to share with your father until I know more about what I've gotten myself into. I knew your dad would ask me a lot of questions, and I don't have the answers. So until I get some answers, mum's the word, okay?"

Jenny made a zipping motion across her lips, catching a glimpse of her watch as she did. "Gosh, it's later than I thought. I promise I'll keep quiet about Tummy Trimmers until you give me permission to talk about it. And I'll be sure Mark does, too. Meanwhile, I've really gotta go. I have to teach a nine-thirty freshman English class, and I can't be late." She gave me a peck on the cheek and sprinted away in the direction of her car, calling over her shoulder, "Tomorrow, same time, and no stalling, Mom, or you won't get to babysit your grandchild-to-be as often as you want." Ha. My smarty pants daughter knew exactly how to threaten me. And even though I was sure she was kidding, I resolved to do better tomorrow.

Of course, I could have continued the walk by myself. But if you've known me for a while, you won't be surprised to learn that I didn't. Instead, I stood on the beach, enjoying the peace and quiet of an early spring morning. It wouldn't be that long before Fairport Beach would be swarming with people—families with young children, tourists escaping from the heat of the city, and other assorted folks, all here to enjoy splashing in Long Island Sound, playing in the sand, picnics, and even the occasional beach wedding.

On impulse, I took off my shoes and socks and waded into the water. Which was a huge mistake. The water was freezing cold, not the warm waters of the Gulf of Mexico I'd so recently enjoyed on my Florida adventure. And I'd completely forgotten about all the stones that our beach is famous for, until it was too late and I was stepping on them.

Enough of this, Carol. Time to get home, shower and make yourself presentable.

I took my own good advice, and headed back to the car, still barefoot. So what if I got sand in the car? I could vacuum it out later. I reached in my sweatpants pocket (I never buy pants without pockets these days if I can help it) and fished out my car keys and cell phone. Yikes. I had five texts, all of them from Nancy, and all with the same message: *Where the heck are you? Call me!*

OMG. While I was walking on the beach with Jenny, something

terrible had happened. I just knew it.

I raced back to the safety of my car (raced being a stretch, which I'm sure you already guessed) and punched in Nancy's number. When I heard my BFF's voice, I didn't give her a chance to speak beyond "Hello."

"Who died? Who's sick? Have you been in an accident? What's wrong?"

I heard a *tsk* at the other end of the phone. A Sister Rose sort of *tsk*.

"Honestly, Carol, you are ridiculous. How did you jump to such a stupid conclusion? Nobody's sick. I'm fine. And nobody's dead. At least, not someone we know."

"So then why the heck did you leave me all those frantic texts?" I demanded. "What was I supposed to think? What's so urgent?"

Typical Nancy, she answered my question with a question of her own. "Where are you? And what are you wearing?"

I looked down at my baggy sweatpants and sandy feet. "If you must know, I'm at Fairport Beach. I just finished a long walk with Jenny, and I'm on my way home to shower and change. I hope you don't want to meet for coffee now, because I look terrible."

"Perfect," Nancy said. "Lori will be thrilled."

"Are you kidding me? What's Lori got to do with this?"

"Honestly, Carol, if you paid more attention to my texts, you'd already know what I'm talking about."

Totally untrue, but I was in no mood to argue with her.

Nancy steamrolled ahead. "We found a property yesterday that Lori just loved. It's a little small, but Lori thinks it'll work perfectly for the Tummy Trimmers program. Not only is the rental price reasonable, it's right in the center of Fairport. Can you guess what I'm talking about?"

"I have no…"

"I can't wait to tell you," Nancy said. "You'll never guess. Lori is going to use the second floor of Maria's Trattoria! Isn't that a fabulous idea?"

"I thought Maria rented that space out for private parties."

"That's what I thought, too," Nancy said. "But it turns out that Maria makes much more money doing off-premise catering than using her own space. She and Lori talked yesterday afternoon and made a deal. Isn't it fabulous?"

"Yeah," I said, "we can overdose on pasta on the first floor, and then work it off on the second floor."

"Huh?" Nancy said, missing my sarcasm completely. Or possibly ignoring it. "So get over to Maria's right away," Nancy ordered. "The photographer is already here. We're waiting for you."

"What in the world are you talking about?"

"We're going to shoot the 'before' pictures for Tummy Trimmers right now."

"But I look terrible," I wailed. "I don't want my picture taken looking like this. I have some pride, you know."

"That's the whole point," Nancy explained. "You need to look terrible in the 'before' photos. So you can look extra fabulous in the 'after' ones. See you soon."

And before I could say another word of protest, she clicked off.

Chapter 12

My goal was to lose 10 pounds this year. Only 15 to go.

I'd never been to Maria's Trattoria when the restaurant was closed. In fact, I never went anywhere near Fairport center, our town's main business district, until at least 10:00, when all the stores and restaurants in the center of town opened for business. Of course, that was also when the area was choked with traffic and the town lots were already full of cars from those early-morning commuters. I know I should make an effort to get errands done earlier every day, but I am the world's greatest procrastinator. Correction: I am the world's greatest procrastinator if there's something on my agenda that I don't want to do. And having my picture taken looking like something the dogs dragged in (we don't have any cats) was right at the top of today's list of things I didn't want to do.

Because it was so early, I found a parking spot right in front of Maria's that I was able to drive straight into, as opposed to struggling to parallel park. I've been known to park my car so far away from my intended destination that I might as well have left it in my driveway if the only convenient parking spot required me to parallel park. Or give up all together and just go home. I had no excuse today, though. Unfortunately.

I checked myself in the rearview mirror. Yuck. I looked terrible, all right. I consoled myself with the thought that a professional photographer could do wonders retouching pictures, and I'd end up looking gorgeous and skinny—let's not forget that part!—when all this was over.

I also had the beginnings of a caffeine-deprived headache, right behind my eyes. I prayed that there would be coffee at the photo shoot. But, why take a chance that there wouldn't be? In a flash, I decided to drive over to the Fairport Diner and pick up coffee for myself, just in case. That'd kill a little more time, and what's a few minutes more when they can't start the photo shoot without the main attraction—me? And while I was at it, maybe I had time to dash home, take a shower, wash my hair, and put on some makeup. *Yes, Carol. Now you're thinking!*

I turned the ignition key and my car roared to life. Right at the same time, Nancy stuck her perfectly made-up face in the open window on the passenger side. "Not so fast, Carol. Where do you think you're going? Everybody's upstairs waiting for you."

Rats. I'd been caught.

"I was just turning off the ignition," I lied, "not turning it on. I'm here as ordered. Let's get this thing over with. And, by the way, why are you outside? You have a very funny look on your face. I haven't seen you look so guilty since we were in high school and you made me take the blame for some stupid stunt you'd pulled. What's going on?"

Nancy looked embarrassed. She yanked open the car door and plunked herself down beside me. "I wanted to talk to you before you went inside," she said. "There's a little bit more to this photo shoot than I realized, and I wanted to warn you in advance. And apologize. And hope you won't hate me for getting you involved in the first place." She took a deep breath, then said, "The photographer wants you to wear a fat suit when he takes your picture, so you'll look even heavier than you really are."

"What?" I squealed. "You're kidding. There's no way I'll do that. I'll be publicly humiliated. I'm outta here."

"I knew you'd be upset about this, Carol," my former BFF said. "And I don't blame you. That's why I wanted to talk to you first. I feel terrible about getting you into this. But Lori promised me your face won't be shown in any of the pictures, so nobody will know it's you. Liam is going to Photoshop in another woman's face in place of yours."

"Liam? Who's Liam?"

Nancy dimpled. "He's the photographer, and he's a real hunk. Wait'll you meet him. He could sell snow to Eskimos."

I laughed. "I haven't heard that expression in years." Then, just because I didn't want Nancy to think I was letting her off the hook so easily, I said, "I still don't want to do this, Nancy. What if something goes wrong? What if word gets out that it's really me in the 'before' picture, and everybody thinks I'm really that fat?"

Nancy crossed her heart and held up her little finger. "Pinky swear, that won't happen."

"Well," I said, weakening a little more.

"So you'll do it!" Nancy squealed. "Oh, thank you so much. Lori is in a position to throw a lot of real estate business my way because she's such a celebrity. I can't afford to let her down." She paused, then said, "And there's a little more I'd better tell you before we go inside. You also have to wear a sweat suit with the Tummy Trimmers logo on it for the pictures. You get to keep the sweat suit."

"I don't mind doing that," I said. "I can always use another sweat suit, especially one that fits me."

"That's the problem, Carol," Nancy said, looking even guiltier than she did before. "It won't fit you. Because you're wearing it over the fat suit, the sweat suit is several sizes too small for you. It's supposed to make you look even heavier." She brightened. "But when you lose the weight, it'll fit you perfectly."

"If that's supposed to make me feel better, it doesn't," I said. "I don't think anything will."

"Oh, pish," Nancy said. "It'll be fun. You'll see. And we'll have a good laugh about it later."

"You've gotten me into some ridiculous situations over the years, but this one tops them all," I grumbled, finally allowing Nancy to lead me into Maria's and up the back stairs to face my fate. This was one close-up that I definitely wasn't ready for.

The next few hours were the most humiliating ones of my entire life (and heaven knows, that's saying something), and I have no intention of sharing any of the details with you. Suffice it to say that most of the time I was wearing a flesh-colored fat suit which Liam kept inflating and deflating until he was finally satisfied with the effect he and Lori were going for. The fat suit was topped by a too-tight purple hoodie and matching purple leggings. Nobody commented on my striking resemblance to Barney of children's television fame. If anyone had dared, I would have decked them, for sure. Throughout the ordeal, I kept my composure and figured the weight must be melting off me because I was sweating like crazy in the darned fat suit. Lori kept gushing at how perfect I looked, and she was *so* grateful that I'd agreed to do this for her. Nancy looked like she was either trying to keep from laughing or crying. Probably both.

When the ordeal was over, Lori gave me a big hug and shoved a piece of paper at me. "My lawyer has asked that you sign this, Carol." I squinted at it and, of course, I couldn't read it because my bifocals were in my purse. Not that I'd admit that to Lori, of course.

"It just clarifies that you've been selected to be the one and only official Tummy Trimmers 'before' model. It will protect you in case anyone else should decide she should have been given the honor instead. Sign here." And like the big dope I am, I did.

While Liam was taking photos of me from every angle, none of them flattering, I realized that there was one good result from this stupid and humiliating photo shoot. It was a perfect excuse for me to dodge today's volunteer stint at the thrift shop.

Chapter 13

When I was young, I let it all hang out. Now that I'm old, it all hangs out, and I can't get it back in.

The next two weeks were a blur of daily walks with Jenny, healthy eating, and more walking for me. Sometimes I took Lucy or Ethel with me, although, because they're dogs, we seemed to spend more time stopping and investigating interesting smells (the dogs' choice, not mine) than walking. Yes, you read that correctly. I actually forced myself to do all the things I should have been doing for the last 20 years. Including portion control for all my meals.

I had an ulterior motive, of course. (I usually do.) There was no way I was going to walk into the very first official Tummy Trimmers meeting in two weeks carrying around any more excess weight than I absolutely had to. I wasn't taking any chances that some smarty pants would figure out that I was the Tummy Trimmers "before" model just by looking at me. I know, that sounds stupid. All my life, I'd wanted to be a model, and now I finally was one, and I wanted to keep it quiet. I remembered that Lori had said something about documenting my weight-loss progress, but maybe she wasn't serious about that. At least, I prayed she wasn't serious.

Jim was impressed with my new-found commitment to a more healthy lifestyle. He didn't even complain when I experimented with foods like tofu and kale. In fact, he was so well-behaved that I suspected that he was secretly going to the Fairport Diner and scarfing down a cheeseburger and fries on a daily basis.

"Explain to me why you have to sign up for the Tummy Trimmers program," he said, pouring so much ketchup on his veggie burger that it looked like it was hemorrhaging. "You're doing great on your own. You haven't looked this good in years. And I say that from first-hand knowledge." He wiggled his eyebrows and winked. "If you get my meaning." Which I definitely did. And proved it by blushing like a high school sophomore.

By the way, in case you were wondering, I still hadn't come clean to my husband about my modeling career with Tummy Trimmers. With any luck at all, I'd never have to.

"Jim, I really need you to support me in this," I said, pushing aside papers that were scattered all over the kitchen table so I could have some room for my own dinner plate. "The Tummy Trimmers program officially launches tomorrow, and I plan to be one of the very first people to sign up. I need to lose at least ten more pounds. Maybe even more. But I know I can't do it all on my own. I need the support of a group of people who all have the same goal, to lose weight and get healthy. I know if I don't join, I'll lose whatever incentive I have and go back to my old eating habits. Don't you understand?"

Jim nodded. "I understand that you want to be healthier, and I think that's great. But one thing I don't understand is why you've been killing yourself to lose a few pounds before the program even starts."

"It's like cleaning up the house before the cleaning woman comes," I said to my husband. I could tell I was confusing him even more. "It's a female thing," I said. "I don't expect you to understand. And besides," I continued, "the founder of Tummy Trimmers is Lori Todesco. Do you remember her from the *New England Rock and Roll Dance Party* television show, back when we were in high school? We all thought she was the coolest person ever. She's here in town. Nancy and I met her a few weeks ago and we both decided to sign up for the program."

"Lori Todesco was at the Fairport Business Association breakfast meeting last week, glad-handing everyone in sight and passing out Tummy Trimmers flyers," Jim said. "I took one, but I threw it away. It had a picture of an extremely overweight woman on the front. Thank God you never let yourself go that much."

If you only knew. I didn't really say that, of course.

Realizing his gaffe, Jim immediately tried to dig his way out of the hole he'd fallen into. "I don't mean you've let yourself go, honey. You've always been gorgeous to me. You know that."

I gave him an icy smile. "You always say the sweetest things." I glanced at the pile of papers that was threatening to topple over onto my plate. "And I don't understand why in the world you insist on using the kitchen table as a desk, when you have an office and a desk of your own." I spied a bright pink Post-it note with my name written on it and grabbed it. "What the heck is this? What does 'CSR.AJ' mean?"

Jim scowled, peered at the note, then said, "It's perfectly clear. It says 'Call Sister Rose and…'" His voice trailed off. "Something that begins with 'A.'"

OMG. I had completely forgotten to check in with Sister Rose and apologize for missing my volunteer stint. Nor had I asked her what happened about the cash Jenny'd found in the pocket of the blue dress. All that walking and healthy food must promote memory loss. I'd probably never get those white Lilly jeans back now.

"When did you take this message?" I demanded.

"I don't remember exactly," Jim confessed. "I'm sorry. I hope it wasn't too important."

"So do I," I said. "I'll bet she's angry at me for not returning her call. Just like she used to be angry with me for not turning in my English homework on time. Or not polishing my saddle shoes." I shivered at the memory.

"You can blame me," Jim said. "After all, it was my fault. I should have told you when she called. I know how Sister Rose can still intimidate you, even after all these years."

I would have argued with Jim about his use of the word "intimidate," except that he was right, darn it. And how many times had I straightened that pile of papers on the kitchen table in the last couple of weeks? At least a hundred. Maybe my subconscious mind (such as it is) had deliberately ignored that piece of paper.

I chose to focus on Jim's apology and the magic words, "It was my fault." I gave him a peck on the cheek and said, "I forgive you, Jim. But now I've got to return her phone call."

"Why don't you text her instead?" Jim suggested.

"That's a great idea," I exclaimed. "Sister Rose can't yell at me if she has to type a response on her cell phone. Although she'll probably answer in all capital letters."

"You may also see her tomorrow at Tummy Trimmers," Jim added. "Sister Rose was at the Fairport Business Association meeting. We sat together. She took a coupon, too."

"Coupon? What coupon?"

"Oh, I guess I didn't tell you about that part," Jim said. "The flyer that Lori whatshername was passing out included a coupon for one free Tummy Trimmers meeting. Maybe I should go with you tomorrow. What do you think? My tummy could use a little trimming, too. And you're always saying we don't do enough things together. The more I think about it, I think that's a brilliant idea."

That's all you need, Carol. Jim shadowing you at Tummy Trimmers and telling you what you're doing wrong, the way he shadows your every move when he's home. And what if Lori introduces you publicly as the Tummy Trimmers "before" model? She said you wouldn't be identified, but she's already passing out flyers with your picture on it without your knowledge.

I felt my stomach clench, and not from hunger pains, either. I searched my brain for a fool-proof way to squelch Jim's so-called brilliant idea asap, without hurting his feelings. And then I had a brilliant idea of my own. "You might want to check the restrictions and terms, Jim," I said. "The coupon Lori gave out at the meeting may be for an initial free visit, but contingent on your signing onto the program as a paying client. Nancy and I are getting a special deal to join, because Nancy brokered a deal with Maria Lesco for Lori to rent the second floor of the Trattoria for the program. Lori was so grateful for Nancy's help that she waived the regular Tummy Trimmers fees, just for us." Notice that I left out the part about my being the official role model for Tummy Trimmers. Jim often has trouble dealing with the whole truth about my antics, and I feel it is my duty as a loving wife to shield him from the facts as much as possible.

I held my breath while Jim processed this information. As much as he loves coupons and rarely passes one up (even if it's for something we'll never use), he hates spending unnecessary bucks on anything. And, I mean, *anything.*

"You're probably right, Carol. But I might go tomorrow anyway, just to check it out. I'll see how I feel in the morning."

Rats. This was the first time that my coupon strategy had failed me. And I still had Sister Rose to deal with before I went to bed. I checked the time—10:00. It was probably too late to text her. But I knew that if I didn't respond tonight, I'd never sleep. Or, even worse, she'd find a way to show up in my dreams.

What the heck. I composed a "mea culpa" text explaining that I'd been dealing with a family emergency (not a lie, since being photographed in a fat suit certainly was an emergency as far as I was concerned), which was why I hadn't been in touch sooner. I did *not* blame Jim, even though he had failed to give me her phone message for heaven knows how long. (I hope I get points for that.) I didn't have the nerve to ask her about the wad of cash we'd found in the pocket of Jenny's dress, either. (More points for me, since I was dying to know.) I pressed Send, and went to bed with a clear conscience. For once.

Chapter 14

Exercise? I thought you said "accessorize."

I decided to walk to the grand opening of Tummy Trimmers the next day, rather than struggle to find a parking spot. And, boy, was I glad I did. I felt sorry for the poor people who planned to enjoy a nice lunch at Maria's Trattoria that day, because there was no way that was going to happen unless Maria was offering valet car parking to her customers. I wondered if she was regretting renting her second floor space for the weight-loss program.

I've never been to a Hollywood movie premiere, but I doubted it was more glamorous than the grand opening of Tummy Trimmers. The sidewalk in front of the building was covered with a red carpet, the Fairport High School marching band was playing a medley of songs they usually reserved for parades, and my least favorite Fairport police detective, Paul Wheeler, had drawn the unlucky assignment of keeping both car and pedestrian traffic flowing. I have to admit I took a certain amount of satisfaction in seeing my personal nemesis relegated to such a lowly role.

There was a huge sandwich board sign outside the restaurant: "Maria's Trattoria Welcomes Tummy Trimmers to Fairport. Twenty percent off menu today only. Come in and see what all the excitement is about!"

Well, that answered one of my questions right away. It looked like Maria Lesco was smart enough to use the weight-loss program as a way to promote her restaurant. I wondered if she'd also tweaked the menu to add more healthy choices. I just hoped she hadn't taken off some of her delicious pasta dishes, like lasagna or vodka rigatoni. My mouth watered just thinking about them.

Onward, Carol.

I felt a tap on my shoulder and turned to see Jenny standing behind me. "Isn't this something?" she said, giving me a quick kiss. "Fairport will never be the same. It's like a circus."

I grinned. "You got that right. I feel sorry for Paul, getting stuck with traffic control. How'd he draw that? And where's Mark?"

"There's a shortage of police right now because of budget reductions," Jenny said, her face looking serious. "It's all hands on deck doing whatever is needed to protect the community until the whole thing gets straightened out. A few of the staff have been temporarily furloughed to save money. But don't worry," she said, seeing the concerned look on my face, "Mark's job is secure and there are enough Fairport police to keep us all safe. There'll be no obvious disruption of services.

"Now," she said, grabbing my arm, "Tummy Trimmers is calling. Let's go."

"Good thing Maria has a back entrance so we don't have to go through the restaurant to get to the second floor," I said, taking a quick peek inside the Trattoria. "The place is filled with customers." I noted that a Stairlift had been installed on the railing leading to the second floor for would-be Tummy Trimmers who might have extra challenges. Fortunately, although I have the usual amount of aches and pains associated with the aging process, I can still make the climb to the second floor without any assistance. It just takes me longer than it used to.

"What's that music I hear?" Jenny asked as we started up the stairs. "It doesn't sound like the Fairport High School band."

"I haven't heard that song in years," I said, laughing. "It's *Tighten Up*. I don't remember who sang it, but it was very popular back in the late Sixties. I guess Lori's using it to get people in the right frame of mind."

"I'm impressed," Jenny said. "What a perfect song for Tummy Trimmers." She gave me a mischievous grin. "I wonder if Lori will have you dance to it today. After all, you are the official 'before' model for the program."

Thank goodness Jim had decided not to come with me today, because I continued to worry about what was in those papers I'd signed. What if I'd given written permission for things I didn't want to do? Well, if I had, there was nothing I could do about it right now. So I squared my shoulders and prepared myself for battle. Although I did make Jenny walk inside the Tummy Trimmers meeting ahead of me. Just in case.

I hardly recognized the second floor of Maria's Trattoria. The place had been totally transformed, and the air was perfumed with the smell of fresh paint. Rows of folding chairs were already filled with Fairport citizens, mostly women of a certain age, giggling like school girls. I was betting many of them were lured here by the chance to meet the formerly famous Lori Todesco of *New England Rock and Roll Dance Party*.

"Carol, there you are," said Lori, scowling as she headed toward us. Uh oh. I could tell from the look on her face that I was already in trouble. "I thought you'd be here earlier, so you could circulate and meet some prospective clients." She stepped back and gave me an apprising look. "What's happened to you? You look different than the last time I saw you. Have you already lost some weight?"

I resisted reminding Lori that the last time she'd seen me, I was wearing an inflatable fat suit. "Just a few pounds," I said proudly. "I've been eating healthier and walking every day with my daughter, Jenny," I said, turning to introduce her to the Tummy-Trimmer-in-Chief.

"You weren't supposed to lose *any* weight until Tummy Trimmers started," Lori hissed in my ear. "You may have ruined everything."

This was a first for me. I'd never been called out for losing weight before. I started to giggle, something that happens when I'm nervous. Of course, that only made Lori angrier.

OMG, you've done it now, Carol. Lori's going to make you put on the fat suit again and stand up in front of everyone and humiliate yourself.

"It's not funny, Carol. I have a lot riding on the success of Tummy Trimmers. A hefty financial investment, my reputation, everything that's important to me. How can I introduce you as my 'before' model now?"

Introduce? Did Lori say "introduce"? I clamped my lips together in an effort to get myself under control. "I had no idea you were planning on introducing me today, Lori," I said, my voice quivering. "You never told me that."

"It's all spelled out in your contract," Lori countered. "The one you signed the day of the photo shoot."

"Contract? I signed a contract? That's not what you called it when you waved that piece of paper under my nose and told me to sign. What else did I agree to?"

Lori flashed a thousand-watt smile and said, "Now, Carol, there's nothing for you to worry about. When you get home, take some time to go over your copy of the contract and you'll understand everything."

You should have done that before you signed the darn thing, stupid.

"If you're going to introduce Mom today, why not say she recently started the program under your personal guidance?" Jenny suggested. "You could call her the first Fairport Tummy Trimmers success story. Or something like that."

Lori thought for a minute, smiled, then said, "That may work. But I have an even better idea." And she scurried away to charm more potential clients.

"Honestly, Jenny, I had no idea Lori was going to introduce me today. She never said a word about it when I was here having my picture taken. And she never gave me a copy of this so-called contract, either. She just waved a piece of paper at me and told me to sign, to protect myself in case some other woman said that she should be the program's 'before' model instead of me."

Jenny steered me toward the third row. "Let's sit and see if we can make some sense of out this."

I waved at Nancy, who was threading her way through the crowd, heading in our direction. "I'm sure Nancy remembers what happened. She was there, too."

"How's my favorite mother-to-be?" Nancy asked, giving Jenny a big hug.

"I'm doing well, Nancy." Jenny patted her tummy. "Baby Anderson and I both are."

Nancy turned her laser vision onto me. "You look different, Carol. What have you been up to?"

Before I had a chance to respond, a woman wearing stylish black yoga pants and a pink and black tee shirt tapped me on the shoulder. "Excuse me, but may I sit with you?" she asked. "It looks like the other chairs are already taken."

"Of course," I said, "but I hope you don't mind climbing over us." I know what you're thinking. I should have suggested we all move over one seat to make it easier for this complete stranger to sit down. But what if Lori did call on me to come up and say a few words about the miracle of Tummy Trimmers? I didn't want to risk tripping over people on my way to a brief moment in the spotlight. And what the heck would I say?

"I'm embarrassed to admit this," the woman said, still standing, "but I'm a teensy bit claustrophobic. Do you mind if I take the end seat?" What else could I do (without being totally rude, something I *never* am, even when provoked, like right now), except move into the center of our row? I hope you're all proud of me, especially those of you who remember that I suffer from claustrophobia myself. My hands were already clammy, and I realized I was a nervous wreck about what could happen next. Although I wasn't sure if I wanted to be pointed out, a part of me (a large part, now that I thought more about it) wanted some public recognition.

"Good morning, Fairport," Lori said, raising her voice to be heard above the voices of the crowd. "I'm excited to see all of you here. So, who wants to look and feel better? Let me hear you." And she cupped her hand to her ear.

People looked at each other nervously, then a brave few answered, "I do."

"I can't hear you," Lori said. "Speak louder. I asked who wants to look and feel better?" Again, she cupped her hand to her ear, and more people spoke up. But Lori still wasn't satisfied with the response she was getting. I figured she wouldn't be until she had every single person in the room committed to signing on to Tummy Trimmers.

"Hmm," she said. "Let me put this another way. Is there anybody here who *doesn't* want to look and feel better? If you do, please stand up." Of course, nobody did.

"All right, so you want to change your life," Lori said. "And you want to recapture the energy and vitality that you had when you were younger. I'm here to help you do it. Are you with me?"

This time, the crowd roared its approval, and I felt like I was at either a rock and roll concert or a religious revival meeting.

"Take a look at this picture," Lori continued, holding a huge poster of me in my fat suit (without my face, thank God) above her head so everyone could see it clearly. "Do you know who this is?" I squirmed in my seat. This was my worst nightmare come true. Although, I certainly looked a heck of a lot better now than I did when that picture was taken.

"You'll never guess," Lori went on. "It's me! Yes, it's me before

I came up with the Tummy Trimmers program. I'm the very first client, and its first success story!" She strutted like a model so everyone could admire her "new" toned body. I was tempted to blow my cover, stand up, and call her out for telling what amounted to a big fat lie. Nancy shot me a look, and I could tell she knew what I was thinking. And she was right.

"Then, what are we waiting for?" Lori asked. "Let's get started! Anyone who signs up today will receive fifty percent off their first month of membership. And to be sure that you start to eat healthy right away, I'm including a delicious cranberry and almond smoothie recipe. I'm thrilled that Tummy Trimmers is on the second floor of Fairport's wonderful restaurant, Maria's Trattoria. In honor of our new collaboration, Maria Lesco is adding several delicious new dishes to her restaurant menu that have been specially designed for the Tummy Trimmers program. I hope you'll all patronize her restaurant and check them out."

Wow. It looked like Lori and Maria were going into business together. Who knew? From the surprised look on Nancy's face, she certainly didn't. I swiveled in my seat and saw Maria standing at the back of the room with a smile on her face.

"Tummy Trimmers sounds great, Mom," Jenny said, standing up and stretching. "I'm going to get in line and at least pick up a flyer. I don't want to sign up until I check with my obstetrician, just to be on the safe side. I hope I can get a sample smoothie, though. Your grandchild-to-be and I are both hungry."

There were two people behind the registration table, struggling to handle the crowd who couldn't wait to put their bodies—and credit cards—into Lori's hands. I immediately recognized one as Liam O'Donnell, the photographer who'd taken those humiliating pictures of me. I noted that when Lori passed behind the registration table to shake hands with her adoring public, she casually caressed his neck on her way by. Hmm. Interesting.

"That Lori certainly is something," the woman in the yoga pants commented as she stood to let Jenny pass her. "Are you and your daughter going to sign up for Tummy Trimmers?"

"You surprise me," I said. "How did you know that Jenny is my daughter?"

"I've seen you walking on the beach together," she said with a smile. "I guess you didn't recognize me without my sunglasses. And please, accept my apology for not speaking to you on the beach.

I get into my own zone, or whatever it is that the kids call it, and stay that way all through my walk. I'm really into meditation. I'm Pat Mathews, by the way."

"Hello, Pat," I said, slightly embarrassed. After all, she'd recognized me, and I had no idea who she was. "I'm Carol Andrews. It's very nice to finally meet you."

There was a discreet cough behind me, and I knew it was Nancy. She hates to be left out of any conversation. "And this is my best friend, Nancy Green," I said, as Nancy grabbed Pat's hand. "I'm with Dream Homes Realty," she said. "If you're looking for any local property to buy, I'd be glad to be of assistance."

"Nancy," I said, and shot her a dirty look. "You're embarrassing me. We've just met Pat, after all. Save the real estate talk for another time, okay?"

Pat laughed. "No worries," she said. "And, to tell the truth, I'm not sure how long I'll be in Fairport. My plans are pretty flexible."

"Well, now that we've said hello, I hope we get to know each other better," I said. "Are you going to join Tummy Trimmers?"

"Definitely," Pat said. "In fact, that's one reason why I came to Fairport. I heard about Tummy Trimmers starting here. Those smoothies sound delicious. It looks like the crowd is thinning out a little." She laughed. "I guess I just made a joke. Anyway, I'm going to get in the registration line now. See you on the beach." And with a friendly wave, she was swallowed up in the crowd.

Chapter 15

I thought growing old would take longer.

"This is the hardest thing I've ever done in my whole life," I moaned. "I've been trying to do this for two whole weeks and I still can't."

"Shhh," Nancy hissed. "You're supposed to be meditating. That means no talking."

I shot her a dirty look and whispered, "That's exactly what I mean."

"Even you can keep quiet for a few minutes, Carol. And I don't know why you're complaining so much. You're not paying anything to participate in Tummy Trimmers, but you have to do every program component. That includes meditation and exercise. Think beautiful thoughts. Imagine you're walking on Fairport Beach." Nancy angled her body away from me just enough that it was clear she was fed up with listening to my complaints.

A woman sitting cross-legged in front of me turned around and gave me an encouraging smile. It was Gloria, the new volunteer at Sally's Closet. "Don't be discouraged," she whispered. "It takes some time to get into this."

"Thanks for the moral support," I whispered back. "And I haven't forgotten about having coffee together."

Come up with a date for coffee and get it over with, Carol. Gloria needs a friend. And having coffee together was your idea. Maybe, by this time, she's already met a few more people and you won't end up joined at the hip.

I sighed and closed my eyes. I hate myself when I let somebody down. I listened for Lori's voice, determined to give this meditation thing the old college try. My eyes immediately snapped open. Destiny, Sister Rose's friend, was leading the group meditation, not Lori. And she was doing a great job.

"Put your mind into a calm, relaxed state so you'll be open to meditating," Destiny said in a soothing voice. "Close your eyes and chant your mantra softly. Ummmmm."

I tried to chant. I really did. But "ummmmm" sounded too much like "yummmmmm," which only reminded me of how hungry I was. I ordered myself to focus on something besides food. For once.

"Listen to your breath," Destiny continued. "In. Out. Inhale. Exhale. Put your worries into a bubble and let it float into the universe. Inhale. Exhale. Breathe in. Breathe out. In, out. In, out."

The next thing I remember, I heard Destiny say, "That was very good, class. The meditation lasted almost fifteen minutes. Now, allow yourself to slowly open your eyes and come back to the world. But always be conscious of your breath. Inhale. Exhale. In. Out."

Wow. I'd actually done it. I didn't remember where I'd gone to, but I definitely went somewhere. Jim would be so surprised when I told him. And amazed that I'd remained quiet for such a long time. I opened my eyes slowly and saw Nancy grinning at me. "I told you that you could do it," she said like a proud mommy. "Destiny is a fabulous leader, isn't she?"

"She must be," I said, "if she got me to meditate."

Gloria flashed me a "V" for victory sign, which I returned. "Thanks for the encouragement," I mouthed, and she nodded.

She leaned back and whispered, "Anybody who can take on Sister Rose can do anything." That made me giggle. I couldn't help myself. Gloria gave me a friendly wave and headed for the exit.

"Who was that?" Nancy asked. She hates to miss anything, and the idea that I knew someone that she didn't clearly annoyed her.

"Someone I met at the thrift shop," I said. "She's a new volunteer there, and new in Fairport, too. She and I are going to have coffee together sometime."

I glanced at Pat Mathews, sitting on her meditation mat to my left, still into what she called her "zone." "Pat told me that she goes to a meditation class several times a week," I said. "Maybe I should, too." Nancy just rolled her eyes. She knows I'd never do that.

SUSAN SANTANGELO

Ignoring Nancy, I rolled over on my knees and pushed myself up to a standing position (with some difficulty). Pat had changed position, and part of her body was now leaning on my own mat, just when I was ready to roll it up and bring it home.

"Pat's still meditating," I said to Nancy. "It's amazing she can do it for such a long time. I don't want to disturb her, but I want my mat. What should I do?"

"Pat's always the last one to come out of a meditative state," Nancy said. "But she's taking much longer than usual today." She turned and beckoned to Destiny, who was deep in conversation with another member of our group. "Destiny, when you have a sec, we'd like to talk to you."

Destiny held up her index finger. "Be right with you," she said. As she headed in our direction, she called back over her shoulder, "Try to meditate for at least five minutes a day until our next class. Okay?" The student nodded. "I'll do my best. You're right. I have to make time for myself."

"You can do it," Destiny said, then turned her attention to us. "Do you need some extra help with meditation, Carol? It's all part of Tummy Trimmers' unique approach to losing weight. Everything begins in the mind," she said, tapping her forehead for emphasis. "If you think you can do it, you can."

"I did pretty well today," I said, smarting a little from being lectured by a girl who was younger than my own daughter.

"I'm glad you enjoyed the class," Destiny said, beaming at me. "And I hope that you'll come back for another one later this week. Practice makes perfect."

Nancy interrupted. "I'm a little worried about Pat Mathews," she said. "It's been at least ten minutes since you dismissed us, and she still hasn't opened her eyes."

Destiny smiled. "I wouldn't worry about her. She's been practicing meditation for so long that she can remain in a deep state for extended periods of time. I'm sure she's fine."

"But she's always ready to leave when we are," I insisted. "We usually walk out together. I'd feel better if you'd check on her. Please."

"Pat goes to meditation classes all the time, Carol," Destiny said, clearly annoyed. "You've only come a few times." She didn't add, "So you don't know what you're talking about." But it was pretty obvious that's what she meant.

98

"I also need my meditation mat back," I said. "Unfortunately, Pat's now leaning on part of it."

"She may not be happy we disturbed her," Destiny insisted.

By this time, I was getting pretty fed up with Destiny. "Never mind. I'll do it myself. After all, it's my mat she's sitting on." And I didn't care if I sounded snippy, either.

I walked across the now quiet room and squatted down next to Pat. "Excuse me," I whispered. "I'm so sorry about disturbing you. But I need my meditation mat. You're leaning on part of it."

There was no response. None.

I plopped my keester down on the floor next to the meditating woman. "Can you hear me?" I asked a little louder. This was getting ridiculous. I gave my mat a gentle tug. And that was all it took for Pat to finally move. In fact, she fell over onto my lap and stayed there. OMG!

I screamed and burst into tears. I could hear Nancy's voice from what seemed like a thousand miles away but was really only across the room. "We need an ambulance!" she shouted into her cell phone. "A woman has collapsed. She may be dead." She rattled off the address of Maria's Trattoria, adding that Tummy Trimmers was on the second floor and to use the rear entrance.

"I have to find Lori right away," Destiny said, standing over Pat and me and looking as shocked and sick as I felt. "I don't know what I'm supposed to do. She never told me anything like this could happen." I could tell she couldn't wait to get out of there. Not that I blamed her. Truthfully, I wanted to run away with her. All I could think about was getting Pat's motionless body off me right away. And before you criticize me, imagine a possibly dead person falling onto you and see how you respond.

"I know this is terrible for you," Nancy said, now squatting beside me and Pat, "but can you be still for a few seconds so I can take a few pictures?" She held up her cell phone and clicked away a few times.

"What did you do that for?" I yelled. "You're wasting time. Help me up. I can't stand her lying on me anymore."

"Since we don't know anything about what happened to Pat, I figured it would be smart to document exactly how she fell," Nancy said. "I learned that from watching a few television crime programs." I was torn between admiration for Nancy's quick thinking and a desire to smack her for wasting time snapping pictures when she should have been helping me up.

"I hope you're finished," I said, "because I've got to stand up. I'll try to do it gently, so as not to disturb Pat's position." I slid myself backward and tried not to look down at Pat. I was afraid I'd lose control again.

"I wish Mary Alice was here," Nancy said, squatting down and holding Pat's head as carefully as she could so I could roll over onto my knees and stand. "Wait a minute," she said. "Pat's breathing, Carol. She's still alive." She put her ear down onto Pat's chest. "There's a very faint heartbeat, but she's still with us. Thank God. Now if the EMTs would just get here, she might have a chance."

I took one of Pat's hands and started to massage it. It was icy cold. "Please, Pat," I said, "stay with us. Help is on the way."

Pat's eyes fluttered open, and she seemed to have trouble focusing. She tried to sit up and failed. "So sleepy," she whispered. Then her body jerked convulsively, like she was having some sort of a spasm. And her skin was now turning pink, almost like a bad sunburn.

In the distance, I heard the wail of a siren. At last. Then the emergency personnel stormed into the room. Nancy and I stepped aside and let them do their work. They bundled Pat onto a stretcher and wheeled her out to the waiting ambulance.

"It's too bad we can't go into a meditative state right now," I said. "After all this, I could use the rest. Just seeing how horrible Pat looked...." My voice trailed off.

"I'm going to text Mary Alice," Nancy said. "I don't know if she's working at the hospital today or not, but maybe she can find out about Pat's condition. With these patient confidentiality laws, nobody will tell either of us anything. I just hope she can make some sense out of my text." She pressed Send, then said, "Come on, let's get the heck out of here. Let Destiny and Lori deal with Maria Lesco. I hope there aren't liability issues for Maria, because Pat collapsed on Trattoria property, even though it is leased to Tummy Trimmers."

"I never thought about that angle," I said.

"That's because I'm a Realtor and you're not," Nancy said. She eyed me critically. "Now what's wrong? Why are you holding up your right foot? You look weird."

"I stepped in something sticky," I snapped back. "And these sneakers are brand new. My mat is sticky, too."

"Roll the mat inside out so you won't get anything on you," Nancy advised. "Let's just get out of here. You can clean everything when you get home." She speed-walked toward the door, then stopped when she realized I wasn't behind her. "What are you doing, Carol?"

"I can't stand to leave the room like this," I said, squatting down on my knees and using a towel someone had left behind to clean up the sticky floor. "I think it's disrespectful to Pat. People will think she was messy."

Nancy gave me a critical eye roll. "What people? That makes absolutely no sense, even for you."

"When I die, I want it to be at home, and everything around me to be neat," I said. "I don't want anybody talking about how messy I was after I'm dead."

"You're completely nutso," Nancy said. "But I promise that, if you go first, I'll hire a cleaning crew to make your house spotless as soon as you die."

"There, that's a little better," I said, tossing the towel into the trash. "I hope whoever left that towel behind wasn't expecting to get it back. The cleaning crew can take care of the rest. Let's go."

"Finally," Nancy said. "It's a beautiful day. Maybe the sunshine will cheer us up."

Ping. I squinted at my phone and saw I had a text from Mary Alice.

Your friend died on the way to the hospital. So sorry. Sending hugs.

Chapter 16

I'm really in favor of exercise, just as long as somebody else does it.

"You still look shaken, Carol. Are you going to be okay?" Nancy asked. "I feel guilty about deserting you like this, but I need to dash home and change. I'm meeting with an out-of-town buyer to show that property on Fairport Beach Road that's been on the market for ages. Of course, it would have sold right away if the seller had priced the property more realistically. It's in such a great location, and the view is fabulous. Plus, it's walking distance to the beach. There's been a tenant in the house for the past few months."

"You're lucky that you have some work to focus on," I said. "I'm not sure what I'll do for the rest of the day. I don't really feel like going home yet. I feel so bad about Pat. And having her fall on me like that." I made a face. "I'll never forget it. What if I could have done something to help her? I'll never forgive myself."

"Carol, this is so typical of you," Nancy said. "Stop blaming yourself for what happened. For all we know, Pat had a medical condition that nobody knew about and that's why she collapsed. It's not your fault."

"But all I could think of was getting her off me instead of trying to help her," I wailed. "That was so selfish. I was only thinking of myself."

"For Pete's sake, Carol, this is really over the top, even for you," Nancy said with more than a touch of impatience. She checked her watch. "I've gotta go. Maybe you should stop by a church and say a prayer for Pat. That might make you feel better. Remember what Sister Rose always told us: Prayer makes everything better." She gave me a quick kiss on the cheek. "I'll call you later." And, pfft, off she went.

I checked my own watch. Was it only 10:00? It felt like a whole day had passed. My cell phone buzzed. At least someone wanted to talk to me. I rummaged around in my bag and pulled it out. There was a text from Jim.

Sister Rose trying to reach you. Says it's urgent. Wants to see you right away.

Yikes. That was all I needed. What a horrible day this was turning out to be. I hoped I wasn't going to be on the receiving end of one of Sister Rose's lectures. But I knew where my next stop had to be—the thrift shop. Then I had another thought. Maybe, just maybe, she was going to surprise me with my pair of white Lilly Pulitzer jeans.

That wouldn't be urgent to Sister Rose, you doofus. Finding those is only urgent to you. I had a brief picture of Sister Rose cavorting around Fairport in white jeans with pink whales embroidered on them. And I kept that ridiculous image front and center in my mind while I made the drive to Sally's Closet. Slowly.

"Hello," I called out. "Is anybody here? Sister Rose?"

A volunteer wearing the thrift shop's trademark purple apron magically appeared from behind a rack of clothing. "Sorry I wasn't on duty at the cashier desk when you came in," she said. "I was trying to organize the clothing racks. Not that anything stays neat around here for long. But if you know Sister Rose, you know that she's very fussy about how things are displayed in the shop."

"I know Sister Rose very well," I said, laughing. "She was my English teacher at Mount Saint Francis Academy about a million years ago. She used to strike terror into me and all my friends way back then. And things haven't changed very much now, either."

"Oh, you're a Mountie girl, too!" the volunteer exclaimed. "What year did you graduate? I'm Betsy Mulcahy, by the way. Class of 1985. I was in the last graduating class before the school closed."

There was no way that I was going to admit to Betsy that I graduated several years ahead of her. And it's no business of yours how many years that was, either.

"It's always nice to meet another Mountie, Betsy," I said. "But I'm kind of in a hurry. Is Sister Rose here? She called and said she wanted to see me. She said it was urgent."

Betsy frowned. "She's in the back room with her niece. There seems to be some kind of family emergency, and she asked me not to disturb them. The niece was very upset."

"Niece? Sister Rose has a niece?" I asked. I was dumbfounded. "I never knew she had any family."

"Well, I didn't come into the world all by myself, Carol," a familiar voice said. "Even I don't have that kind of power." Betsy immediately scurried away and busied herself folding clothes as far away from Sister Rose as possible.

I snapped to attention. Then, I did a double-take. Sister Rose had another person with her. It was Destiny.

Chapter 17

Water is essential to life, because without it,
you can't make coffee.

I was still trying to come to terms with Sister Rose and Destiny's family connection without making one of my usual snappy comments when I heard her say, "Now, Destiny, I know you've had a terrible experience, but no one can hold you responsible for what happened today at Tummy Trimmers. I'm sure even Carol will agree with me about that. Am I right, Carol?"

I nodded like a bobblehead doll. "Of course you're right, Sister." *You always are. And even if you're wrong, you never admit it.*

I didn't say that last part, of course.

Sister Rose frowned. "Although I must say that it's quite remarkable to me that, according to Destiny, you were also present today when this terrible incident occurred, Carol. Tragedy seems to follow you around like a magnet. Why do you think that is?" And she fastened her laser vision onto me, making me squirm. Holy cow. Did Sister Rose think Pat Mathews collapsed just because I happened to be there, too? Talk about being unfair!

Not giving me a chance to defend myself, Sister Rose gave Destiny a hug. "Now, my advice to you is to hurry back to your job and have a long talk with your boss. I'm sure your job is secure. And I'm also sure that the woman who collapsed will recover completely. It was probably just a brief fainting spell. I'm told that strenuous exercise can do that to a person."

"But there was no strenuous exercise today," Destiny said. "I was leading a meditation class."

"I don't know much about the Tummy Trimmers program," Sister Rose answered with a disapproving sniff. "My daily meditation consists of conversations with the Lord. I don't need to be in a group setting to do that. Now, run along, dear, and don't worry. I'll call you later to check on you."

Looking unconvinced but calmer, Destiny nodded. "I'm sure you're right. Thank you for being there for me."

"Any time, Destiny. You know I'm always here for you." Sister Rose patted Destiny's cheek and repeated, "We'll talk later."

The good sister waited until the thrift shop door had closed behind Destiny, then said, "Betsy, will you be all right here by yourself for a few more minutes? I need to talk to Carol privately."

"Yes, Sister," Betsy said, exchanging a sympathetic glance with me. She obviously remembered from our high school days that a private chat with Sister Rose usually meant the other person was in Big Trouble. "I'll be fine."

"Use the buzzer to call me if necessary," Sister Rose added. She gestured around the thrift shop. "I've noticed that the clothes on these racks look very messy. If there are no customers in the shop, you can use the time to straighten them out."

Betsy flushed. "Of course, Sister. Right away."

I returned her sympathetic glance with one of my own, since Betsy was already doing that very thing, and followed Sister Rose into the back room. "We're short-staffed again today, as you can see, Carol." Left unspoken were the words, "And you were supposed to come in and help out recently, but didn't show up. I haven't forgotten about that." I still heard those words, even if Sister Rose didn't say them aloud.

Don't let her intimidate you. She's not your teacher any more. You're both adults, and you're friends, too. Sort of. Take over the conversation yourself, before she does. Make her apologize for saying such unfair things to you.

Of course, I just opened my mouth when Sister immediately switched gears on me, something she's perfected over the years which she used to keep hundreds of Mount Saint Francis students off balance. "I owe you an apology, Carol, for being so hard on you in front of Destiny. I'm sorry."

Say what? I thought I had misheard. But if this was a bona fide apology, I was going to take full advantage of the situation.

"I'm not exactly sure what you mean," I said. "What in particular are you apologizing for? Unfairly suggesting that the accident at Tummy Trimmers was due to the fact that I was there? That it was my fault that another woman in the meditation class collapsed? Is that it? Is that why you wanted to see me so urgently today? To ream me out in front of Destiny, so she'd feel better?" I paused to take a deep breath. But I wasn't finished with the good sister. Not by a long shot.

"And, by the way, Sister Rose, the woman who collapsed at the meditation class today had a name. It was Pat Mathews. She was a friend of mine. She collapsed on top of me. It was a terrible experience, one I'll have nightmares about for a long time. And she died on the way to the hospital. I suppose you're going to blame me for that, too."

Enough, Carol. Don't say any more things that you'll probably regret later.

Sister Rose made the Sign of the Cross and bent her head in prayer for a moment. "I deserved that, Carol," she finally said. "All the things you said. And I'm so sorry that poor woman died. God rest her soul. I've always been overprotective of Destiny. I had to be. But I was wrong to use you this way. I hope you can forgive me."

I let the silence build between us, hoping she'd tell me more.

"Destiny is my younger sister, Violet's, daughter," Sister Rose finally said. "Our mother loved flowers, and she named us after two of her favorites. Violet always was the wild one, and Destiny had an unconventional upbringing, to put it mildly. And then there was the other trouble." Sister clamped her lips shut. "But I'm not going to talk about that. It's all over and done with now. Destiny finally had something positive in her life, and then this had to happen."

The nosy part of me (my dominant side) was dying to find out more about Sister Rose's family. But I could tell by the expression on her face that I wasn't going to get anywhere by peppering her with any more questions right now. Besides, I was still angry about the way she had treated me in front of Destiny, even though she had apologized. I wasn't letting her off the hook that easily. Especially since it was probably a once-in-a-lifetime occurrence.

"I understand from Jim that you've been trying to reach me," I said, hoping she took note of my frosty tone of voice, so like her own. I was darned if I was going to apologize for taking so long to get back to her.

"Oh, yes," Sister Rose said, looking a little flustered. A good look for her. "But when I called you this morning, I had no idea about what had just happened at Tummy Trimmers. It was an unfortunate coincidence, but I can certainly see why you might have trouble believing that. I need your advice about an entirely different matter. There's no one else I can talk to except you."

Well, this was an unusual turn of events. Sister Rose needed my help. Too bad Nancy, Mary Alice, and especially Claire, weren't here to witness it. They'd never believe it.

"You know that I don't often ask people for advice. I prefer to give it," Sister Rose said. That admission made me smile a little, and I bit back the sarcastic comment that immediately flashed into my mind. I hope you're all proud of me.

"But in this case, I really don't know what to do," Sister continued. "I thought maybe you'd have a suggestion." She pulled a man's tuxedo off a clothing rack and handed it to me. "This came in as part of a donation yesterday."

"I don't understand," I said. "Are you're asking me if Jim needs a tuxedo? Because he doesn't. The days of black tie events are over for us."

"No, Carol. That's not it. Check the inside breast pocket. Reach way down to the bottom." I put my hand deep inside, as instructed. And pulled out a wad of cash.

"Holy cow!" I said. "How much is here?"

"I counted it myself twice after I found it," Sister said. "There's over two thousand dollars here. Two thousand four hundred and twelve dollars, to be exact."

"Holy cow," I repeated.

"Exactly," Sister said. "You were the only person I could think of to call." At my puzzled look, she clarified, "Because you have a policeman in the family, I thought you could ask him, unofficially, what I should do about this money. And you did offer to talk to him when Jenny found that other money in her dress, in case you don't remember."

"Sister, I wasn't serious about that," I said. Me and my big mouth had gotten me into trouble again.

"Perhaps you weren't," Sister said. "But since this is the third time a substantial amount of cash has been found in one of our donations in the past few weeks, it can't be a coincidence. And each time, there's more money. I don't want there to be any cloud of suspicion hovering over the thrift shop, but I'd be a fool not to realize that something suspicious is going on. Possibly even criminal. We can't afford any negative publicity."

"I remember when Jenny found the money in the dress pocket," I said. "You're telling me there was another time?"

Sister Rose gave me one of her famous withering looks. "You never were good at math, were you, Carol? Of course there was another incident," she snapped.

I dropped the tuxedo and turned to leave. No way was she going to talk to me that way, especially after the day I was having. She could damn well figure this thing out all by herself. Sister placed a restraining hold on my arm. "Please, don't leave. My nerves are just so strained right now, and I'm taking everything out on you. I'm sorry. I really need your help."

"Okay," I said, sitting back down at the sorting table. "Let's go through this all over again. In chronological order." I pulled a piece of scrap paper toward me. "I'll make a few notes, so I can keep everything straight in my mind." Then, I laughed. "I sound like Claire. She's always the note-taker in our crowd. I guess because she's married to a lawyer."

"I may need advice from a lawyer before all this is over," Sister Rose said. I looked at her closely and realized she was dead serious.

I found a pen in my purse and prepared to scribble some notes. "All right, Sister. When was the first incident?"

"The first one was when Jenny found cash in the pocket of that dress a few weeks ago," Sister Rose said. I nodded and made a note.

"The next one was last week. One of our *regular* volunteers found eleven hundred dollars in a donated purse." She frowned. "I believe it was a Vera Bradley purse, but I can't be certain of that."

"Can you remember the exact date for that one?" I asked. "If I'm going to talk to Mark about this, the more specific information you can give me, the better."

Sister Rose thought for a minute, then said, "It was last Tuesday. Yes, I believe that's right. Gloria Watkins was the cashier. She comes in to help most days, and she's turning out to be a real treasure."

Humph. Good for her. I made another note—last Tuesday, in Vera Bradley purse.

"And then I found this money in a man's tuxedo late yesterday afternoon. I didn't sleep a wink last night, worrying about it."

"You have no idea who donated any of these items?" I asked. I found it hard to believe that Sister Rose, who ran the thrift shop like a drill sergeant, the same way she used to run our high school English class, could have been so lax in getting donors' identities. I knew for a fact that there was a donation intake form kept right by the back door, and each donation was meticulously logged in by whichever volunteer had received it.

Sister Rose shook her head. "I'm embarrassed to admit that I have no idea. The dress that you bought for Jenny was part of a donation we found in a paper shopping bag on the back steps." At my questioning look, Sister clarified, "This happens way too often, especially if the donor is bringing in items that should really be taken to the town dump and they're embarrassed. They just want to get rid of items. We usually don't even bother going through donations like that. We just put them in a tub that we reserve for recycling. I remember we made an exception for that donation because the shopping bag it was in was in good condition and from an upscale local shop. But please, don't ask me which shop," she said, forestalling my next question.

"Okay," I said, "let's move on to the purse. What can you tell me about that?"

Sister Rose closed her eyes. "I'm trying to remember the details about that one." Her eyes snapped open. "That came in as part of a very small donation that was in a plastic bag. You know, the kind some grocery stores still use."

I nodded. "Did you happen to be in the back room when that donation came in?"

"No, I was in the front of the thrift shop re-doing a window display. But I remember that the volunteers told me that several people came in with donations at the same time, and they had trouble keeping track of which items were from which person."

"That's interesting," I said. "If I was writing this in a mystery book, I'd have the donor wait until there was a flurry of people bringing in donations at the same time, and then sneak in with mine."

"This isn't one of your mystery books, Carol," Sister Rose snapped. "But I must admit, that idea makes a lot of sense."

"What about the tuxedo?"

"I checked yesterday's donation list," Sister Rose said. "And I called the volunteer who was in charge of in-take." She shoved the sheet toward me. "She can account for every single donation except the tuxedo. She has no idea when it came in. She claims she just found it hanging on the men's clothing rack here in the back room."

For the first time since I've known her, Sister Rose looked completely overwhelmed. "I just don't know what to do next. I've locked all the money in our office safe. I used separate envelopes for each and dated them. I know we can't keep the money, and I don't know what to do with it." She took a deep breath, then continued, "I don't often ask for help. And I know I'm very hard on you. I admit it. But I have nobody else I can ask. I'm depending on you to figure this whole thing out." She smiled. "And I know you can do it. You are, after all a Mount Saint Francis girl."

I'm a sucker for flattery, probably because I don't receive it that often. And there was absolutely nothing I could do for the late Pat Mathews, except attend her memorial service and pay my respects to her loved ones. But helping Sister Rose was something positive I could do. So I went home, got my saddle shoes out of the closet, and started sleuthing.

Chapter 18

Sometimes I open my mouth and my mother comes out.

First things first, Carol. You can't just go barging into Mark's office and make him stop whatever he's doing to listen to the tale of Sister Rose and the appearing money. He doesn't appreciate being interrupted, as he's made abundantly clear to you on the numerous times you've done exactly that.

But on the other hand...sometimes the element of surprise can work best. Especially if you have an honest-to-goodness excuse for dropping in. And a plea for help from a nun is about as honest-to-goodness an excuse as a person can get.

I sat back in my kitchen chair, pondering my plan of attack, and took a long, satisfying swallow of my pineapple smoothie. "I never knew fruit could taste so good," I said to the dogs, who were circling around me, hoping for a treat. Lucy gave me a dubious stare, which made me laugh. "Don't worry," I assured her. "No way am I going to substitute a piece of fruit for a dog biscuit. Besides, I heard that some fruit is poisonous to dogs. Like grapes."

Of course, at the magic word "biscuit," even Ethel snapped to attention. "Okay, you win," I said, tossing each of my canine companions two biscuits apiece. "Now, will you back off a little, please? I need to think." Lucy gave me one of her, "You've got to be kidding" looks and padded off in the direction of her dog crate, Ethel following right behind her.

My stomach growled, indicating that a single pineapple

smoothie, no matter how delicious, wasn't sufficient to quell my hunger pangs. "Listen," I said, looking down at my tummy, "you'd better quiet down. Tummy Trimmers says a daily fruit smoothie is plenty of food for lunch. I'm sorry if you disagree. We're in re-training mode now. You can't always have what you want. And I know exactly what you want. A burger and fries from the Fairport Diner."

I suppose you think I'm really losing it, now. First, I talk to my dogs out loud. And now, I'm talking to a body part. Oh, well, you can think what you want. I don't care.

I checked the time on the kitchen clock. Man, this day was really crawling by. It was only a little past one o'clock, and I was exhausted. Of course, having a woman collapse on top of you can really wipe a gal out. Take my word for it.

What I needed was a hot shower and a plan to approach my darling son-in-law with Sister Rose's problem. And, while I was at Mark's office, I could also make discreet inquiries about the sudden death of Pat Mathews at the Tummy Trimmers class this morning. (You didn't really think I was going to let that one go, did you?) And if Mark hadn't heard about that, I'd be glad to fill him in.

I was leaning more and more toward a surprise visit, but I needed an angle. A ruse to get me beyond the gate keepers who do their best to stand between me and a heart-to-heart talk with my son-in-law. As I was rinsing the shampoo off my hair, I had one of my truly brilliant ideas. The way to a man's heart is through his stomach, right? And what do policemen love more than any other food in the world? Donuts! And if a small part of a glazed donut just happened to break off, and I picked it up and popped it in my mouth, well, who could fault me? After all, one teeny piece couldn't hurt, right? Of course, right. But maybe I should bring along the blue sunglasses, just in case I was tempted to eat the whole donut.

Chapter 19

*God promised men that good and obedient
wives would be found in all corners of the
earth. Then He made the earth round, and
laughed, and laughed, and laughed.*

For the benefit of those of you who've never had the pleasure
of visiting the Fairport Police Station, perhaps a brief description
would be in order. The kindest way to describe this bastion of truth,
justice and the American way would be to say that it looks like it
was designed by someone with no knowledge of architecture at all,
except what he (or she) retained from playing with Tinker Toys or
Legos as a child. The old police station had been housed in a red
brick structure on Fairport Turnpike, smack in the middle of our
town's main shopping district and conveniently adjacent to our
courthouse. When it became clear that a new building was needed,
the town fathers, in their infinite "wisdom," and without any input
from the residents, decided to move the police station to a vacant
piece of land smack near an entrance ramp to Interstate 95. The
land had been vacant for years, for that very reason.

Six months after the new police station opened, there had
been several attempts by its overnight "guests" to boogie out of the
station in the direction of the oh-so-convenient highway entrance.
The town fathers realized they'd made a huge mistake. A big mea
culpa from the first selectman, our town's fancy term for mayor.

And he wisely chose not to seek re-election.

After a brief stop at a local bakery to pick up a dozen assorted donuts as a gift for my son-in-law, I took my sweet time driving to the police station. It isn't often that I get to inhale the wonderful aroma of just-baked pastry, and I wanted to make the experience last as long as possible. By the time I rolled into the parking lot, I felt almost giddy. I'm ashamed to admit that I made sure all the car windows were up before I locked it, but not for safety reasons. After all, I was parked in the police department parking lot—the safest place in town. No, I made sure the windows were all closed to keep as much of the intoxicating donut aroma as possible in the car for me to inhale on my ride home.

The point of entry for visitors of the non-criminal variety to the Fairport Police Station is a uniformed receptionist seated behind a protective glass window. Most of the receptionists are volunteers who are graduates of the Citizens Police Academy, a free three-month series of lectures presented to teach the many aspects of police work to interested members of the community. I've heard that it's a wonderful experience, but I never felt the need to sign up for it, myself. After all, when you have a star detective in the family, opportunities to learn about police work abound, especially if you're a curious (some would say, nosy) person such as myself who is blessed with a natural flair for sleuthing.

Since I've helped our local police crack some cases that had them stumped, it was no surprise to me that the volunteer receptionist on duty recognized me right away. "Hello, Mrs. Andrews," she said, giving me a big smile. "How nice to see you today. How can I help you?"

Because I am such a modest person, I allowed myself to blush, just a little. "Why, Marlene," I said, squinting just a bit to read her name badge, "I'm surprised that you recognized me."

"Oh, Mrs. Andrews," the woman said, "you're pretty much a legend around here. We all know who you are."

My, my. How times have changed from the first time I visited the police station to be grilled about the untimely death of someone in our house several years ago. I was so nervous then. And now, well, I'm an in-house celebrity. Yes, even a legend.

I reined myself in. "Is Mark Anderson in?" I asked, lifting the box of donuts so that Marlene could see them. "I come bearing gifts for my son-in-law."

"I believe he's still in the weekly detectives meeting with the chief," Marlene said. "Want me to check?"

I resisted a snappy comment. "Why, yes, I'd really appreciate that."

Marlene nodded and disappeared into another room. Which I thought was odd. After all, there was a phone right there, on her desk. With a lot of difficulty, I managed to overhear part of her conversation. "Yes, sir, I did." Pause. "No, I tried that, too. But she's insisting on seeing you. I have a feeling she won't take no for an answer." Pause. "Yes, you're right about that." Laughs. "I certainly can see what you mean, now." Pause. "Okay, I'll send her in."

Well! It seemed that I wasn't as welcome here as I thought I was. Not that I'd give Marlene the satisfaction of knowing I'd figured that out.

Marlene returned and gave me another bright smile. "The meeting's just breaking up." She pressed a buzzer on her desk, and I heard the door to my left click open. "Go on back," Marlene said. "I'm sure you know where his office is."

I returned her smile. "Yes, I certainly do." I held up the box of donuts. "Want to have first pick? I'm sure that once the box gets to the break room, it'll be empty in about a minute."

Marlene laughed. "You're tempting me, but no, thank you. I'm trying to watch what I eat. I'd like to lose a little weight. Sitting at this window for hours gives me too much of an opportunity to snack on things I shouldn't, and not enough time to exercise off all the extra calories." She leaned forward and confided, girlfriend to girlfriend, "I'm even thinking of joining that new program in town, Tummy Trimmers. Have you heard of it?"

"I certainly have," I said, standing a little taller and making an effort to suck in my own tummy. "I joined it myself. In fact, I'm pretty much of an expert on it. Here." I scribbled down the Tummy Trimmers contact information on the back of a napkin and handed it to her. "Give Lori Todesco a call. Tell her that you've met me. I'm sure she'll be more than happy to tell you all about it. I'm the program's number one success story."

Marlene took the napkin and surveyed me critically. "Well," I laughed, "I'm working hard on being the number one success story." And, bearing my box of donuts and a positive attitude, I went in search of my son-in-law.

"I promise I won't keep you long," I said, giving Mark a quick peck on the cheek, then standing back and taking a good look at him. "You look tired. Are you getting enough sleep?"

Mark grimaced. "Let's put it this way. Jenny spends a lot of the night tossing and turning. When she doesn't sleep well, I don't sleep well. Sometimes she gets up in the middle of the night and I find her sitting in the living room with her eyes closed. The first time this happened, I figured she'd fallen asleep so I left her alone. But then she'll come back to bed, and immediately start to toss and turn again. I can't figure out what's going on. And I lie awake in the dark, worrying about her, and frustrated that I can't go back to sleep." He ran his hand through his buzz cut—the latest hair style for members of our police force—in a gesture of frustration.

"She should meditate if she can't sleep," I said. "That's one of the things we learn to do at Tummy Trimmers. It calms a person down. Believe me, it works. Why don't you suggest it? Maybe she can teach you to do it, too, and you can both get a good night's sleep."

"I never thought of meditation," Mark said, nodding at my suggestion. "I'll talk to her about it tonight."

"Don't tell her the suggestion came from me, though," I advised. "Make it seem like it was all your idea. Trust me, you'll get husband points for being extra sensitive." I nudged the box of donuts in his direction. "And, meanwhile, you look like you could use a little sugar boost. So I brought you these to share. Help yourself."

Mark's face lit up. "You always knew how to make my day, even when I was a kid. Did I ever tell you that I felt more at home at your house than I did in my own?"

I chose to ignore that remark, although Mark's relationship with his parents has always been a mystery to me. I think his father had been chief of detectives here many years ago, and as for his mother, well, I don't think I ever laid eyes on the woman, even when the kids were in school.

"I don't want to waste your time," I said, "and I do have an official reason for stopping in today. Two of them, in fact."

Mark gestured for me to continue while helping himself to another donut. I noticed that he had a blob of jelly on his chin, but resisted the urge to lean forward and wipe it off. Points for me, right? Instead, I got down to business. Finally.

"There's something really odd going on at Sally's Closet. That's the local thrift shop Sister Rose runs to benefit victims of domestic abuse," I clarified for Mark, in case he didn't recognize the name. Not every husband is on top of his wife's retail purchases as much as Jim is. "Did Jenny tell you about the money she found a few weeks ago in the pocket of that cute little dress I bought her?" Without giving Mark a chance to answer, I plowed ahead with my story. "I saw Sister Rose today, and she told me it's happened two more times. Finding money in clothing donations, I mean. I know sometimes I'm not exactly clear." Mark rolled his eyes, which I pretended I didn't notice.

"Sister Rose doesn't know what to do about the money, so she asked me to talk to you. It amounts to over four thousand dollars. She's such an honest person, and she'd really like to return the money, but she has no idea who brought in the donations. She's also worried that something criminal could be going on that could reflect badly on the domestic violence program. What do you think?"

"That is a little odd," Mark said. "But it doesn't sound like anything criminal. Maybe someone wanted to make an anonymous monetary donation. The shop does benefit a worthy cause."

"Three separate times? I don't think so," I said.

"Now, Carol," Mark said, his manner changing from loving son-in-law to official detective, "don't start letting your imagination run away with you. It's probably just a coincidence."

"I'm not letting my imagination run away with me," I countered, a little annoyed at his cavalier attitude. "Sister Rose is the one who's upset about this. And she's certainly not a person with an overactive imagination."

Mark wiped his hands on a napkin. "So, what exactly are you asking me to do, Carol? My case load is already more than I can handle alone. Your pal Paul Wheeler is on furlough for the next two weeks because of department budget cuts. I know you don't think too much of him, but he and I work well together and I could really use my partner right now. It's just lousy timing."

Ooooh. Wow. Mark needs a partner for the next two weeks. And here you are, sitting right in front of him, the absolutely perfect choice.

Before I could open my mouth to make him an offer he couldn't refuse, Mark beat me to it. "And don't go getting any funny ideas about offering yourself as my unofficial partner while Paul's away," Mark said, shaking his finger at me like I was a naughty child. "There's no way that'll work. And the chief would have a fit."

"It never even entered my mind," I fibbed. "Even though it's a great idea." I resisted reminding him about all the times I'd helped him solve a crime in the past. Instead, I switched gears. "I know your time is limited, especially right now, but I wondered if you were investigating what happened at Tummy Trimmers this morning." I held up my hand to forestall Mark's concern. "Don't worry. Jenny wasn't there. But I was. Another member of the group collapsed right on top of me and died." My eyes filled up, remembering. "It was horrible."

"I've been told nothing about this," Mark said. "I'm very sorry that it happened, and that it involved you. Perhaps she had a health issue that nobody knew about."

"I don't believe that for one second," I said. "Jenny and I see…" I corrected myself, "saw Pat Mathews speed-walking on the beach every morning. There's no way she could have a heart condition, or whatever else you're suggesting, and be able to do that. Besides, this happened after a meditation class. Hardly a strenuous activity."

"Jenny knew her?" Mark asked. "I hope you don't plan on discussing this with her, Carol. It'll only upset her, and I want to protect her as much as I can."

"So do I," I said, surprised at his implication that I would intentionally do anything to raise Jenny's stress level. "I'm her mother, after all. I love her, too."

Mark sighed. "I'm sorry. I didn't mean to jump down your throat. I'm just tired, and overworked. But I know you sometimes have good instincts, Carol. And I know you won't leave here until you tell me exactly what happened to you today. So, go ahead. But just the facts. No opinions, please."

Not my preferred way of telling a tale, but I forced myself to comply. And besides, my rational side agreed that Pat Mathews' death was just a tragic accident. Which, unfortunately, had involved me. When I'd finished—I'll spare you the details, since you already know them if you've been paying attention—Mark said, "That must have been terrible for you, Carol. I've never heard of anything like that happening before. Talk about being in the wrong place at the wrong time."

"I thought you should know exactly what happened while my

memory for details was intact," I said. "Just in case it turns out that Pat's death wasn't accidental. I'd be happy to make a formal written statement, if you want."

Mark raised his eyebrows. "You're doing it again, Carol. Letting your imagination run away with you. But to die on top of you." He shuddered. "Awful."

"Well," I admitted, "she didn't exactly die on top of me. She collapsed on top of me, and I thought she was dead. She died on the way to the hospital."

I could see from the skeptical expression on my son-in-law's face that my unintentional exaggeration had destroyed any credibility in his eyes. I knew it was time to vamoose while the vamoosing was good.

"I'm glad we had a chance to catch up a little," I said. "Jim and I are looking forward to our family dinner this Sunday. And Sister Rose would appreciate hearing from you if you come up with any theories or suggestions about the mysterious money. Meanwhile, I guess she'll just keep it locked up in the filing cabinet. I hope the rest of the force enjoys the donuts."

I gave him a quick kiss on the cheek and hurried out of his office. It had suddenly occurred to me that, even if Mark didn't think it was necessary to write down the details of Pat's death, I did. And the sooner I wrote them down, the better. My short-term memory isn't as sharp as it used to be. (Truthfully, it never was that great, even when I was a lot younger.) Perhaps some of you can identify with that. Since my sleuthing skills are called upon so often by the local police, I like to be prepared. And while I was on the computer, I'd email Sister Rose a summary of my meeting with Mark on her behalf.

It was time I concentrated on my own life, for a change. I had a weight loss goal and, by golly, I was going to reach it, even if I never saw those darn Lilly Pulitzer jeans again.

Chapter 20

It's a proven medical fact that hearing loss affects 100% of married men. The longer the marriage, the greater the loss.

I am not an "obituary junkie," like some other people I know. They're the ones who skip reading the front page and even the funnies and jump right to the obituary page to see who the latest additions are. And let out a big sigh of relief if they don't recognize any names. Not that I'm criticizing, understand. I would never do that. I just find that habit morbid. And, although it's really none of your business, I'll confess to you that I skip the headlines myself and go right to the daily horoscope, so I can decide how to live my day. I also try to keep up with the goings on in town via our local paper, because I hate to miss anything.

So I was surprised that several days had passed after the terrible event at Tummy Trimmers and there had been absolutely nothing in our local paper about it. Nada. Zip. No obituary for Pat. No local news story about Tummy Trimmers, either. I thought the lack of public information about a sudden death like Pat's was very unusual and, yes, weird.

By the way, in case any of you are wondering what I shared with Jim about Pat's death and my inadvertent involvement in it, rest assured that I gave Jim the basic facts in a low-key, non-emotional way. No tears. No histrionics. I didn't even say, "It was so terrible, Jim, having Pat collapse on me like that," and burst into tears.

Although it was horrible, and I wanted to burst into tears. Jim restricted his response to patting me on the hand, then asking, "Who's Pat?" When I clarified—again—he added, "How sad." Which, of course, it was.

I even resisted the temptation to ask Jim to find out why there'd been nothing about Pat's death in the local newspaper. He spends a few hours a week at the newspaper office in high-level (his words) meetings with his editor, deciding which town department or commission has committed a major enough faux pas to merit being the subject of his "State of the Town" column. (Hey, it's not much, but it gets him out of the house and makes him feel important.) Yes, Jim was in a perfect place to do some undercover snooping for me. The old me would have asked him to in a skinny second. But the new me was fixated on becoming skinny herself. So I forced myself to concentrate on my own life rather than nose around in other people's.

Mindful of making healthy eating choices, especially where my pregnant daughter was concerned, I turned my attention to selecting the menu for our upcoming family dinner on Sunday. I decided on a roasted chicken, one of Jim's favorites, so he couldn't complain that I was starving him to death. Plus a variety of veggie selections. I decided against "mashed potatoes" that were really steamed, whipped cauliflower in disguise. I'd tried the recipe on Jim a few nights ago. He took one forkful of the cauliflower, tasted it, grimaced, then said, "What the heck is this?" For Sunday's dinner, I decided to serve real mashed potatoes and just give myself a small portion. Brilliant, right?

I also took a tip from the Tummy Trimmers "Guide to Dining and Healthy Eating," and would only use smaller, luncheon size plates when I set the table for dinner. And I'd serve thick fruit smoothies as dessert. I'd read somewhere that the thicker the smoothie, the fuller a person feels, and I wanted to test out that theory on my husband. The nicest thing of all was having the four of us together, sharing a meal and catching up on our lives. That's what families are all about, right? Of course, right.

Our family dinner started off just the way I'd planned it,

although Jim couldn't resist pointing out that for once, he was eating "real food" instead of one of my low-fat healthy concoctions. I was in such a good mood that even his teasing didn't get the usual rise out of me. "Just imagine," I said, beaming at my now really pregnant-looking daughter and her handsome husband, "in another year, we'll need to add a high chair when we get together for a meal."

Jenny shook her fork at me. "Don't jinx it, Mom. I still have a ways to go before I introduce you to the world's most perfect grandchild." She smiled. "But it will be great. You're right. Believe it or not, even Mike is excited about becoming an uncle for the first time. He plans to fly home right after the birth, to give little Punky his official stamp of approval."

"Punky?" I repeated as I passed Jim the basket of whole wheat rolls for the third time. "Don't tell me that's what you're naming the baby."

"Why, Mom, you don't like it?" Jenny said with a perfectly straight face. She glanced at her husband, who was trying not to laugh. "So far, it's the only name Mark and I can agree on. Especially since we don't know whether it'll be a boy or a girl." She waited just a beat, then said, "I wish I had a mirror so you could see the expression on your face right now. It really is priceless. You have to know that I'm kidding, right? Although we call the baby 'Punky' all the time."

"That was my idea," Mark interjected. "I'd ask Jenny how she was feeling, and she'd always answer, punky. It took me a little while to figure out that she meant she wasn't feeling up to par, not that she was a member of a rock band of pregnant women."

"So we started calling the baby 'Punky,' " Jenny finished. "And now that I'm starting to feel some movement, I can say that I really 'feel Punky.' Get it?"

I didn't, and I could tell by Jim's expression that he didn't, either. I didn't bother to check with Lucy and Ethel, who were in their favorite spot under the table and available to catch any morsels of food that might come their way.

"Now that I'm getting more sleep, I feel much more energetic than I did before," Jenny continued. "My doctor is encouraging me to walk more. I bet Pat is wondering what happened to me. Want to meet at the beach tomorrow morning around eight?"

I was afraid to look at Mark, even though this shift in conversation was definitely not my fault. "Um, sure," I said. "That'll be nice."

"You don't sound very enthusiastic, Mom," Jenny said. "Did I say something wrong?"

I finally looked at Mark, and he gave a slight nod, which I interpreted as permission to tell Jenny about Pat's death. At least, I hoped that's what he meant.

"About Pat," I began. "We won't be seeing her on the beach anymore." *Or anywhere else, for that matter.* "She passed away rather suddenly at a Tummy Trimmers meditation class."

"She's the one who collapsed on top of you and died, right?" Jim asked. Good old Jim. Open mouth, insert both feet.

"What?" Jenny exclaimed. "When? Why didn't you tell me about this? What happened?"

"Now, Jenny," Mark said, putting his arm around her, "don't get upset." She shook off his arm and glared at her husband. "I'm pregnant, Mark. Like millions of other women before me. I don't need to be coddled or protected like some fragile flower." Then, addressing me, "What the heck happened to Pat?"

"I really don't know how to answer that," I said, looking toward Mark for some help, which was not forthcoming, unfortunately. I cleared my throat, then began, "We were doing a meditation exercise. Nancy was there, too. She was on one side of me, and Pat was on the other. We were all sitting on the floor on mats, and our leader was encouraging us to go to a serene place in our mind. I had a lot of trouble doing that, and whispered to Nancy that this was the hardest thing I'd ever done in my life."

Jenny started to look impatient. I knew I was taking too long to get to the point of my story. "Anyway, I was able to put myself into a meditative state for a few minutes, and I was surprised when the leader began to bring us out of it. I stood up to leave and tried to pick up my mat, but Pat was leaning on part of it. I squatted down and tried to move my mat, and she rolled over on top of me." My eyes filled up. "I couldn't get up. It was terrible. Nancy called 911 right away. And the EMTs came and took Pat away. That's it." I looked at Mark again, but he had his poker face on, so I couldn't tell if he was pleased with the way I told my story or not. Either way, at least it was out there. Sort of like an unwanted guest at the Thanksgiving dinner table.

Jenny reached for my hand and gave it a loving squeeze. "I'm so sorry you had to go through that, Mom. It must have been terrible for you."

I nodded. "It was awful. Of course, it was a lot worse for Pat than it was for me. Poor soul. But I'm sure she's in a better place now." Which reminded me of a question I had that had been niggling away at me ever since the incident.

"You may not know the answer to this," I said, addressing Mark directly for the first time. "But how can I find out about Pat's funeral? Which funeral home is handling the arrangements? And if there's going to be a wake first, I really feel I should attend. There hasn't been anything in the paper about it, unless I missed it. I read the local obituary page every day."

Mark took his time answering. I could tell by the way he was concentrating on eating his salad instead of looking at me that I had inadvertently asked a loaded question. Finally, he said, "I was hoping to avoid this conversation and have a pleasant family dinner tonight. But since you've raised the question, Carol, I have to confess that our department has been asked for assistance in the matter of Pat Mathews' death." He raised his hand to forestall the barrage of questions he knew I was dying to ask. "Not in the way you think, Carol. The medical examiner is satisfied that there's no question of foul play involved. But so far, no final arrangements have been made because no next of kin has come forward to make them. There even was an announcement in the legal ads section of the paper asking for help, but there've been no responses to that, either. That's why we've been called in to assist in the search for next of kin, but so far, we've come up empty. It's like Pat Mathews never existed at all."

Chapter 21

I ate salad for dinner. Mostly croutons and tomatoes. Really, just one big round crouton covered with tomato sauce. And cheese. FINE. It was a pizza. I admit it. I had pizza for dinner.

Jenny immediately spoke up. "How could you say anything so ridiculous?" She saw the hurt look on her husband's face and softened her comment. "I'm sorry I was so blunt, honey. But, of course Pat Mathews existed. Mom and I saw her walking on Fairport Beach every morning. And she sat with us at the opening of Tummy Trimmers, remember, Mom? That was the first time we actually talked to her."

"Calm down, Jenny," Mark said, patting her hand like she was a child. Which was exactly the wrong approach to take. I should know. Jim's tried that approach with me over the years, and all it ever does is make me more upset. And angry.

Jenny pulled her hand away. "I'll calm down when you say something that makes sense," she said. "So far, you're batting zero in that department." She crossed her arms over her tummy.

I knew that I had to diffuse the situation fast, before Jenny said something she'd regret later. Like mother, like daughter.

"We saw someone walking on Fairport Beach every morning who introduced herself as Pat Mathews," I countered. "But that may not be who she really was. It must be unusual that no one has come forward to claim her remains. What happens if no one can be found to take responsibility for her funeral, Mark?"

"The town of Fairport will have to do it," Mark answered. "There's a small contingency fund in the town budget for this kind of situation. But it's rarely been used."

"Poor Pat," Jenny said. "That is so sad." She leaned her head on her husband's shoulder. "I'm sorry for what I said to you before. I got a little carried away." She patted her tummy. "You can blame Punky for that."

"I can't imagine dying and having no one care," I said. For a millisecond, I focused on what I wanted my funeral to be like. I hoped it was standing room only, and instead of singing hymns, the mourners would sing Broadway show tunes. One of my all-time favorites is *What I Did For Love* from *A Chorus Line*. I made a mental note to write some of this down to make it easier for the loved ones I'd be leaving behind. I wanted my funeral to be a great time for everybody, even if I wasn't there to enjoy it.

"It does happen, Carol," Mark said, bringing me back from planning my funeral to the present. "Especially during the cold winter months. Unfortunately, we have some people in town who have to rely on the homeless shelter for housing. And if the shelter is full, and it's a cold night, well, you can fill in the rest."

Jenny shuddered. "What a horrible thing."

"But Pat wasn't homeless," I insisted. "I'm sure she lived near Fairport Beach."

I could see the wheels in Jenny's head turning. "What about her Tummy Trimmers registration, Mark? I remember it asked for an address."

"That's right," I said. "I remember that, too. Did you check that?"

"She gave a post office box as her official address," Mark said. "It turned out to be a non-existent number."

"What about putting a story in the *Fairport News*?" I suggested. I turned to Jim, who so far hadn't involved himself in the conversation. "Would the paper run something? Maybe you could write the story."

Jim shook his head. "Even if the paper did an article, that's not the kind of story I'd ever be assigned. All I write is my column. I'm not a regular reporter."

"But you know the editor," I insisted. "Couldn't you talk to him? You could do a feature—something about a mystery woman dying and ask readers for help in identifying her." I hope you're all noticing that I'm now doing the exact thing I had decided *not* to do. But the poor woman deserved a decent burial. Was I the only person in the whole town who felt that way?

"That's a great idea," Jenny said, backing me up. "What about it, Dad?"

Before Jim could respond, Mark interrupted. "Do you have a photo of Pat Mathews, Carol? We certainly wouldn't want to photograph her now."

I shook my head. "The only thing I can suggest is to check with Lori Todesco. She's the Tummy Trimmers founder," I clarified. "Maybe Pat's in a picture that was taken at the grand opening. I think someone was circulating with a camera, snapping candid shots."

Mark made a note on his phone. "Good idea. We'll check that out. We never thought of that."

"But what about a feature story in the newspaper, Dad?" Jenny asked, putting her father on the hot seat once more. "Can't you do something to help? We're not talking about a stranger. This is someone Mom and I knew. And she was a nice woman. She deserves a proper funeral." Her eyes filled up. "Please, Dad. Can't you do something?" The tears she'd been struggling to hold back spilled down her cheeks.

I started to cry, too. In a second we were both sobbing, while our husbands looked at us like we were both nuts. "If nobody else wants to give Pat a proper funeral," I said between sobs, "I'll do it myself." Of course, I knew that threatening to pay for Pat's funeral out of the Andrews family bank account was the one sure way to guarantee Jim's cooperation. I haven't been married to him for more than thirty-five years without figuring that out. And combined with Jenny's and my tears, I knew I'd hit a home run, for sure.

"All right. All right," Jim said. "I surrender. Two crying females is more than I can take. And there's no way we're going to pay for a funeral for somebody we barely know. I'll send the editor a quick email tonight and see what he says about doing a feature story." He held up his hand. "But no promises. If he says no, then that's it. I'm going to do it right now, so no one will have to keep reminding me about it." And he gave me a pointed look, which I ignored.

"Dad, you are the best," Jenny said, smiling.

"I don't know about that," Jim said. "But I'm a sucker for tears. Just ask your mother. Whenever she's losing an argument, she turns on the waterworks." And with that parting shot, he headed toward the family room and the computer.

"Don't you want dessert?" I called out after him.

"Not if it's one of your healthy ones," he said. "Those smoothies just don't do it for me. If you have some ice cream with fudge sauce, or a brownie, that'd be great."

"But tonight I'm trying a new flavor smoothie," I protested. "You should at least try it. I swear, it tastes just like ice cream, but with a lot less fat. It's much better for your heart."

"No way, Carol. Nothing tastes like ice cream but ice cream," Jim said.

"Suit yourself," I said. "But if you have a heart attack while you're sending off that email, don't blame me." Jenny looked alarmed, so I added, "Just kidding. He's really eating healthier than he ever has. He just doesn't realize it. And don't tell him either, okay?"

"You really are too much," Jenny said, laughing.

"Is there anything I can do to help you track down information about Pat Mathews?" I asked Mark. "You've already done an Internet search, right?"

"Of course," Mark said. "That's where we started. And I really don't want you," he looked at Jenny, "either of you, involving yourself in what's become a police matter."

"But we're already involved," I insisted. "Jenny and I actually knew Pat. Or," I said, conceding the point, "the woman who called herself Pat. And she did collapse on top of me, remember." Jenny looked a little green when I said that, and I mentally cursed myself for being so thoughtless. But I was making a point.

Mark pulled out his cell phone to take some notes. "Okay," he said. "Tell me what you remember about her. Maybe it'll help us. Who knows? Any chance you know where she lived?"

"I know it must have been walking distance to the beach," Jenny said. "Because when we drove to the beach in the morning, there were no other cars in the parking lot." She looked at me for clarification, and I nodded.

"Fairport Beach Road has some pretty fancy houses on it," I said. "I doubt that she lived in any of those. Most of them are summer homes, and they're closed up this time of year. The owners don't open them until closer to Memorial Day."

"But there are smaller bungalows when you get closer to Lantern Point," Jenny interjected. "A lot of students from the college rent those, though. I doubt if Pat lived around there."

"Do you remember what direction Pat walked from?" Mark asked. "That might be helpful." At my puzzled expression, he continued, "Did you both walk the same way every morning? In other words, did you get out of the car and turn left on the beach, to head toward the Point, or right, to head toward the marina? And was Pat walking toward you, or the same way?"

"But Mark," I said, "what possible difference could that make? She could have walked in one direction, and then turned around and gone the other way."

Mark looked embarrassed. "You're right. I hadn't thought of it that way."

"Nobody's a genius all the time," Jenny said. "But I love you anyway."

I suddenly had a brainstorm. "You know who could help figure out where Pat lived?" I asked. "Nancy! She's a real estate agent. I bet Pat was renting a place near the beach. Maybe Nancy could search current rentals in town and find out who the tenants are. What do you think? Should I call her right now?"

Mark's phone pinged. He took one look at the incoming text and stood up so quickly that he almost knocked over a kitchen chair. "That's a great idea, Carol. Hold that thought. Right now, I have to leave. There's been a break-in at Sally's Closet."

Chapter 22

If it wasn't for stress, I'd have no energy at all.

"Wait, Mark," I yelled, grabbing my purse and chasing after him as fast as I could, which wasn't very fast. "I want to come with you." But his car was already gone.

"Mom, take it easy," Jenny said, coming up behind me and nearly scaring me to death. "You're going to give yourself a heart attack."

"But did you hear what Mark said?" I asked, panting a little from my sudden burst of exercise. "There's been a break-in at Sally's Closet. Who in the world would want to rob a business that only sells second-hand clothing? It doesn't make any sense."

"I'm more worried about Sister Rose than the shop itself," Jenny said. "What if she was at the shop and surprised the thief? She could be hurt."

"Your imagination is even more active than mine," I said, dismissing an idea that I'd already had and was too frightened to share aloud. "There's no reason why she'd be at the shop on a Sunday night. Even if she had paperwork to catch up on, she'd wait until Monday." I looked at my daughter for affirmation. "She would, wouldn't she?"

"I have no idea," Jenny said. "You know her better than I do. But there's no point to us standing here worrying. Let's take your car and drive over there to see what happened."

"Won't Mark be angry at us and say we're interfering?" I said, beginning to chicken out. "For once, maybe I should do the sensible thing and stay out of a situation that really doesn't concern me."

"Mark will probably be mad at first," Jenny said. "But he won't stay that way for long." She patted her belly. "Punky and I will sweet talk him around. Don't you worry about that. And you know you really want to do this."

"I swear, you're beginning to act just like me," I said. "I don't know whether that's a compliment or not."

"Let's just say that I inherited my snooping gene from you," Jenny said. "We're good friends of Sister Rose, and we want to be sure she's all right. I'll bet he'll even be glad to see us, because she's bound to be upset."

"This is Sister Rose we're talking about, remember? She doesn't lose her cool."

"There's always a first time," Jenny said.

"What about your father? He hates it when I'm snooping."

"He's busy on the computer," Jenny said. "I bet he's determined to find Pat Mathews' real name and next-of-kin, even if it takes him all night. He won't even notice that we're gone." She handed me my car keys. "Quit stalling and let's go."

Like I've said before, like mother, like daughter.

"It must be a slow night for crime in town," I said as we turned the corner and the thrift shop came into view. "There are three police cruisers here, plus Mark's car."

"There's a parking spot you can drive right into at the end of the block," Jenny said. "No parallel parking required."

"Good," I said. "I'm so nervous now that I'd probably total the car if I tried anything that required dexterity." As I cruised into the spot, my headlights picked up the figure of a pedestrian heading our way. I realized it was Maria Lesco.

"What's going on?" she asked. "I heard sirens while I was at the restaurant. And why are you both here?" Now, I could have asked Maria the same question. But I didn't. Still, it seemed odd to me that Maria would leave her busy restaurant on a Sunday night to investigate emergency sirens. Especially since sirens were not an uncommon occurrence in Fairport, sad to say.

"There's a problem at the thrift shop," I answered, telling the truth but not the whole truth. I hesitated to use the word "break-in." I have no idea why.

By this time, the three of us had reached the side parking lot of Sally's Closet, which is protected by a chain link fence and padlocked when the shop is closed to discourage any after-hours donations. The padlock was on the ground, and a police photographer was taking pictures of the scene. As we watched, a patrolman, wearing gloves, scooped up the padlock and secured it in a plastic evidence bag. "Sorry, ladies, you can't stay here," the patrolman said, catching sight of us. "This is an active crime scene. No civilians allowed."

"We're not civilians," I said, looking the patrolman squarely in the face and giving him the mommy look that I used to strike terror into my kids when necessary. "My daughter is married to Detective Mark Anderson. We've been asked to assist in the investigation because we're very close friends of Sister Rose. Where is she? Is she all right?" Okay, so I stretched the truth a little. Okay, so I stretched the truth a lot. But it was for a good cause, right? Of course, right.

"Where is Detective Anderson? I'm sure he'll vouch for us."

"Who are you?" he asked Maria.

"I'm Maria Lesco, and I'm also a good friend of Sister Rose," she said. "I own Maria's Trattoria, right around the corner. I heard the sirens and followed the police cars here. I was worried."

The patrolman looked skeptical, but before he could tell us to leave again, I caught sight of Sister Rose being led out of the side door of the shop, supported by Mark. They both spotted us at the same time. One person was clearly not happy to see us. I bet you can figure out who.

Not wasting any time, I ran toward Sister Rose. "Sister, are you hurt?" I asked. "What happened?" She shook Mark's arm away when she saw us. "I'm really all right, just a little shaken up. I don't need to go to the hospital."

Mark frowned. I wasn't sure if it was because Sister Rose had refused medical attention, or because he'd seen Jenny and me. I took a step back and let Jenny handle her husband. "Don't be mad at us for coming here, honey. You know how close Sister Rose and Mom are. We were worried about her."

Mark sighed. "I guess I'm not really mad. And I'm not surprised, either, knowing the two of you."

I focused on Sister Rose. "Are you sure you don't need to go to the hospital to be checked?" Truth to tell, the good sister looked terrible. Like she'd aged ten years, at least. "Don't try to tell me what I should do, Carol," she snapped at me. "I'm fine. I just need a place to sit down and collect my thoughts for a little while, that's all. Preferably alone."

Well, that certainly put me in my place. But for once, I didn't mind her harsh tone.

"Why don't we go back into your office," I suggested.

"No! I can't bear looking at what the shop looks like right now." And to my complete amazement, I saw tears in Sister Rose's eyes. Or maybe it was just a trick of the light.

"Why don't we walk over to the Trattoria," Maria Lesco suggested, speaking up for the first time. "You can have a nice cup of tea, or maybe a glass of wine. On the house. You and Jenny are invited, too, Carol."

Jenny stifled a quick yawn. "I'm afraid I have to say no, as tempted as I am. Punky and I have decided to call it a night. Mark, are you finished here? Can we go home now?"

"Of course, honey," the father-to-be said, putting his arm around Jenny and starting toward his car. Looking back at Sister Rose, Mark called out, "Plan to come into the police station tomorrow morning and make a statement. The police photographer will be here for a while, taking pictures inside the shop. I'd appreciate it if you didn't try to straighten anything up until we've told you it's all right."

Sister Rose nodded. "I understand. I don't think I could face going back into the shop tonight, anyway. It's too upsetting." She turned to Maria Lesco. "I think I'll take you up on that offer of a glass of wine. Carol, are you coming with us?"

"As soon as I say a quick good night to Jenny and Mark," I said, hanging back a little. "You two go on ahead. I'll catch up."

When the two women were safely out of sight, I decided to take a quick peek inside the thrift shop. Just to satisfy my own curiosity. Not to meddle or interfere with the police investigation, of course.

"I'm Carol Andrews, a close friend of Sister Rose," I said to the patrolman who was stationed at the front door. "She asked me to remind you to lock up the shop when you're through. She wants to be sure nobody can get inside to steal some of the inventory."

The policeman gave me a look that would melt stone. "You must be kidding. I don't think you or Sister Rose have to worry about that. Nobody could find anything to steal in there right now."

"She just wanted to be sure," I said, inching my way around him so I could get a better view of the inside of the shop. It was complete chaos. Clothes were thrown everywhere. It looked like someone had torn through the place in a complete frenzy. I was shocked.

"Who could have done this?" I said to the policeman. "I've never seen anything like this before."

"Lady," the policeman said in a patronizing tone of voice, "consider yourself lucky. It was probably someone who wanted quick money to buy drugs. There's more of that going on in Fairport than you realize. And when they can't find cash right away, they flip out. I've seen a lot of places that were trashed even worse than this one."

"I had no idea," I said. "That's very scary."

"Just be sure that you keep your valuables in a safety deposit box," the policeman advised. "And don't keep a lot of cash in the house. One more thing. If you don't already have a burglar alarm at home, get one installed pronto."

I thought about our personal burglar alarms, Lucy and Ethel. I wondered how effective they'd be in protecting us from a burglar. I knew they'd bark—at least, Lucy would. But how much good would that do?

"I'll reassure Sister Rose," I said. "And talk to my husband about installing an alarm system." Then I sprinted around the corner to Maria's Trattoria. And I'll admit that I stopped to look over my shoulder a few times. Just in case.

Chapter 23

A thief broke into my house last night. He was looking for money, so I got up and looked with him.

"I wish I could tell you what happened," Sister Rose said, cradling a glass of merlot so tightly I feared she'd break it. "Unfortunately, I can't. I still can't believe it."

Sister Rose and I were sitting at a quiet table at Maria's Trattoria. The dinner rush was over, and there were only a few diners left, lingering over dessert and coffee. Rather than order a glass of wine for myself, I settled for a cup of espresso. I wanted to keep my mind clear, and I figured it was going to be a long night. Because if I knew Sister Rose, and I did, after she finished her glass of wine, she'd insist on going back to Sally's Closet and straightening up the carnage, no matter what Mark had said. And if she did, I planned to go with her.

"Thank goodness you weren't hurt," I said. "Did you actually see the person who broke into the shop?"

"The police asked me the same thing," Sister Rose said. "I saw someone running down the street toward the train station. But I couldn't tell if it was a man or a woman. All I saw was the person's back."

I took a sip of my espresso. Ugh. It was so bitter. What I really needed was something sweet. A sugar fix, to give me a burst of energy. I wanted to resist the siren call of the cannoli, but I could feel myself weakening. Especially because the waistband on the jeans I was wearing was a little looser than it was the last time I'd worn them. And everyone cheats on a diet, right? Of course, right.

Be strong, Carol. Don't give in.

I forced my attention back onto Sister Rose. "Don't you agree, Carol?"

"That's one way to look at it," I said, hedging, since I had absolutely no idea what Sister Rose had just said.

"There's no way to tell if the person I saw running down the street was the same person who broke into the thrift shop," Sister Rose reiterated. "It could be just a coincidence. I don't want to get an innocent person into trouble with the police."

"I suppose the person you saw could have been rushing to catch a train," I said. "But you have to admit that's a remarkable coincidence." I paused, then added, "I took a quick peek inside the shop before I walked over here. Whoever broke in must have been desperate. Or very angry. The whole place is torn apart."

"That's what I'm really worried about," Sister Rose confessed. "We can straighten up the shop and put the merchandise that's salvageable back on the shelves. But what if it was a person trying to threaten the domestic violence program itself or one of our clients? Thank God we keep the address of our safe house totally confidential to protect them."

Wow. That was something that had never occurred to me. And that made a lot more sense than the policeman's theory of a thief breaking into the shop for quick cash.

"Before we jump to any conclusions, something I'm really good at," I said, bringing a quick smile to Sister Rose's face, "how about if you go over everything you can remember with me in chronological order? You're going to have to do that tomorrow for the police, and it may help crystalize things in your head. Let's start with why you went to the thrift shop on a Sunday night. Do you often do that?"

Sister Rose took a tiny sip of her wine, then pushed the glass away. "No," she said, "but when we closed Saturday I didn't have a chance to tally up all that day's sales and enter them into the computer. I like to keep a daily account, and keep track of what sells and what doesn't. We're constantly changing what donations we'll accept, and when. And, during our big sale time, it gets harder to track our inventory. I don't like to postpone work, Carol, as you know."

I nodded and ignored the implied criticism, since I have a black belt in procrastination.

"Did you come into the shop by the front or the back door?" I asked.

"The front," Sister Rose said. "I remember being surprised that the lights in the main part of the shop were out. We always leave some on, even when the shop is closed. I flipped the main switch by the door, and that's when I saw the mess the shop was in."

"Don't you have a burglar alarm or something?" I asked, mindful of the recent lecture I'd received from one of Fairport's finest.

"We've never needed one," Sister Rose said. "After all, we sell used merchandise. There's not that much of value to steal. But there's no question that we'll have to install something now."

"Did you hear or see anything else when you came into the shop?" I asked.

Sister Rose closed her eyes and thought for a minute. "Yes. I distinctly remember hearing something from the sorting room, like something had fallen onto the floor. And then the back door squeaked opened and closed. I keep meaning to get that door fixed." She shivered. "I guess someone was still in the shop."

"And then what did you do?"

"I was afraid to go into the back of the shop," Sister Rose admitted. "I went out the front door. And that's when I saw a person running in the direction of the train station. It must have been the thief."

"Thief?" I repeated. "Something was stolen?"

"Oh, yes, Carol. The filing cabinet in my office was broken into. Saturday's receipts were in there. And the other money."

"Other money?"

"Yes," Sister Rose said. "The money we found hidden in those donations. All that money was stolen." She took a large swallow of her wine. "Yes, that must have been it. It was a random break-in, not someone targeting one of our clients. They found the money and then ran away."

"That's the theory the police seem to favor," I said. "At least, that's what the officer I talked to said. He said people looking for quick cash to buy drugs are breaking into properties all over town."

But there was one thing about that theory that really troubled me. Why did the thief cause such carnage in the shop itself, rather than head straight to the office where the chances of finding cash would be better? I didn't voice my concern to Sister Rose, though. The wine seemed to be having a calming effect on her, and I didn't want to upset her any more by voicing some of my frequently harebrained theories.

Unfortunately, my imagination doesn't take orders from my mind. The more I will myself to stop thinking about something, the more my imagination refuses to let it go. So when I finally made it back home and crawled into a bed already crowded with Jim and two canines—all of whom were snoring and oblivious to my late arrival—I lay awake in the dark for a long time, going over the events of the night. It was like watching the same rerun of an old television show, over and over again.

Then I "switched channels" and replayed the dinner conversation with my son-in-law and Jenny about Pat Mathews. I tried to envision Pat walking toward Jenny and me on Fairport Beach. Was she always coming from the same direction? Did that mean anything at all?

I guess I finally fell asleep. But I had a terrible dream that Sister Rose and I went to the thrift shop late at night and had a violent confrontation with the thief. And no matter how hard we tried, and how much we fought, we couldn't see the thief's face.

Chapter 24

I love being a senior citizen. I learn something new every day. Unfortunately, I also forget five others.

When I finally dragged my body out of bed after a night of too much tossing and turning and too little sleep, I found that my darling husband had neglected to leave me even a drop of coffee at the bottom of the pot. There was a series of yellow sticky notes taped across the kitchen table, ending at a clean coffee mug. I squinted to read them without my bifocals. "I was up early and drank all the coffee. There's a fresh pot all ready to start. I know you hate old coffee. I'm meeting with my newspaper editor this morning about your deceased friend. Still looking for information about her." The word "your" was underlined three times, in case I didn't understand that Jim was doing me a huge favor. "Where the heck did everybody go last night? And without telling me???" The last note was signed with an upside down smiley face.

He was right, of course. Jenny and I pretty much forced Jim to try and convince his editor to run a story on the mystery woman we knew as Pat Mathews. And we did bolt out of the house without telling him where we were going, or why, both cardinal sins in the Andrews household. I had to figure out a way to atone for last night's sudden disappearing act.

"You're lucky you never got married," I said to Lucy and Ethel. "Sometimes having a husband is exhausting." Lucy gave me one of her withering looks. "I know," I responded. "I never even let you date. I'm sorry. But it's too late for you now." Her Highness responded by padding over to the cupboard where the dog food was kept and sitting down in front of it. She then strolled to the refrigerator, sat, and stared at me. Ethel, of course, followed and did exactly the same thing.

"I don't get it," I said. "I know you're trying to tell me something, but I don't understand what you mean."

Lucy sighed deeply at my stupidity, then the canine pair repeated the process. First they went to the dog food cupboard, then to the refrigerator, then both turned and stared at me. A lightbulb, curiously shaped like a dog bone, went off in my mind. "Now I get it!" I said. "I should cook a nice dinner tonight, too, instead of serving what Jim calls diet mush. Maybe steak and baked potatoes. If I use an extra lean cut of meat, that'll still be healthy." My taste buds jumped up and down with joy at the very thought of such a sumptuous repast. It had been a long time since we'd had beef for dinner. If I only had a small portion, how many calories would I consume? I figured saving my marriage was worth the risk. And I could always eat while I was wearing my blue sunglasses. Assuming I could find them.

My stomach growled, reminding me that dinner was a long way away and it wanted some sustenance right now. First, I needed to perk the coffee that Jim had thoughtfully left for me. And maybe that would perk up my little grey cells, too.

"Since we're already having this human-to-canine chat," I said to the dogs, "I wonder if either of you have any thoughts about Pat Mathews. I'm sure you were eavesdropping last night while Mark and Jenny were here, so you heard that nobody has claimed responsibility for her funeral. And that it's possible Pat Mathews isn't her real name."

Lucy yawned. Clearly, this topic of conversation was of no interest to her at all. But I persisted. Sometimes she has pretty impressive insight. She just needs some coaxing.

"I know you never met Pat. So you have no relationship with her, like you do with Nancy, Mary Alice, or Claire." Both dogs looked a little more attentive now, especially since I'd tossed them each a dog biscuit.

"How could someone have no relatives or friends who care about them?" I asked. "Even you have litter mates, and you know who your breeder is, and your parents. Your AKC papers give all that information." I frowned. "Of course, you can't read them yourselves, but if you want to know, just ask and I'll be glad to read them to you."

I remembered that the AKC papers also gave official registration names for each canine. Lucy and Ethel were just the house names that Jim and I called the dogs. "Your official name is Pineridge English Cockers 'Toast of the Town,' " I said to Ethel. "And yours is Pineridge English Cockers 'Life of the Party,' " I told Lucy. Both dogs looked really alert now. They love it when I talk about their family history. "Both your sire and your dam were champion show dogs," I continued. "That's why you're both so gorgeous." Don't try and tell me that the dogs hadn't understood a single word, because when I told them they were gorgeous, they responded by licking my hands, and I wasn't even holding any food.

"Maybe Pat was in the Witness Protection Program," I mused, pouring myself a cup of steaming coffee and continuing my rambling. "That's a pretty good reason to have a brand new identity, don't you think?" This produced still another withering look from Lucy. "Okay, that's a stretch. But maybe I can do a little poking around myself and see what I can find out. Not everything is available through Google. Sometimes some good old nosy questioning will do the trick. And I'm a champ at that. Even Mark says so. Although I don't think he always means that as a compliment."

Hmm. What an interesting thought. Maybe Mark really wanted me to poke around, but he just couldn't ask me officially. He just set out the bait and he knew I couldn't resist. The more I thought about that, the more it made sense. On the other hand, that was the sneaky method that I've also employed to get my own way. I didn't think my son-in-law was that devious.

But on the other hand—as I've said before—like all of you, I only have two hands. And there were other, more pressing matters to attend to today. Tops on my list was the break-in at the thrift shop. So while I was having my low fat, healthy breakfast, instead of what I really wanted—a Western omelet with cheese, home fries and several slices of crisp bacon—I sent Sister Rose a quick text.

Me: *Good morning. How are you?*
SR: *Exhausted. Angry. On my way to police station.*
Me: *Can I help? Maybe I can help clean up shop later today?*
SR: *Straightened everything up last night. Couldn't sleep.*

Me*: What can I do then?*

SR*: Figure out the money mystery. I'm depending on you!*

I sat back in my chair. Rats. Cleaning up the shop would have been easy compared to the task Sister Rose handed me. Although I was pretty sure that the mysterious money and the break-in were connected.

My phone pinged with an incoming text, informing me that I had one event scheduled for today, my weigh-in meeting at Tummy Trimmers. Double rats. I felt like I was being called to the principal's office for another infraction, because if I was being totally honest with myself, I was positive I hadn't lost any weight since the last time I weighed in. My whole day was ruined; I was a complete fat failure.

Maybe I should take a moment here to clarify the unique approach Tummy Trimmers has to the weigh-in process. Well-respected weight loss programs like Weight Watchers have regularly scheduled weekly meetings which members attend to chart their weight loss progress—or lack—on a carefully calibrated scale, listen to an inspirational talk by a certified Weight Watchers leader, and share helpful information among themselves. For those people who don't want the in-person touch and reinforcement provided by attending weekly meetings, Weight Watchers is available online as well.

The Tummy Trimmers program has a whole different way of checking a member's weight loss—the surprise attack. At least, it was a surprise to me, since I never bothered to read the entire Tummy Trimmers registration form I had agreed to and signed. The best way I can explain it is to liken it to a pop quiz that we used to get in school—something you could never anticipate, so you could never study for it. The Tummy Trimmers program guidelines stipulate that active members will be required to attend a single weigh-in meeting within every two week interval. But, cleverly, the guidelines do not give specific weigh-in meeting times. Instead, as a way to ensure that members are constantly monitoring their food intake and exercise, we receive a text the day of our weigh-in meeting and must attend or risk being dropped from the program. Talk about stress!

I had no choice. I had to attend the meeting. I wondered if Nancy would be there, too, not that she really needed to monitor her weight. She's always managed to keep her figure just as slim as it was in junior year of high school. It was a good thing we were

BFF's or I would sincerely hate her. She and I hadn't spoken since the day Pat Mathews died, and we had a lot to catch up on.

I checked the time of the weigh-in meeting and realized it was at noon today. I could easily make that. And if I was really lucky, maybe Lori Todesco herself would conduct the meeting, giving me a golden opportunity to observe the Tummy Trimmers founder in action. Perhaps I'd even be able to throw in an innocent question—or two—about Pat's tragic and unexpected death.

I felt a lot more optimistic now about attending the meeting, no matter what my traitorous scale reading was. Bring it on. I was ready! And no matter what, I was going to treat myself and Jim to a delicious dinner tonight, even though I had to cook it myself. And maybe, even, have dessert.

Chapter 25

I wear a non-activity tracker on my wrist. It's called a sit-bit.

"Congratulations, Carol," Destiny said to me in a low voice. "You're down two pounds since your last weigh-in."

Whoa. This was big news. I was so surprised that I almost corrected her. The Tummy Trimmers scale didn't register the same as my brand new bathroom scale, which had shocked me this morning by announcing that I weighed one pound more today than yesterday at the same time. Note to self: be sure to give new bathroom scale a stern lecture on importance of accuracy at earliest opportunity. Oh, by the way, in professional weight-loss parlance, one never uses the terms "gained or lost" a certain number of pounds or ounces. Instead, the gentler, "You're up" (or "down") is the preferred method of delivering the good or bad news. Just in case you didn't know that.

Destiny gave me the newest Tummy Trimmers motivational handout and a nametag with a cartoon drawing of a smiley face. This subtly announced to fellow Tummy Trimmers that the lucky person wearing it had lost weight. There was another nametag, which I secretly called the Tag of Shame. This one had the cartoon drawing of a face with tears cascading down its cheeks. Because you're all such smarty pants, I bet you can figure out what that one signifies. And it's none of your business whether I ever had to wear that one or not.

I affixed my smiley face nametag in a prominent position on my shirt and took a seat in the center of the front row. If Lori was conducting the meeting, I wanted to be able to eyeball her without anyone blocking my field of vision. Not that I'm criticizing anyone, but several of my fellow Tummy Trimmers had enough meat on their bones to fill out my view completely and then some. Which was, of course, why they were coming to Tummy Trimmers in the first place.

I busied myself looking at the latest Tummy Trimmers marketing flyer, which featured another dazzling picture of Lori Todesco on page one. Our fearless leader was wearing a black leotard and yoga pants which were so tight that they proved without question that she didn't have even an ounce of extra fat on her lithe dancer's body. Her red hair was styled in a casual ponytail. The photo caption read: "I did it! And you will too! Let's take the journey together!"

I sincerely hated Lori at that moment, because I knew without a shadow of a doubt that I would never grow six inches taller, nor shed enough body fat to be caught dead or alive in a form-fitting outfit like that, much less allow myself to be photographed wearing one.

Look on the bright side, Carol. At least you're not on the brochure cover in your fat suit, as the Tummy Trimmers "before" model.

Suddenly, all conversation in the room stopped. The *Tighten Up* song came blasting through the sound system. One person, then another, then another, began to clap, until everyone in the room (except me, because I had no idea what was going on from my front row vantage point) was cheering. I turned and saw Lori making a grand entrance, similar to what the president does at his annual State of the Union address to Congress, stopping to greet one person after another as she made her way to the front of the room. She was dressed in a similar outfit to the one she wore for the new marketing piece, except that she had added a matching black wraparound skirt.

When Lori saw me, sitting front and center, she faltered a little. But not for long. She pulled me to my feet and maneuvered me into a position right beside her. "Ladies and gentlemen," she said, "this is the true face of Tummy Trimmers. Not me. When Carol Andrews first contacted me, desperate to lose weight, she was in complete despair. She had tried countless other programs, and failed at every single one of them. Can any of you identify with that?"

"Yes! Yes! Yes!" everyone yelled. Well, everyone except me. I was so mortified that I wanted to crawl into the nearest hole and stay there forever.

"But Carol found Tummy Trimmers," Lori continued with a huge smile. "And look at the nametag she's proudly wearing today. Carol is wearing a smiley face! She's losing weight! Tummy Trimmers has succeeded where other diet programs have failed!" She grabbed my hand and raised it up high. "If someone as overweight as Carol was can do it, so can all of you! And you will!" Then, she hissed in my ear, "Smile, Carol. We're having our picture taken." I looked toward the back of the room and saw Liam documenting my so-called Tummy Trimmers victory.

Cue more cheers and clapping from the crowd. Cue Carol wanting to break free of Lori's viselike grip and slink back to her seat. Cue Carol, hearing a familiar male voice coming from the back of the meeting room. "Ms. Todesco, I'm Jim Andrews from the *Fairport News*. Would you care to comment on the sudden death of one of your members, Pat Mathews, at one of your classes?"

Cue Carol wanting to get the hell out of there.

Chapter 26

If men are really from Mars, can we send some back on the next space shuttle?

"I don't see what you're so upset about, Carol," Jim said. "I was doing exactly what you asked me to do. I had the meeting with my editor about Pat Mathews, just like you wanted. He was intrigued by the fact that this woman had died and no one had come forward to give her a proper funeral. He assigned me to the story, just like you hoped he would. It's not my fault that he wanted me to get some background quotes from people who'd had some contact with Pat Mathews to add some meat to the story. You want people to read it and respond, don't you? Why aren't you answering me? Say something."

We were standing eyeball to eyeball on Fairport Turnpike in front of Maria's Trattoria, too public a place for me to say what I was really thinking. And, to be clear, I love my husband. Always have. Always will. But sometimes, he makes me nuts, especially when he's completely clueless. Like, right now. And I tend to snap at him with a nasty reply that I instantly regret. After all, despite all Jim's good points—and there are many—he is first, last and always A Man. So, he can't help being clueless. Or, to be more accurate, his wave length isn't my wave length. Never has been. Never will be. If you've been married for any length of time, you understand what I mean. And if you haven't been, well, read on and learn.

"Jim," I said, glancing around to be sure nobody was close

enough to overhear us, "I don't want to argue with you. And, you're completely correct. You did do exactly what I asked you to do. Thank you." Jim's expression changed from confused to happy. Swear to God, he looked like Lucy and Ethel when I praised them for their potty habits and rewarded them with dog biscuits.

"You see, dear," I continued, "I'm not quarreling with what you did. My problem is with the public way you did it. You embarrassed me. You blindsided me. Why didn't you let me know in advance that you were coming to the Tummy Trimmers meeting to grill Lori Todesco? You should have texted me first." My voice was getting higher, and louder, despite my best efforts.

"Do you want me to write the story or not?" Jim asked me. "And for your information, Carol, I was not *grilling* Lori Todesco. I asked her for a comment on a tragic situation that involved Tummy Trimmers and, by extension, involved her, because she is the founder of Tummy Trimmers. I repeat, what the heck are you so mad about?"

For a split second, I really envied Pat Mathews. Not the fact that she died. I'm not totally crazy. I envied her ability to put herself into a deep meditative state. I closed my eyes tight, took a few deep breaths and willed myself to a calm place. But no way was my mind going to cooperate. No part of me was going anywhere.

This is a teaching moment, Carol. For you and for Jim. Don't waste it. Calm down and behave like an adult, not a screaming banshee. You're only making Jim madder, because he's frustrated and doesn't understand your reaction. All the screaming in the world won't change that. So let it go. And, for Pete's sake, don't start crying.

"I'm sure you agree how important it is for us to communicate with each other," I said in a more reasonable tone of voice. Which took a lot of effort, so I hope I get points for that.

"Of course I do. Which is why I was so mad last night when I came into the kitchen after doing fruitless research on a dead woman *I don't even know* and you, Jenny and Mark were all gone, without telling me you were leaving, where you were going, or when you'd be coming back." Need I tell you that, by this time, Jim's voice had gotten louder and higher? No, I didn't think so.

I had to admit the situations were eerily similar. It was the classic husband-wife standoff. Who would blink first? Me, of course. The peacemaker. And every wife worth her wedding band knows it's always a lot easier to get her own way with sweet talk than with shouting.

I looked properly contrite. "We're both at fault, Jim. Me for last night, and you for today. And I know you were doing what I asked you to do. You just surprised me, that's all."

"Speaking of surprises," Jim said, "I was sure surprised to see you standing in the front of the meeting with Lori Todesco. What the heck was that all about? And the way she was holding up your hand, and everyone was clapping. She sure can fill out a leotard in all the right places. You know, she really looks familiar. But I can't figure out why."

Squelching down a brief pang of jealousy, I said, "I told you before that she was on that old television show, *New England Rock and Roll Dance Party*. And you saw her at a Fairport Business Association meeting, remember?" Honestly, Jim's short-term memory is getting to be as bad as mine.

"No, Carol, that's not what I mean." He shook his head. "Maybe it'll come to me. Anyway, it's probably not important. But why were you in the front of the Tummy Trimmers meeting with her? The way she was holding up your hand, you looked like you'd just won a big prize."

"Not exactly a big prize," I said. "But I am pretty proud of myself." I pointed to my smiley face nametag. "Do you know what this means?"

Jim shook his head. "No idea. Should I?"

"It means I've lost weight, Jim," I said. I twirled around in front of him, so he could admire my shrinking body. Okay, it was only a few pounds. And I had a long way to go before I'd be in Lori's league, but I was definitely heading in the right direction. "All those meals that you refer to as diet mush are paying off. And I feel better, too. I definitely have more energy. Although I need to exercise more."

Jim gave me a familiar look. "I've got an idea about some exercise we can do together," he said, taking my hand. "Let's go home and I'll show you." I had to laugh. Jim was so predictable. But I knew how lucky I was that my husband still found me attractive after all these years.

"I'll see you at home," I said, giving my paramour a playful pat on his posterior. "And then we'll...."

Wait a minute. I don't have to tell you about that.

Chapter 27

The only therapy I'm interested in is the retail kind.

You all know that I don't like to brag. But after years of driving two kids to sporting events, dance lessons, sleepover parties, scout meetings, school outings, and who knows what else, my knowledge of shortcuts in our fair town of Fairport is superior to Jim's. Although, to give the guy his due, after years of commuting to Manhattan for his job, he knows much more about navigating around the Big Apple than I do. He can even find his way around SoHo and the West Village, two areas of town that are mega confusing to a lot of people. Including me.

So it was no surprise that when I pulled into our driveway, there was no sign of Jim's car. Yay. That gave me some time to make myself more presentable for our midday date. I was mentally flipping through my choice of appropriate ensembles as I speed-walked toward my kitchen door. And stopped short as I caught sight of a woman sitting on the side steps. Not just any woman. It was Sister Rose.

Oh, boy. There's nothing like the sight of a nun to wipe the mind clean of any potential afternoon delight. I flattened myself against the back of the house and considered my options.

Maybe she didn't see you, Carol. Maybe you can head off Jim and the two of you can slink away somewhere without her catching on.

I'm not proud of the way my mind was working, so I hope you

won't judge me too harshly. But then, reality kicked in.

You must be kidding, Carol. This is Sister Rose you're talking about. She'll know. She always knows. And besides, don't you want to find out what happened at the police station today?

So I sighed, squared my shoulders and pasted what I hoped looked like a glad-to-see-you smile on my face. "This is a surprise, Sister. I didn't see your car. How did the police interview go?" I took a closer look. Sister Rose was not happy.

"I walked from the thrift shop," she replied. "I thought a long walk around town would clear my head. And then I found myself in front of your house. Maybe the Good Lord was guiding me. Who knows? And to answer your question, things did not go well. At least, not from my point of view. I can't believe what I did."

I unlocked the kitchen door and shooed the dogs away. "Later, girls. Let us in. And, please, show Sister Rose that you have some manners. Don't jump all over her, even though that's the way you usually greet people." I turned to the good sister and asked, "Would a cup of coffee or tea help?" I know it's stupid, but in moments of crisis, and clearly we were headed in that direction, I tend to fall back on tried-and-true clichés to diffuse the situation.

"Just some water, please, Carol. I don't want to put you to any trouble. In fact, I probably shouldn't have come at all. Maybe I should just leave."

Now, I was torn. Part of me wanted to nod my head and say, "Yep, that's exactly what you should do, Sister. Vamoose before Jim gets home and you completely ruin our afternoon plans."

But the good girl part of me was made of kinder, gentler stuff. To say nothing of the fact that I was absolutely dying of curiosity. I poured bottled water from the refrigerator into two glasses. "Why don't we talk in the dining room, Sister," I said, "Lucy and Ethel won't bother us in there." I gave them a stern look. "Will you, girls?"

Not waiting for an answer, I led the way to the dining room and placed the glasses on my mahogany table. (Of course, I gave each of us coasters, in case you were wondering.) "Now, Sister, why don't you tell me what happened." *And don't leave any little detail out.* I didn't really say that last part, of course.

"I'm in the midst of a moral dilemma, Carol. What's the penalty for lying to the police?"

Oh, boy. Holy macaroni. Holy everything. This was uncharted territory, even for me. I have been known to embellish the truth on occasion. All right, on several occasions. But I've never, ever lied to the police. Not even to that twerpy Paul Wheeler when I was working on clearing Jim of his retirement coach's murder.

But I digress. Forgive me.

I took a slow sip of water and considered how to respond to Sister Rose's bombshell question. It was clear to me that the only reason Sister Rose would tell a lie was to protect someone. Perhaps it was a former student from her teaching days at Mount St. Francis Academy. Or one of the clients from the domestic violence center. That second idea made the most sense to me.

Then, a completely outrageous idea popped into my head. Did Sister Rose lie to protect herself? Was that even remotely possible? *Oh, Carol, you're losing it now. No way. Right?*

"I have no idea what the penalty for lying to the police could be," I said. "Maybe you didn't really lie, though. Maybe you just didn't tell them the whole truth. I mean, if the person who interviewed you didn't ask the correct questions, you didn't need to add any information. I believe there are laws against self-incrimination."

"You don't understand, Carol," Sister Rose snapped. "As usual, you've jumped to the wrong conclusion. Not that I blame you. I haven't explained myself very well." She took a deep breath, then said, "I went to the police station this morning to give my statement about the break-in. I was very nervous. I wasn't sure who was going to interview me. I was so relieved when your son-in-law was the one who met me. He took me to his office so we could have some privacy."

"That was so nice of Mark," I said. "He's a real sweetheart."

"Yes, he is, Carol," Sister Rose said, "but I'd really appreciate it if you'd let me tell my story without interrupting me."

"Of course," I said. "I'm sorry. Jim says that interrupting people when they're talking is one of my worst faults." I zipped my lips shut and willed them to stay that way.

Satisfied with my self-imposed silence, Sister Rose continued her tale. "Mark began to take me through the sequence of last night's events. He was making notes that he said would be compiled into a statement for me to sign at the end of the interview. And one of the questions he asked me was…"

Yes! Yes! I leaned forward in my chair. Now we were getting to the heart of the matter. And that's when I heard my darling husband calling to me from the kitchen. "Carol. Carol! Where are you? Are you hiding? Wait till you see my surprise! It's guaranteed to get you in the right mood."

Chapter 28

I just burned 10,000 calories. That's the last time I leave a pan of brownies in the oven and decide to take a nap!

Oh, no! Jim was home with a surprise for me, no doubt one related to our planned afternoon activities. With Sister Rose sitting right here. I had to head him off before he burst into the dining room and embarrassed himself and me. And probably gave Sister Rose a coronary.

"Carol, are you in the dining room? What are you doing in there? We never use that room unless we have company."

"Jim!" I screeched, jumping up so fast that I knocked over my chair, "stay there. I'll come in." I gave Sister Rose an apologetic smile and said, "I'll be right back."

But Jim was too quick for me. He burst through the door with a big smile on his face, holding a bouquet of red roses. Thank God, at least he was still completely dressed. The last time he surprised me, he was wearing nothing but a bow tie and a smile. He skidded to a stop when he caught sight of Sister Rose. And blushed a furious shade of red, either from frustration that his afternoon plans had been ruined or embarrassment. Probably a little of both.

"You didn't tell me you were expecting anyone, Carol."

"Sister Rose surprised me," I said. "Isn't that nice? We were just having a lovely chat. Weren't we, Sister?"

I gave Jim a chaste peck on the cheek. "How lovely that you

remembered our anniversary, dear. Thank you so much for these roses. You know that they're my favorite. Haven't the years just flown by? You haven't brought me flowers since Mike was born."

Jim looked at me, clueless. Then I guess a lightbulb must have gone off in his brain. "Happy Anniversary, Carol."

"I didn't realize I was interrupting a private family moment," Sister Rose said, clearly uncomfortable. "Perhaps it would be best if I left. We can talk another time, Carol."

"No, please don't go," Jim said. "I'll just put these flowers in water and give you two time to finish your chat." And he telegraphed a husbandly look. *Don't take too long.*

Satisfied that we'd be left alone for a little while, I tried to get Sister Rose back on track. "You were saying that Mark was asking you questions about the break-in."

Sister Rose took another sip of water. Then sighed. "This is a true moral dilemma for me, Carol. Is lying a lesser sin than betraying someone you care about? I don't know. But I had to make a snap decision, and I made it. I lied. And now, I don't know if I did the right thing. And I'm afraid of the consequences of my actions. Both for me and the other person involved."

Whoa. We were getting into issues that were clearly over my head. I've never been much into examining moral dilemmas before. But Sister Rose was clearly so miserable that I had to do something. And she had come to me—me, of all people!—for advice, which showed how desperate she was.

I took her hand and squeezed it. "Sister, do you want to tell me what you lied about? Sharing something that I'm upset about with a person I know I can trust usually makes me feel better. You can trust me. I won't share what you tell me with anyone else."

"Perhaps you're right. Well, here goes. Mark asked me if I had any idea who had broken into the thrift shop. And I said I didn't. I said I never saw the person. But that was a lie." By this time Sister Rose was gripping my hand so hard that I was afraid she'd break it.

"Just to be clear, you saw the person. And you recognized the person. But you didn't tell Mark that. Is that correct?"

"Yes, Carol. You see, I couldn't tell him. The person I saw was Destiny. My niece."

Poor Sister Rose. No wonder she was so upset.

"I'm so sorry, Sister." I took a big chance, and decided to ask a few more questions. She could always shut me down if she didn't want to answer me, and she was, after all, in my dining room, so that gave me the right to be curious, right? Of course, right.

"Are you absolutely sure it was Destiny you saw? It must have been pretty dark in the shop."

"Of course, I'm sure," Sister Rose said, looking even more miserable. "And I couldn't sleep all night worrying about her."

"Forgive me if you think I'm pushing you too hard," I said, "but how do you know it was Destiny? Did you see her face?"

"No," Sister Rose admitted. "But I saw her jacket. It's a very distinctive design. I gave it to her for Christmas last year, and she wears it all the time. Maybe you've even seen it on her? It's bright red and it says 'We're all sisters!' on the back. I had it made especially for her."

I shook my head. "Nope. I can't say I've ever seen it." To me, this sounded like flimsy circumstantial evidence, not real proof of Destiny's guilt. If there's one thing I've learned from all those mysteries I've read over the years, it's that circumstantial evidence can be deceiving. Of course, this was real life, not fiction. I paused and let my brain find another track for my questions. Means, motive and opportunity. The big three that pop up in all those books. While I was pondering these possibilities, I was all too aware that Jim could put in another appearance at any moment. I had to hurry my interrogation along.

"Why would Destiny break into the shop, trash it and steal money?" I asked. "She has a regular job that pays her a salary. That just doesn't make sense to me."

"That's because I haven't told you a lot about Destiny's background," Sister Rose replied. "She could have a desperate need for money. And that means only one thing to me. She's back on drugs again."

"Oh, no," I said, shocked. "Are you sure?"

"I'm not sure," Sister Rose admitted, looking sadder than I'd ever seen her before. "But it's entirely possible. Destiny was never taught to make good life choices. I already told you that my sister, Violet, never provided her with a normal family life. Destiny ran away several times, and got in with the wrong crowd, which is all too common. She got hooked on drugs and...." Sister Rose's eyes filled up. "She completely dropped out of sight. Violet finally contacted me and told me what had happened. She begged me to help her find Destiny. And, thank God, because of some contacts I'd made over the last few years, I was able to track her down last year and help her. She loves her job at Tummy Trimmers, and told me she had a serious boyfriend now. She was so excited. She insisted I meet him, and I must say that Liam seemed quite smitten with her. I liked him very much."

I tried not to show my surprise. Of course, there could be more than one person named Liam in the town of Fairport. But not working at Tummy Trimmers. But I couldn't forget the intimate caress Lori had given him at the grand opening of Tummy Trimmers. If what I suspected was true, I feared that Destiny was going to have her heart broken.

"I thought Destiny finally had her life heading in the right direction," Sister Rose continued. "But when I saw her last night running out of the thrift shop, I realized I was wrong. Addiction is an illness, and she's still sick. She needs professional help, and I'm going to see that she gets it. But no matter what, I'll never betray her to the police. Never."

Sister Rose had her face set in the "don't argue with me" look that I knew so well. I started to speak but she cut me off. "Thank you for listening to me, Carol," she said, handing me her water glass and preparing to leave. "Talking this out with you has convinced me that, even though I told a lie, it was for a very good reason. I hope God understands that, and forgives me."

I had a brief agony of indecision. Part of me really wanted her to leave asap. The other part knew that she had made a huge mistake and hadn't really considered the possible consequences of her actions. I found myself in the surprising—and very uncomfortable—position of playing mother confessor, judge and jury to my high school English teacher.

"Sister, please wait a minute," I said, jumping to my feet and pulling at her sleeve.

"I have to leave," Sister Rose said. A small smile played at her lips. "And I think your husband is waiting to start celebrating your wedding anniversary."

I blushed. I couldn't help myself. But then I realized that by turning the spotlight back on me, she had successfully dodged any chance of my voicing my opinion. Well, she wasn't going to get away with it.

"Sister Rose," I said in my firm mommy voice, "you need to sit down again. This conversation isn't over." And I pulled out her chair and gestured to it. "Sit."

Sister Rose glared at me. But, finally, she sat down. "This is the second time you've talked to me in that tone of voice, Carol," she said. "I don't care for it."

"That's unfortunate, Sister. Because you asked for it, both times." Oops. I couldn't believe I'd just said that to Sister Rose. I slapped my hands over my mouth. "I'm sorry, Sister. That just came out. My mouth sometimes speaks before my brain has a chance to stop it. I know you're under a lot of stress. I want to help you, if I can."

I was suddenly distracted by a wet doggie nose nudging my leg. Lucy, of course, had figured out a way to get into the dining room, where she and Ethel were forbidden. And her canine cohort was right behind her.

"Lucy," I said, taking her collar and leading her back toward the kitchen, "you're a little devil. You know this room is off-limits."

"Let them stay, Carol," Sister Rose said. "I find it comforting to be around dogs. And I don't have the opportunity often enough." She settled herself back into a chair and snapped her fingers. Within a millisecond, both dogs had gravitated to her side. I was amazed at their response, especially because Sister Rose didn't even have any food to offer them. And, truth to tell, I was just a tiny bit jealous, too. But with their sudden appearance, the dogs had managed to diffuse the tension in the room, and for that, I was grateful. I made a mental note to reward them with a handful of extra kibble in their dinner bowls tonight.

"You both can stay," I said, addressing my canines, "because Sister Rose said it's okay. But don't get used to being in here. This room will be off-limits to you again as soon as Sister Rose leaves." Lucy gave me a look which telegraphed that she didn't believe me for one single second. I let it go. I hate to have a public argument with her. Especially since she usually wins.

"Now that we're friends again," I said, hoping that was true, "what were you saying about Destiny, Sister?" I hope you're all impressed with the masterful way I took over the conversation.

"I was telling you that I was afraid she was back on drugs, Carol," Sister Rose said. "Weren't you listening to me?" And she gave me one of her famous evil eye looks. But this time, I didn't mind as much as I usually do.

"Of course, I was listening, Sister," I said. "But I was shocked at what you told me about Destiny. How long ago did she have a problem with drugs?"

"She's been clean...I believe 'clean' is the correct word...for over a year," Sister Rose replied. "At least, that's what she told me. And I had no reason to doubt her word. But now, I wonder." She looked thoughtful. "I've only seen her on a few short occasions until recently, when she moved to Fairport. Maybe she never was off drugs completely."

"The poor girl," I said. "I wish there was something I could do to help." *Careful, Carol. Haven't you got enough on your plate right now, with Jenny's pregnancy and Pat Mathews' death?*

As soon as the words popped out of my mouth, I knew I'd made a big mistake. It was almost like I could see them hanging in midair between Sister Rose and me, with a furious Jim looking at us. Oh, boy. If he found out I was sleuthing again, he'd read me the good old riot act.

"Carol, dear, thank you so much," Sister Rose said, now giving me a huge smile. "I feel so much better now that you've agreed to figure this whole situation out and clear Destiny. After all, as you said, I could be completely wrong. Perhaps it wasn't Destiny I saw at all. You are the epitome of a true Mount Saint Francis graduate, always wanting to help others." She glanced at her watch. "Mercy, is that the time? I must leave. Please keep in touch, and if you have any more questions I can answer, you know where to find me."

And just like that, she was gone, leaving me sitting in shock at my very own dining room table. *Yes, Sister, I do have one question. How did I get myself into this? Oh, and here's another one. Is this what you wanted from me all the time?*

I didn't really say that out loud, because it was too late. I had been snookered, plain and simple.

Chapter 29

The only crunches I like are the Nestle kind.

The following day I awoke to the sound of my husband warbling in the shower. It could have been *Some Enchanted Evening*, but I couldn't swear to it. My goodness, but he was in a good mood today. Come to think of it, I was too. I stretched and realized that my neck wasn't hurting today. I couldn't remember the last time that happened.

My freshly showered husband appeared, a towel wrapped around his middle, and gave me a quick peck on the cheek. "Shower's all yours," he said. "I'll take care of the dogs and start the coffee. Unless you have any other ideas." And he raised his eyebrows suggestively.

"Coffee sounds perfect," I said, ignoring the hint. "I'll see you in a few minutes."

My good mood was obliterated by the ping of an incoming text. I squinted to read it without my glasses. Oh, boy. It was Sister Rose.

SR: *Have you found anything to help Destiny yet?*

Me: *Huh?*

SR: *Destiny! You promised you'd help her.*

Me: *I did? I mean, I did. But I'm just getting up. I'll text you later, okay?*

SR: *Fine. Good luck.*

Good luck. That's exactly what I'd need. Or perhaps, a minor miracle. And then I realized I had my personal miracle man, who fancied himself the king of Internet research, in the kitchen making coffee for me. Maybe I could suggest he do some cyber sleuthing about Destiny, as background for the story he was writing about Pat Mathews. After all, Destiny was present when Pat collapsed at Tummy Trimmers, and the only information I had about her was from Sister Rose, who was not the most objective of sources. Maybe Destiny wasn't the innocent young woman Sister Rose believed her to be. I figured that the more I knew about Destiny, the better. Does that make sense to you? Well, it does to me, and that's all that counts.

The only problem was that Jim rarely takes work-related ideas from me. Just look at all the tears Jenny and I had to shed to talk him into pitching the story about Pat Mathews to his editor. But he was in an extra good mood this morning, thanks to a combination of a lovely chardonnay, a delicious takeout meal from Maria's Trattoria (my idea, of course), and...well, I don't have to tell you everything. But, trust me, my timing could not have been better. Feeling confident that I could pull this off, I took a quick shower and dressed in record time. As I was applying a brief spritz of Jim's favorite perfume, my phone pinged again. "Give me a break, Sister," I muttered. "I haven't even had breakfast yet."

I was torn between checking the text and ignoring it. Then another ping, and another, and another. Lordy. But because I am constitutionally unable to ignore a ringing telephone, doorbell, or, multiple text messages, I gave in. After all, it might be something important. Like Jenny, needing motherly advice. Or else, God forbid, going into labor prematurely. I grabbed the phone and squinted at the text. No, not Jenny, thank God. Nor Sister Rose. It was Nancy, all three times.

Text 1: Want 2 have an adventure 2day?

Text 2: Carol, are u there?

Text 3: Carol, for Pete's sake, call me right away. This is important!

Sheesh. Why did everybody seem to be on my case today? My good mood vanished, replaced by a large helping of annoyance. But, still. Nancy did mention an adventure. She knew that'd intrigue me.

I punched in her number from my "favorites" contact list. "This better be good," I said to her.

"There you are. I was worried when you didn't respond to my texts."

"Some of us have other priorities besides answering texts," I said.

"Oooooh, that sounds provocative," Nancy said. "Under any other circumstances, I'd ask you to spill all the details. But not this morning. Are you dressed?"

"What does that have to do with anything?" I paused, then added, "Yes, I'm dressed."

"Can you be ready to leave the house right away? Mary Alice and I are coming to pick you up. We're going to have an adventure. I promise you, you'll love it."

"I already have plans for today," I said. "I have something to take care of for Sister Rose. She texted me before you did this morning."

Nancy laughed. "Poor you. What a way to start the day. But this adventure will cheer you up. And we won't be gone too long, I promise. You'll be back home by lunch. Promise."

"This adventure doesn't have anything to do with Tummy Trimmers, does it?" I asked. "It better not be another addition to the program which requires me to be photographed using some horrible machine to lose more weight. I know how you love working out, but I hate it, in case you've forgotten."

"No, Carol," Nancy said. "It's not a new Tummy Trimmers workout. But it does have something to do with Tummy Trimmers. Sort of. Get a move on, girl. If you quit asking me questions and get off the phone, we can be on our way in fifteen minutes and you can see for yourself."

"Well…" I said, weakening. "Make it twenty minutes. I have to talk to Jim, first. I'm delegating part of Sister's Rose's assignment to him. Except he doesn't know it yet."

Nancy chuckled. "There's nothing new about that. Most of the time, Jim has no idea what you're up to. I'm so glad Bob and I don't live together any more. Dating your husband is so much more fun than being with him twenty-four/seven. See you in twenty minutes. And we'll bring coffee."

"New car?" I said, settling myself into the passenger seat of a cream-colored Mercedes Benz convertible. I reached into the back seat and gave Mary Alice's hand a loving squeeze. "I'm glad you got corralled into this adventure, too, Mary Alice. I figured that if you were along, our designated driver wouldn't make our adventure anything we could get arrested for. You always keep us on our good behavior."

"Now, that's just plain silly," Nancy said. "You're the one who comes up with the outlandish schemes, Carol, not me."

"Pardon my back seat comment, but as I recall, you each come up with an equal share of outlandish schemes," Mary Alice said, laughing. "But my life has been pretty dull lately. I've been working too many hours. I never knew retirement could be so exhausting. And boring. At least, for me. So I'm up for whatever Nancy has in store." Long pause. "I think."

"As far as this new car is concerned," Nancy said, flooring the accelerator and achieving a speed I was sure would land her a ticket, "it's from Bob."

"Bob?" I repeated. "Bob your sort-of husband? Maybe Jim and I should try your married-but-dating lifestyle, too, if the fringe benefits include presents like this. And by the way, where are we going?"

"I'd like to know, too," Mary Alice said. "You're being very mysterious, Nancy." She yawned. "It's a little early in the day for a mystery."

The Mercedes tires squealed as Nancy turned a corner. I closed my eyes and began to pray.

"Bob didn't exactly give me the car," Nancy said.

"Oh my gosh, Nancy, it's not stolen, is it?" Mary Alice said. "And, for Pete's sake, and mine, will you please slow down a little? Your driving is making me nervous."

Nancy eased up on the accelerator a little. "The car isn't stolen, silly. Bob's getting into car sales, and he loaned this beauty to me to test drive. He wants me to see how it performs under a variety of conditions."

"It certainly passed the speed test," I muttered. Daring to open my eyes, I looked around and read a street sign. "We're going to the beach," I said. "Why the heck didn't you just say we were going for a walk on the beach in the first place?"

"We're not going for a walk on the beach," Nancy said. "We're going to look at a house."

"Oh, no," I protested. "Don't tell me you're going to try and get Jim and me to sell our house and move. The last time you listed our house for sale, we ended up with a dead body in our living room. We're staying put, thank you very much."

"Honestly, I don't understand why everyone always thinks I have an ulterior motive when it comes to real estate," Nancy said, pulling into the seashell driveway of a gorgeous home on Fairport Beach Road with uninterrupted views of Long Island Sound. "We're here. Everybody out."

"Nancy, this is fabulous," I said, drooling in spite of myself. "It looks like something from HGTV. Jim and I could never afford this."

"I know that," Nancy said. "That's not why I brought you here. It's a rental house. With a recently deceased tenant. Pat Mathews."

Chapter 30

Another day, another donut.

"You were right, Nancy," I said, hopping out of the car and admiring the spectacular water view. "This is an adventure. But why didn't you tell me this before?"

"Before what?" Mary Alice said, joining us on the front steps. "Who's Pat Mathews? The name sounds vaguely familiar."

"Pat Mathews is the woman who collapsed at a Tummy Trimmers meditation class," I said.

"That's only part of the story," Nancy said. "She collapsed on top of Carol."

"Oh, Carol, how terrible." Mary Alice gave me a hug, then said, "I remember now. You texted me about her, right? And she died on the way to the hospital. But I had no idea you were so closely involved."

"So, what's the story with this house?" I asked. I could hardly wait to get inside and check it out.

"It's a listing our office has been trying to sell for a long time," Nancy said. "Do you remember, Carol, the day Pat died, I had to dash off because someone wanted to see it? Of course, that showing didn't produce an offer, either. The owner will not consider a price reduction. It's just ridiculous." She punched a series of numbers into the lock box on the front door, which remained stubbornly closed. "This sticks sometimes, because of the salt air. Getting it to open may take me a little while. But I guarantee you, it's worth the wait."

"I hope so," I said, my curiosity being blown away by a sharp wind coming off the water. "It's cold out here."

"I'm doing my best, Carol," Nancy said through gritted teeth as she tried the lock box again. "Anyway, I knew the property had a tenant, and every time I wanted to show the property to a prospective buyer, I had to be sure the house would be empty. I did that through the agent who handles the rental. I never knew the name of the tenant. There. Finally," Nancy said, holding the front door key in her hand. "Let's go inside."

"I still don't understand how you figured out that Pat was the tenant," I said.

"I noticed last night that the status of the rental listing changed to 'active,' " Nancy said. "I wondered why. So I texted the agent and she told me the tenant had recently died. When she gave me the name, I almost fainted. I wanted to call you right away, Carol, but I figured it was too late and you'd already be in bed."

True.

"I'm glad I called you for a coffee date this morning," Mary Alice said. "I've been out of the loop with all of this. And I love looking at houses, especially those I know I could never afford to buy."

Nancy laughed. "You and a million other people," she said. "Come on in and take a look at this one."

"Wow," I said. "The outside of the house is gorgeous, but the inside. Wow. Just, wow." I was blown away by the open floor plan and the state-of-the-art kitchen with custom cabinets that must have cost a fortune.

"Told you it'd be worth the wait," Nancy said. "I call it 'California style meets New England beachfront' on the listing sheet. It's 2,700 square feet, with four bedrooms and three baths, but the high ceilings and the loft make it seem even bigger. Plus, the owner decorated it entirely in white, so that adds to the illusion of more space. Take a look around. The master bedroom on the second floor is guaranteed to knock your socks off."

"You don't have to ask me twice," I said, grabbing Mary Alice's hand. "Let's go."

"Are you sure this is okay to be here?" Mary Alice asked. "I feel like we're trespassing."

"We're not trespassing, Mary Alice," Nancy assured her. "This is my listing, remember? Take a look around. I'll wait in the great room and admire the view."

"Come on, Mary Alice," I said, "let's go check out the second floor. I don't know about you, but I'm ready to have my socks knocked off." Mary Alice laughed and followed me up the stairs to the master bedroom.

"How'd you like to wake up to this?" I asked, plopping down on the king size bed, positioned so that it faced a sweeping view of Long Island Sound. "I might not ever leave."

"If you think the bedroom's great," Mary Alice called, "come look at the master bath. It's all marble. With a multi-head shower and a sunken tub. I've never seen anything like it."

I hopped up and smoothed the wrinkles out of the bedspread. "Pretty impressive," I said. "But I'd hate to keep all this clean. I can just imagine Lucy and Ethel shedding all over the white bedspread."

"I wonder how much it would cost to buy this house," Mary Alice said as we checked out the other bedrooms.

"Why? Are you interested?" I asked with a grin.

"Interested, sure. In a fantasy," Mary Alice replied. "But I can dream, can't I? Speaking of which, I want to take one more look at that master bedroom and bath, since I doubt I'll ever see something so spectacular ever again except on television. You go on ahead. I'll be down in a minute."

I nodded and made my way to the main floor, imagining what a great staircase this would be for a bride to make a grand entrance on her wedding day. Like, possibly, my grandchild-to-be, assuming Jenny had a girl, of course. Hey, I can dream, too, can't I?

"So, Nancy," I said, rejoining my BFF in the great room, "we've seen the house and it's gorgeous. What's the asking price? Mary Alice may want to make an offer."

Nancy's eyes widened, then she realized I wasn't serious. "The house is listed for three million dollars," she said. "But you can rent it, fully furnished, for a mere ten thousand dollars a month. And it's pet friendly."

"Not to my pets," I snorted. "That's a lot of money for a rental. I didn't realize renting could be so expensive."

"It's the location," Nancy explained. "Waterfront property is prime. And, by the way, the rental doubles in cost during the summer. Ten thousand dollars is only the going rate for September through May."

My goodness. No way Jim and I could ever afford this place,

even as a rental. And I wondered how in the world Pat Mathews could. She never seemed like an ultra rich person to me.

Honestly, Carol, you barely knew the woman. You have no idea how healthy her bank account was. For all you know, she was an heiress.

"If Pat Mathews was an heiress, wouldn't there be at least one person who'd step forward and arrange for her funeral?" I said aloud.

"Pat Mathews was an heiress?" Nancy repeated. "I didn't know that."

I waved my hand. "Don't listen to me. I was just speculating about how she could afford to rent this place. And I guess I speculated out loud. I have no idea if Pat was rich or a pauper. But she'd need to have big bucks to afford the rent on this place." I sank into one of the plush white chairs facing the stone fireplace. "Ooh, this fits my back just right. I may stay here for the rest of the day."

"Don't get too comfortable," Nancy warned. "Here comes Mary Alice. It's time for us to leave. I need to lock up the house."

"Not quite yet," Mary Alice said. She placed a cardboard box in the center of the glass coffee table. "I confess that I did a little more snooping upstairs. I wanted to check out the walk-in closet. It's big enough to be another bedroom, by the way. I saw this box hidden in a corner on the very top shelf. Everything else has been cleaned out. I thought I'd better bring it down to you, Nancy."

Nancy's expression wavered between curiosity and annoyance. "The rental agent was supposed to clean out all the tenant's personal effects before the listing went to 'active.' They're in a secure storage locker until Pat's next-of-kin comes to claim them. How could she have missed this box?"

I cleared my throat. "Actually, no next-of-kin has been located, and nobody has claimed responsibility for Pat's funeral. As a matter of fact, the town may have to take care of Pat's final arrangements if they can't find anyone else. Isn't that the saddest thing? Can you imagine someone dying and having nobody care?"

"But that means…"

"That means, maybe it's okay for us to open this box and see what's inside," I finished for Mary Alice. "There could be personal contact information in there. And maybe whatever we find will help the town save some money. And give Pat Mathews a proper send-off. As concerned citizens who found the box in the first place, it's our duty to check it out first and decide if we should turn it over to the police. Don't you think?" Hey, I can justify almost anything. I've had years of practice.

"I don't know," Mary Alice said. "That doesn't feel right to me."

I turned to Nancy, who was now holding the box. "It's your call. You're the 'official' person here. Mary Alice and I are merely your guests."

"Are you practicing what you'll say in case we get in trouble for this?" Nancy asked. "Just like you did in high school?"

"As I recall, you were the one who got us into trouble in high school, and I was the one who always got caught and had to shoulder the blame," I said. "It's your turn, now. Open the box."

"All right, already. I'll do it. But do you think I should wear gloves? I don't want to leave any fingerprints," Nancy said.

"You're being ridiculous," I replied. "You have every right to be here and you know it. Give me the darn thing. I'll open it."

The box was taped shut. "I hate this stuff," I said, using Nancy's car key to loosen one corner. "I'll bet that, when I finally get the darn thing open, there'll be nothing important inside."

"It must be important," Mary Alice said. "Otherwise, why would Pat Mathews have gone to so much trouble to hide it?"

"True," I agreed. At last the corner opened just enough so that I could slip my hand inside and free the entire top of the box. "Here goes nothing," I said, and spilled the contents on the coffee table.

"I don't know what I was expecting, but this looks like a lot of junk to me," Nancy said. "It's just some old photographs."

I flipped through the photos, checking the backs for any clue as to who was in them or where and when they were taken. But there was nothing.

"We might as well put everything back in the box," Nancy said, holding out her hand. "I can take it back to the office and put the box in storage along with everything else that's been cleaned out of the rental."

"I have another idea," I said. "How about if I show the box to Mark? He told me the police have been asked to help locate Pat's next-of-kin. Who knows? There may be something in here that we've missed. And if he doesn't want it, I'll drop it by your office, Nancy. Is that okay with everyone?"

"Works for me," Nancy said, and Mary Alice nodded.

I scooped up the box contents as best I could, and stuffed them back inside. There was still a car key on the table. Honestly, that

Nancy. She's getting so forgetful in her old age about a lot of things. "Hey, Nancy," I called, "aren't you forgetting something?" I waved the car key. "We won't get too far without this."

Nancy stopped and reached inside her coat pocket. "You had me going there, Carol. I thought I left my key on the table after you used it to open the box. But here's mine, right where it should be." She waved it back at me. "See?"

"Then, whose is this?" I asked, staring at the key.

"Not mine," Mary Alice said. "I wear mine on a lanyard around my neck so I always know where it is. Carol, it must be yours."

"Nope," I said. "I left the house so fast this morning that I didn't even bring my purse." I thought for a second, then said, "I bet that key was in the box. I'll take it with me and give it to Mark."

But before I paid a visit to the Fairport Police Station to see my son-in-law, I had a stop to make at home first. I wanted to see how Jim was doing with his Internet sleuthing. Not that I'm criticizing the ability of Mark and the entire Fairport police department to do the same thing, understand. But I suspected that finding someone to assume responsibility for burying poor Pat wasn't at the top of their to-do list.

And while I was home, I planned to make copies of the photos in the mysterious box before I handed the contents over to Mark. Because you never know when that might come in handy, right? Of course, right.

Chapter 31

The more you weigh, the harder you are to kidnap. Be safe. Eat dessert!

"Hello. Anybody home?" The house was eerily quiet. "Where is everybody?" Jim was gone, and so were Lucy and Ethel.

"What did you expect?" I said aloud, putting the cardboard box on the middle of the kitchen table. "You ran out on Jim without even giving him a goodbye kiss. And on top of that, you've told him to find out everything he can about two people that he doesn't even know. *Told* him, not asked him nicely. What a way to kill the chances for another romantic interlude. You have to stop taking Jim for granted. And you have to stop talking to yourself all the time."

As if that would ever happen. There was something comforting about the sound of my own voice. It was like I had a special friend, or a twin, who thought about things the same way I did. And who let me talk about my darkest, deepest fears and wildest ideas and never criticized me. I know. Weird.

I felt the beginning of a caffeine-deprived headache forming right behind my eyes. Not surprising, since I was so excited about being able to nose around Pat Mathews' rental house that I never touched the coffee Nancy had provided.

"First things first," I ordered myself. "Coffee. Food. Photocopying." I laughed. "My personal version of *Eat, Pray, Love.*" I spread the contents of the box on the table, which was, amazingly, not littered with Jim's clutter. Since he's retired, he tends to take over any available spot as an office, which drives me crazy.

"I guess Jim isn't really mad," I said, spying the coffee pot that was all ready to perk. As I pressed the button to start the magic brew, I saw a note in Jim's familiar scrawl taped to the counter. "Off to interview Lori Todesco for _your_ story. Took dogs with me and will give them long walk before I come home. XXOO."

I had an irrational flash of jealousy, then told myself I was being stupid. Jim had never strayed in all our years of marriage.

Remember what he said when he saw Lori yesterday? That she filled out a leotard in all the right places. He's never said that about you.

Oh, shut up. And stop being so ridiculous and immature.

I gave myself a mental slap, filled a large mug with steaming high-test coffee, and settled myself at the kitchen table, determined to make order out of the pile of photos. And maybe, if I was lucky, pick up a clue as to who Pat really was and why she died so suddenly.

I admit that I am not the most organized person in the world. I usually operate on pure instinct as opposed to my friend Claire, for instance, who organizes every single aspect of her life until she squeezes all the excitement out of it, in my opinion. Not that I'm criticizing her, understand. Claire just approaches life differently than I do.

"What would you do if you were faced with all these photos, Claire? I wish I could channel you right now."

"How about giving me a cup of coffee instead?" said a familiar voice outside my kitchen window.

I jumped up and raced to the door. "Claire! When did you get home? Do Nancy and Mary Alice know you're back?" I pulled the poor woman into the kitchen and hugged her without giving her a chance to answer.

"Larry and I got home late yesterday," Claire said. "Nobody else knows we're back yet. I wanted to see you first. Nancy's been keeping me in the loop. I understand you're up to your old tricks."

Ignoring Claire's jibe, I pulled out my phone. "We have to set up a lunch date asap. How about Maria's? Is it too late to do it today?"

Claire stopped me. "No, Carol, don't call anybody else now. It's not that I don't want to see Nancy and Mary Alice. Especially Mary Alice, since she never made it to Florida over the winter. But when the four of us are together, we all talk at the same time. It's hard to have a real conversation. I decided on the long drive home from Florida that one of the gifts I'm giving myself this year is quality time with each of my best friends. And you live the closest to me, so I came here first. Catch me up."

"You drove north from Florida?" I repeated to be sure I hadn't misheard. "How come? You always leave a car in Florida and fly home."

"You may not believe this," Claire replied, "but my husband, the uptight lawyer, seems to be having a late-in-life crisis and..."

"Oh no, Claire," I said, immediately thinking the worst. "He's not cheating on you after all these years, is he? Oh, my God, I can't believe it."

"Leave it to you to jump to the worst possible conclusion, Carol," Claire said, laughing. "Larry has discovered a new love, but it's not a woman. It's a car. A vintage car, to be precise."

"Thank goodness," I said, relaxing back in my chair.

"Actually, a girlfriend might be cheaper," Claire said. "This new car is already costing us a fortune. It's a 1966 Shelby Mustang, and it's extremely rare. And valuable. Larry always wanted one. There are so many people in Florida who drive vintage convertibles all year long because the weather is so good, and Larry started doing research on the Internet to see if he could find the car of his dreams. It took him some time, but he finally found one in mint condition and bought it. We drove it back north and it's resting from its long journey all covered up in our garage." She smiled. "It's a real beauty, and Larry is thrilled with it. Wait'll you see it. It's candy apple red with a white stripe. I have to confess, I love it, too. But I'm afraid to drive it. If I get so much as a single scratch on it, Larry'll probably divorce me. You can come visit it in the garage. Maybe he'll let you sit in it, too."

"Men and their toys," I said, shaking my head.

"Let's get to more important news," Claire said. "How's Jenny feeling?"

I beamed. I just couldn't help myself. "She's great. She's at that glowing stage of pregnancy. Remember that part? When the morning sickness finally goes away and you get some of your old energy back?"

Claire laughed and accepted the coffee mug I'd put in front of her. "This really hits the spot. And as far as the glowing state of pregnancy is concerned, I must have skipped that part. Or if I glowed, I don't remember it."

Now it was my turn to laugh. "At first, Jenny was worried about losing her flat tummy," I admitted. "But she finally accepted that that's all part of being pregnant. She's also been having some trouble sleeping, but I think she's better now."

"Speaking of weight," Claire said, eyeing me critically as only she can, "you look different, Carol. Are you losing weight?" She covered my hand with her own. "You're not sick, are you?"

"Good heavens, Claire, I'm not sick. And I've only lost a few pounds so far. I've been walking more, and trying to eat right. I figured that if I'm going to have a grandchild to chase after pretty soon, I better start taking better care of myself."

"I'm impressed," Claire said. "Good for you. Nancy didn't tell me about that." She frowned for a minute, then added, "Come to think of it, Nancy did say you were trying to lose weight. Something about blue sunglasses?" She shook her head. "I must be remembering wrong. I couldn't understand what the heck she was talking about. What could sunglasses have to do with weight loss?"

Not much, as it turns out. I really didn't say that out loud, of course. This was one part of our conversation I didn't want to get into. Claire would have told me I was nuts. And, in this case, she would be right.

"I'm surprised Nancy didn't mention Tummy Trimmers, especially since she's the one who got me involved with the program in the first place."

"Tummy Trimmers? What the heck is that?"

I sighed. "It's long story," I said. "And it sort of leads into what you referred to as my getting up to my old tricks."

"I've got loads of time," Claire said. "I'll bet Larry hasn't even noticed I'm gone. He's probably in the garage with his new love. So, what's Tummy Trimmers?"

I thought back to how my weight-loss obsession began, and realized I was sitting in the exact same chair I'd been in when Jenny said she knew she would gain weight while she was pregnant, but she just didn't want to end up with a permanent post-partum tummy bulge like I had. Or words to that effect. Even now, remembering those words, they still hurt my feelings a little.

I took a deep breath, then said, "Well, it all really started with Jenny's pregnancy." And I went on and on. And on. I didn't leave anything out—not the blue sunglasses, meeting Lori Todesco and her offer to make me the official Tummy Trimmers poster child, the horrible photo shoot and me wearing the humiliating fat suit,

my walks on the beach with Jenny and meeting Pat Mathews, and....
Well, I hope you were all paying attention, and I don't have to go
over everything else with you as well as Claire.

My friend responded in typical Claire fashion. She never once
interrupted me, not even to ask a question. But she did pull out
a notebook from her purse and began to scribble some notes as I
was talking.

I also threw in the strange goings-on at the thrift shop, since
Sister Rose's niece, Destiny, worked for Tummy Trimmers and was
the leader of the meditation class where Pat keeled over onto me. I
left out the part about Sister Rose misleading the police about the
break-in at the shop, though. I didn't want to break her confidence.

When I'd finished, I sat back in my chair, exhausted and badly in
need of some liquid to quench my dry mouth. I took a swig of cold
coffee and grimaced. It tasted lousy, but it was better than nothing.

I could almost hear the wheels in Claire's head as they turned
around and around, trying to make sense of all I'd told her. Finally,
she said, "Well, Carol, I have to say that your life is never boring.
And you sure have a knack for being in the wrong place at the
wrong time."

"How was I to know that a woman was going to collapse on me
after a meditation class that was supposed to help me relax and lose
weight?" I protested. "Nancy was in the same class. It was just a fluke
that I was sitting next to Pat when she collapsed and not Nancy."

Claire looked skeptical. "It's just that you seem to attract dead
bodies like some sort of a magnet."

"But only since Jim retired," I shot back. "If you want to blame
anybody, blame him. My life was perfectly calm until he decided to
hang around the house all the time. I had to come up with a whole
new set of interests that get me out of the house."

This was so blatantly ridiculous that both of us burst out
laughing. In fact, we laughed so hard that I had to pay an emergency
trip to my bathroom, if you get my drift.

When I got back to the kitchen, Claire had spread all the photos
out on the table and was regrouping them into piles. She looked
up at me, guilt written all over her face, and pushed the photos
in my direction. "I'm sorry, Carol. I didn't mean to be nosy. These
are your pictures, not mine. I guess you're organizing them into
some sort of order. Although you must have been leading a secret
life when we were growing up. There isn't a single one of any of us.

In fact, I don't recognize anyone in these pictures. Who are they?"

"They're pictures Mary Alice found this morning at one of Nancy's real estate listings," I said. "The house itself is gorgeous, but that's not why Nancy took us to see it. We had a real adventure. Too bad we didn't know you were home. You could have come with us."

"I don't understand," Claire said. "Why would Nancy want you to see a listing of hers? Don't tell me you and Jim are thinking of moving again? Especially after he spent so much time and money remodeling this house for your twilight years. I thought you loved it here."

"Now who's jumping to conclusions?" I asked. "It turns out that Nancy's listing had also been a rental, and the tenant was none other than the late Pat Mathews."

"Pat Mathews? Oh, your most recent dead body." Claire picked up a photo and scrutinized it, then handed it to me. "Is Pat Mathews in any of these pictures?"

"I don't know. I haven't had a chance to look at them yet. I was interrupted," I said, glaring at Claire. It hadn't taken too long for us to fall back into our old familiar pattern. Claire always knows how to push my buttons, and I always react the same way—overly defensive. You'd think that, after all these years, I wouldn't be so sensitive. If anything, the older I get, the more sensitive to criticism I seem to be. And Claire gets more critical the older she gets. And the dance goes on.

But this time, my old friend must have realized she'd gone a little too far. "There I go again, Carol," she said, looking embarrassed. "I didn't mean to be so snarky. I'm sure that your experience was terrible. I bet you even had nightmares about it. Forgive me?"

"Of course," I said, relieved that Claire had apologized so quickly.

"I volunteered to turn over these photos to Mark," I said. "They may help the police trace Pat's next of kin. So far, nobody's come forward to claim responsibility for her funeral. If nobody does, the town of Fairport will have to do it. Isn't that a terrible thing, to die and have no one care?"

Claire shook her head. "I never heard of such a thing. That's so sad." Then she gave me a hard look. "But you, being you, are planning on going through everything first for clues about Pat, before you head to the police station to see Mark, right?"

Busted.

"You know me too well," I said. "Of course I am. Not that I expect to find anyone who looks familiar, but if I don't look, I won't know."

"And what's this?" Claire said, picking up the key and scrutinizing it. "It looks like an old car key."

"The key was in the box, too. I have no idea how to trace it, or even if it's important."

"I'll bet Larry can help with this," Claire said. "After all, he's into vintage cars now, remember. He made contacts all over the country when he was looking for his Shelby." She thought for a minute, then added, "I remember he mentioned some guy in La Jolla, California, who was an expert on classic Mustangs. In fact," she said, wiping some of the grime off the key and giving it an even closer look, "I think there's a Mustang logo on this. And there's something scratched on the back that looks like a date. How about if I take the key and show it to Larry? He could contact his source in California. Who knows? It may be helpful."

"I have a better idea," I said. "How about if you take a picture of the key instead?" I waited a beat, then added, "I'm afraid you might lose it."

I know. That was childish. But as you know, sometimes I just have to have the last word.

Chapter 32

I don't mean to brag, but I finished my
14-day diet in 3 hours and 20 minutes.
Unfortunately, I didn't lose any weight, but I
hope I get points for speed.

Talking with Claire, as annoying as she can be sometimes, did focus me, no pun intended, on organizing the batch of photos I had spread across my kitchen table. I decided to separate the ones that were in black and white from those that were in color, figuring that the black and whites were probably taken earlier. Next, I separated the black and whites by size. I had forgotten that, when I was a kid, photographs sometimes were smaller and square in shape. How technology has changed since those days.

I realized, after finally putting on my bifocals and scrutinizing each of the piles, that some of the older photos also had dates stamped on them. The earliest ones went back to 1959, and were mostly shots of a few young girls in poodle skirts mugging it up for the camera. I decided, in a burst of channeling Claire, to file each of my piles in envelopes and label them, so when I finally got around to turning them over to the police, there'd be some semblance of order.

I then tackled the color photos, many of which were yellowed with age. Some of them were of groups of teenagers at the beach. How funny those bathing suits looked now. Two pictures in particular, fastened together by a rusty paper clip, caught my eye. The first showed two girls sitting on the hood of what boys call a "muscle car." Both the girls were mugging it up for the camera—or perhaps showing off to impress the handsome guy standing on the right side of the car. I had to giggle as I remembered those innocent days. The second shot showed one of the girls behind the steering wheel of the car, pretending to drive it. The boy had his hands to his face in mock horror, and the other girl was laughing. I separated these two out from the rest and put them into an envelope marked "Beach/car pics."

That left me with one pile of color photos still to go through. I could tell from the clothes and hairstyles the girls were sporting that these were from the late 60s and early 70s. Ugh. Not the best era for fashion. For once, I was glad I had to wear a Catholic school uniform back in those days.

It seemed to me that the reason Pat saved these old pictures was that they were of very dear friends from her younger days. She could even be in some of them herself. It was even possible that, if I could identify anyone from one of the photos, I could give that information to Mark, he could contact him or her, and that person could take over Pat's funeral. Wow. What a great idea. And still another example of how much the Fairport Police depend on me for invaluable assistance, whether they realize it or not.

Another crazy thought skittered across my mind. Was it possible to take some of the people in the photos—the two girls posed on the car, for instance—and age them thirty or forty years, to see how they'd look today? Maybe there was a website for that.

Sure enough, after I typed "How to age people in photographs" into my smartphone browser, I got two promising suggestions from the Google genie. One was for a free app called, believe it or not, "AgingBooth." The same site also featured apps called BaldBooth, BoothStache, and UglyBooth. I burst out laughing at the myriad of possibilities, then calmed myself down. No way did I need another app on my phone. I already had way too many, and I wanted to save a prominent space on my screen for the picture of my soon-to-be-born first grandchild.

The other Google genie suggestion was Photoshop. At least I had heard of that one, so I tapped into that website. There was a tutorial which suggested that I use a full-face photo of myself for practice. Humph. Like that would ever happen. My own aging process was speeding ahead with no help from Photoshop, and I had no desire to see what the end result would be. But just for ha ha's, I clicked on the "how to age" instructions. It looked way too complicated for a non-geek like me.

Then I had another brilliant idea. If I couldn't do this myself, I had two other resources I could call on. One was my darling and very techie son. Mike and I hadn't been in touch for a while and this would be a perfect excuse—I mean, reason—to contact him. And the other was Liam, the Tummy Trimmers photographer. I was sure that one or both of them would be able to solve my dilemma.

All I had to do now was choose a few pictures and copy them. Or, better yet, maybe I could capture the images with my smartphone camera. That way, I could manipulate the size of the faces, and text or email them if I needed to. Maybe I was finally coming into the twenty-first century after all.

Chapter 33

My get-up-and-go just got up and left.

"Why are you taking pictures of pictures?" Jim asked, giving the top of my head a hello kiss. He picked up one of the photos and squinted. "Am I supposed to recognize any of these people? Because I don't."

"I don't either," I said, leaning down for some doggy love from Lucy and Ethel. "That's why I'm copying the pictures."

Jim shook his head. "I'm not even going to bother trying to understand you this time," he said. "In fact, I've decided I'll never understand women. Period." He pulled out a chair and settled in at the table. "Is there any coffee left? I could sure use a jolt of caffeine right about now. That Lori Todesco sure is something else." And he smiled.

"Yes, I recall your saying something like she knows how to fill out a leotard when you saw her at Tummy Trimmers," I said, trying not to let the green-eyed monster take over my thoughts. "I gather you still think so." I resisted the urge to pour the coffee onto my husband's head. I hope you're all proud of me, because it wasn't easy.

"How did the interview go?" I asked. "What did she have to say about Pat Mathews? Did she dodge your questions, the way she did at the meeting?"

Jim regarded me over his coffee mug. "I am a seasoned interviewer, Carol, as you well know. There was no way I was going to let Ms. Todesco off the hook, no matter what kind of feminine tricks she tried on me."

I raised my eyebrows. "Care to explain that part about the feminine tricks, dear?" I asked. "I'm just dying to know."

Jim blushed. No kidding, he really did. "Well, she didn't take her clothes off and invite me into her boudoir," he said. "But she did talk a lot about how lonely she is now that her last divorce is final. And she did put a hand on my knee at one point. It was obvious that she found me attractive."

I willed myself to let Jim continue without interrupting. I took a deep breath, then another.

"But I knew what she was doing," Jim said, oblivious to the effect this conversation was having on me. "She didn't want to answer any of my questions about Pat Mathews. And she was doing everything she could to get me off track. So I switched tactics and asked her about her early life, when she was on that television dance party show. I wanted to get her to relax and let her guard down."

"Just as long as *you* didn't relax and let your guard down," I said through gritted teeth.

"No way was I going to let her control the interview," Jim continued. "You would have been proud of me. She talked on and on about her days on television, how she continued dancing after the show ended, her marriages, her divorces, and how proud she is of Tummy Trimmers. I told her how much you're enjoying the program. I laid it on really thick, and told her how proud I was of you for all the weight you'd lost." He held up his hand to stop me. "And before you get the wrong idea, I am proud of you. For sticking to the program, and for losing some weight. Even though I haven't told you before."

"Thanks," I said, mollified. "It hasn't been easy, just in case you think it has been. And, by the way, how many times has Lori been married?" I was interested despite the fact that I now truly hated this woman who had tried to seduce my husband. The nerve!

"I don't know," Jim said. "Several. And she has one child. A son, I think. By that time, I was so bored, I was zoning out on what she was saying. And waiting for the right time to get to the point of why I was there in the first place."

"Speaking of getting to the point, Jim...."

"I know. I'm rambling on. But by this time, Lori was practically eating out of my hand. Figuratively speaking, of course."

I nodded. Of course.

"I brought the conversation back to you and Tummy Trimmers," Jim said, beaming at his own cleverness. "I told her how traumatized you were by Pat Mathews' death, especially since you were so intimately involved in it. And how upset you were that so far, there hadn't been a funeral because it seemed like nobody cared enough about the poor woman to plan one. I bragged a little about how you helped the police solve some of their toughest cases in the past, and said you'd been asked to help them find out more about Pat Mathews because of her sudden, mysterious death. I made you sound like a cross between Joan of Arc and Miss Marple. Lori was fascinated. She never knew all that about you before. She thought you were just a small-town housewife. But I set her straight, all right. And you'll never guess what happened then." I was still processing what Jim had told Lori Todesco about my detective skills, so I almost missed what he said next.

"Lori said that you had enough to do already without worrying about a funeral for a woman you barely knew. She said Tummy Trimmers would cover the entire cost of Pat's service and the burial. Isn't that something?"

"Yes," I echoed, "that's something." I thought for a minute, then asked, "Why? I mean, why now? Why didn't she just do it in the first place?"

"Who knows?" Jim answered with a shrug. "Lori also said she blames that young woman you asked me to check out, Destiny, for not acting professionally when Pat Mathews collapsed after her meditation class. She's thinking of firing her." Jim held up his hand to stop the question he knew was coming from me. "I haven't had a chance to research anything about Destiny yet. Maybe later today."

I knew enough not to push Jim any further right now. But I was positive that Sister Rose would really be on my case if Lori fired Destiny. Not only would she expect me to keep Destiny out of jail, I'd also have to find her a new job. No way was that going to happen if I had anything to say about it. And, you know me, I always have something to say.

"That is completely unfair," I said. "Destiny is young, yes, and clearly she'd never had anything like Pat's collapse happen to her before. Her immediate reaction was to call Lori, who is her boss, for instructions on what to do. If you want to blame anybody, blame the lovely Lori for not responding professionally, not Destiny.

Remember, Nancy and I were both there." I thought for a second, then said, "Maybe Gloria was still there, too. I bet she'd be happy to defend Destiny's actions if necessary."

"Who's Gloria?" Jim asked. "A new member of your posse?"

"Very funny," I said. "Gloria is a new volunteer at the thrift shop. She's very nice. But, speaking of my posse, Claire surprised me this morning. She and Larry just got back from Florida. Larry bought a vintage Shelby Mustang and they drove north in it. Claire said Larry's always wanted one. She called it his late-in-life-crisis purchase."

"I guess he can afford it," Jim said. "Larry must have made big bucks as a lawyer. But he never struck me as a Mustang type of guy. I wanted one, too, but never could afford it. Speaking of which," Jim reached for one of the photos I was copying onto my phone, "there's a Mustang in this picture, too. These two bathing beauties are sitting on the car hood."

"That might explain the key," I said, my mind racing with new possibilities. At Jim's quizzical look, I continued, "I found a car key in this box along with all these old photos. Claire thought Larry might be able to identify it."

"Well, I don't know how a Mustang key got into a box of our old pictures, but I'm glad you're doing something productive, Carol, instead of nosing around and trying to solve another mystery. After what almost happened to you in Florida, I worry about you. Not that I take back all the glowing things I said to Lori Todesco about you," Jim said, forestalling what he knew would be a snappy comeback from me. "I have to admit that you're pretty good at unraveling mysteries. But going through our old pictures and copying the ones you want to save onto your phone is a lot safer use of your time. I just hope that, if you run across any of my pictures, you won't toss them out without asking me first."

"But Jim, these aren't..." I stopped myself. No way did Jim need to know where these pictures came from. Instead, I gave him a big smooch and said, "That's a thank you kiss for worrying about me. And for being a good boy and resisting Lori's feminine wiles."

"Now that Lori Todesco will be organizing Pat Mathews' funeral, you don't have to be involved anymore," Jim said. "And I probably won't have to write a story about the poor woman's death, either. But just to be on the safe side, I'm going to write up my interview notes while I can still decipher them. If you want to try your feminine wiles on me, feel free to interrupt me."

Honestly, that Jim.

I scooped up the photos and filed them in their carefully labeled envelopes. It was time to turn them over to Mark. And at the same time, I could find out how my darling daughter was feeling. I am not one of those overly hovering mothers who calls or texts her offspring every single day. In fact, in the interests of family harmony—that would be Jim telling me to back off, in case you didn't get that reference—I sometimes let three or four whole days go by without contacting Jenny and Mike. Not that Mike ever responds to a text with anything but a smiley face, but at least that showed me he was still alive. And as for Jenny, well, we do live in the same town and she is pregnant for the first time and I am her mother and I know all about being pregnant so I want to…. Oh, wait, I'm hovering, aren't I?

As a matter of fact, Carol, you're acting about Jenny the same way Sister Rose is about Destiny. So back off and stop being so critical.

Hmm. Maybe, on the way to the police station, I should stop into Tummy Trimmers and have a little chat with Destiny about job security. In a very subtle way, so she won't feel threatened. Just make a few harmless suggestions about how her job at Tummy Trimmers has prepared her for an interesting career path, and maybe she should think about getting a resume together. Or going back to school to get a degree of some kind.

Good idea, Carol. And if you're really lucky, maybe Liam will be there, too, and you can show him the photos and ask him about aging some of the people in them. Brilliant!

I love it when I can multitask.

Chapter 34

Every time I hear the word "exercise" I wash my mouth out with chocolate.

Real life never works out the way you want it to, of course. At least, mine doesn't. If I was writing this in a novel, both Destiny and Liam would be at Tummy Trimmers when I stopped in. Destiny would be overjoyed and grateful at my helpful suggestions, and Liam would take the mysterious photos and—presto—in an instant the laughing teenagers would be transformed into senior citizens.

Instead, by the time I got to Tummy Trimmers, the main meeting room was empty. But I heard music coming from the smaller room that Lori uses as her office, so I decided to investigate. My hand was on the knob when I heard voices above the sound of what I now recognized as Chubby Checker inviting people to "twist again like we did last summer." One of the voices was definitely my happy homewrecker-wannabe, Lori Todesco. The other (not counting Chubby) was definitely male and familiar, though I couldn't quite identify it.

I have a master's degree in snooping with a minor in eavesdropping 101, so I pressed my right ear to the door to listen in. And boy, did I ever get an earful. First, I heard Lori say, "This is a great workout dance to trim the tummy. Let's definitely add this to the Tummy Trimmers curriculum."

"The word 'curriculum' is misleading, don't you think?" the male voice asked. "You didn't come up with any of the program components yourself. Every single thing you're touting as your own and unique to Tummy Trimmers you copied straight off the Internet. One of these days, some bright person's going to figure that all out and nail you for it. Just you wait and see."

I heard the sound of a snort and figured it was Lori. "As if," she said, laughing. "Some people have tried, but nobody's succeeded. Remember, I am the undisputed queen of the bandstand ballroom. My adoring fans would never believe anything negative about me."

Wowser. Lori Todesco, and by extension, the entire Tummy Trimmers program, was a big fat fake. Well, maybe not fat. But definitely fake. I didn't want to miss a single word, so I pressed even harder against the door.

"You almost got caught when that poor woman collapsed in your so-called meditation class," the male voice persisted. "I thought that was the end of Tummy Trimmers, for sure."

Lori laughed. "Not to worry. That was just a momentary hiccup, and nobody can ever blame me for what happened. It was just an unlucky accident. And you're making money out of this, too. Don't forget about that important piece of information in case you get a sudden attack of conscience, Liam. And if anybody starts to ask questions about that incident, like that nosy Carol Andrews, we've always got Destiny to blame."

By now I was so mad with what I was hearing that I wished I could march right in and make a citizen's arrest. Poor Destiny. She'd be nothing but a convenient scapegoat, and her whole life would be ruined. And that Liam. What a rat.

"Promise me you won't involve Destiny, Mom," Liam said. "You know how I feel about her."

Mom? Did Liam call Lori "Mom"? Holy macaroni!

You are so stupid, Carol. You should have recorded this conversation on your phone and brought it to Mark. Then Lori would be busted, once and for all, and Destiny would be in the clear.

"You worry too much, Liam," Lori said. "But all right, I promise. If everything goes according to plan, your girlfriend won't be involved. I expect that Jim Andrews will make me look like Mother Teresa in his newspaper story since I'm picking up the cost of Pat Mathews' funeral. I had him eating out of my hand today when he interviewed me. The funeral will be great marketing for Tummy Trimmers. I bet we get a slew of new sign-ups after it's over. That's the only reason I agreed to do it. Pat always was…"

"Pat always was... what?" Liam asked. "Did you know her before? What were you going to say?"

"I knew her a long, long time ago, before you were born," Lori said. "That's all I'm going to say, because you don't need to know any more. How about one more dance before we lock this place up for the night? Something upbeat. You pick the song." The next thing I heard was Danny and The Juniors belting out one of my favorite oldies, *At the Hop.* I took the hint and hopped right out of Tummy Trimmers before I got caught snooping.

I sure had a lot to think about. Too much, in fact. Isn't odd how there are days that nothing interesting happens, and other days that are so jam-packed it's impossible to deal with it all. This day definitely fell into the latter category. I needed a nap. But before that, I needed my son to age some people in a few of those photographs, since there was no way I could ask Liam now. I don't know what surprised me more from my latest exercise in eavesdropping—that Liam was Lori's son or that Lori admitted that she knew Pat Mathews way before Tummy Trimmers started. I filed both away in my brain to think about later.

I checked my watch. It was now 3:30, a good time to reach Mike. He should already be at Cosmo's, the trendy restaurant he co-owns in Miami's South Beach, getting ready for another successful night wining and dining all his wealthy customers. Heaven forbid I should call him, though. Being a modern guy as well as a swinging bachelor, he only responds to texts these days. And because of our recent "adventure" in Florida, where Mike and I were at odds over a girl he was crazy about (who turned out to be crazy, herself, in the literal sense), I hadn't asked him for help in a while. Now, I had no choice.

Fortunately, there was nobody honking at me to move my car so they could have my parking space, so I hunkered down in my temporary "office" and fired off a text.

Me: *I need your help. Emergency.*

I sat back and waited. He responded within seconds.

Mike: *What emergency? Jenny ok?*

Me: *No. Sorry. Jenny's fine. I'm texting you pictures. Important that you look at them.*

Mike: *No time.*

Me: *Make time!*

Mike: *Sheesh. Ok. Go ahead.*

Me: *Thanks. Here they come.*

It took me a few minutes to figure out how to attach pictures to a text message. I'm a pro at email, but texting is still somewhat of a mystery to me. I was finally able to fire off two photos of the girls and the car. And just for the heck of it, I sent pictures of the car key, too.

Me: *Did you get them?*

Mike: *Yes. Cool car.*

Me: *Can you age it?*

Mike: *What? The car?*

Me: *No, the people. Can you make them look 40 years older?*

Mike: *Can this wait? I gotta meet with a supplier now. I'll fool around with these in an hour or so. And you better tell me why.*

Me: *I will. I promise. Can you i.d. the car key, too?*

Mike: *Mom, come on!*

I smiled. Mike was protesting, but I knew he'd come through for me. He always did. Like Jim, sometimes it just took a little persuading.

Me: *I love you. Thanks. Over and out.*

Chapter 35

How to prepare tofu: 1. Throw it in the trash.
2. Grill some meat.

My brain was in overdrive even more than usual so, rather than go directly to the police station, I headed straight home for a calming cup of herbal tea. I'd read somewhere that gazing into tea leaves can tell the future. Maybe gazing into a soggy tea bag would have the same effect. There was Tummy Trimmers and Lori Todesco, Liam and Destiny, and Pat Mathews' death. Even though I now knew that Tummy Trimmers and Lori were big fakes, nothing she had done was really criminal. At least, I didn't think so.

There was also Sister Rose and the thrift shop break-in. Although I hated to admit it, there was a common link between Pat's death and the break-in: Destiny. But I couldn't figure out why. It just made no sense.

I needed a fresh perspective, preferably someone who already knew the key players so I didn't have to start from scratch. I'd ruled out Mark first, because even though he's my son-in-law and sometimes (grudgingly) has accepted some assistance from me in solving a case, all I had were questions and no answers. He didn't have time for that. I knew I was stalling for time as far as he was concerned, too. When I talked to Mark, I'd have to turn over the photographs. He'd want an explanation about how and why I had them, and I still had no idea where they fit into this. No sense in confusing him before I had the answer.

I ruled out talking to Jenny, Nancy and Mary Alice, and Claire was trying to research the mysterious car key. That left me with Lucy and Ethel or my darling husband. Now, the dogs give me unconditional love but they both think I'm brilliant and I hate to disillusion them. That left my husband, by process of elimination (but please don't tell him that). Jim is the most rational person I know. Sometimes critical, yes. But always rational. After all these years of marriage, I'd learned that the best way to approach him was to put together a summary of events and a timeline and present it to him for comment. He always responds to something in writing, from all his years in corporate America.

Satisfied that I had a winning strategy, imagine my disappointment when I arrived home to find the only ones who greeted me were Lucy and Ethel. My husband had vamoosed again. This time, however, there was a note on the kitchen table in huge letters: "MEATLOAF FOR SUPPER?? GROUND TURKEY IN REFRIGERATOR. HEALTHY!" Next to the note was a recipe Jim must have found on the Internet. I opened the fridge and the ground turkey package was decorated with a big blue gift bow and a tag that read, "PLEASE COOK ME."

"Did you two help Jim pick out this present?" I asked the dogs, who were sniffing the package with undisguised interest. "Down, girls. This isn't for you. But here." I tossed them a couple of Milk Bones, which seemed to satisfy them, at least for a little while.

If meatloaf's what Jim wanted, that's what he'd get. "And he does get points for scouring the Internet and coming up with this healthy recipe," I said. "Too bad he couldn't find one for a healthy low-fat chocolate cake while he was at it."

Lucy gave me a dirty look, clearly telegraphing that chocolate wasn't good for dogs, so it shouldn't be for humans, either. She feels very strongly that anything that's served in the Andrews house should be safe for all of us to eat, especially her.

"I get it, Lucy," I said. "But chocolate comes from a tree, so it's really a fruit. Eating chocolate is like eating a sweet salad. And remember what Forrest Gump's mama said, 'Life is like a box of chocolates, because you never know what you're going to get.' "

I thought about that for a minute, then added, "Of course, that's not really true. If you eat a box of chocolates, you know what you're going to get. You're going to get fat. Turkey meatloaf is much healthier."

I scanned the list of ingredients and was satisfied that I had almost everything the recipe called for. And if I had to substitute one spice for another, well, Jim would never know the difference. I washed my hands, donned a rarely used apron, and set to work.

"I'd forgotten how much fun this is," I said to the dogs, who were now sitting beside me, plaintive looks on their faces. I added a beaten egg and bread crumbs to the mixture and mixed it together with my hands. "Out of my way, girls," I said, shooing them away. "I have to chop an onion and that always makes me cry. And I don't want to take the chance of dropping a tiny piece of onion near you. Onions aren't good for dogs, either."

My eyes started to water as I peeled and chopped, reminding me, for reasons I'll never be able to explain, of the day Pat Mathews died. And how glassy-eyed she looked while she was trying to get her breath. And how her skin was such an odd color.

"Stop it," I ordered myself, wiping my eyes with a clean paper towel. "Add the onion and mix the turkey loaf. Focus on making dinner, and nothing else." As I continued to knead the turkey mixture together, I thought about how amazing it was that a variety of unrelated ingredients can be put together to make a yummy meal. All that was needed were the proper ingredients in the proper proportion. Too much salt, for example, would make some dishes taste terrible. But each ingredient had a purpose, if the cook could only see it. I slid the turkey meatloaf into a 350-degree oven and set the timer for 45 minutes.

I squinted at Jim's recipe again and learned I also had to make a low-calorie sauce to pour over the meatloaf, so I pulled some other spices out of a kitchen cabinet. I was feeling so...domestic. So at peace with myself. I was cooking a healthy meal for my darling husband. Weird, huh? No kidding. Because a domestic goddess I certainly am not. But there was something so orderly about putting together ingredients and knowing what the final outcome would be. Unless I burned it, of course. There was always that chance, as I'm so easily distracted. Like now, for instance.

And then, it hit me. I had all the necessary ingredients to figure out the riddle of Pat Mathews' death as well as the thrift shop break-in. All I had to do was to figure out the proper proportions. The two events were connected—I was absolutely certain about that. One event was the meatloaf—the primary one—and the other was the sauce. I mixed a can of fat-free turkey gravy with some white wine in a saucepan, added some sliced mushrooms and the spices, and began to stir.

Which came first, the break-in or the death? *Stir, stir, stir.*

The death was first, and the more important of the two events, of course. So Pat's death was the meatloaf. So to speak. *Stir, stir, stir.*

Except...I suddenly realized that something weird had happened at the thrift shop even before Pat's death and the break-in—Jenny finding a stash of cash hidden in a pocket of the dress I bought her. Was that added to the meatloaf or the sauce? Or did it belong with neither one?

I pondered all the possibilities through dinner, which was a big success. I gave Jim full kudos for searching out the turkey meatloaf recipe. Being a guy, he wiggled his eyebrows at my praise, and suggested I could show my thanks later that evening, after the dishes were done.

"Oh, sure," I said, my mind a million miles away. "Whatever you want."

"I know you're not really paying attention to what I'm saying," Jim said, waving his hand in front of my face. "Mission Control to Carol. Come back to Earth from wherever you are, please."

"Oh, that's fine," I said, rising to clear the table. "You go right ahead. I'll clean up the kitchen." I think I heard him sigh as he headed toward the family room and the comforting presence of the remote control.

Much later, as I drifted off to sleep, it occurred to me that I'd never heard back from Mike about the pictures.

Chapter 36

Maybe I should just slap an "Out of Order"
sticker on my forehead and call it a day.

My son-in-law showed up, unannounced, at my kitchen door the next morning when the sun and I were struggling to rise and shine. When I saw his haggard face, I tried very hard not to jump to conclusions, the way I always do. And failed. If you've ever had a pregnant daughter, maybe you'll understand.

Calm, Carol. Take deep breaths. Let the poor guy talk. Please, Lord, don't let it be bad news.

"What a lovely way to start the day," I said, trying to smile and failing. "Come in and have some breakfast. Jenny didn't tell me you were working nights this week. You look exhausted." My voice shook when I said my daughter's name, and I hoped Mark didn't notice.

"Jim'll be glad to see you, too," I continued. "He's in the shower right now. But he made the coffee this morning. You know he makes it much better than I do."

Mark raised his hand to stop my babbling. "I'm glad for the coffee. And I know I look lousy. But Jenny's fine. At least, she will be. I know that's what you really want to know. I'm sorry if I scared you." I set a coffee mug in front of him and waited. And prayed. "That's why I've come so early. I need your help, Carol. We had a little hiccup last night. Jenny hadn't been feeling well all day, and she had some unexpected...." He stopped. "Well, without going into too much detail, her doctor has ordered her to take things much easier until the baby comes. She's going to take a leave of absence from teaching. That's where you come in."

By this time, Jim had joined us. He took my hand, which was shaking, and squeezed it. "You can count on both of us to do whatever we can to help," he said. I nodded, tears threatening to spill over onto the linen place mat.

"Of course you can," I said. "We're her parents, and we love her, and you, very much."

"So, what do you want us to do?" Jim asked.

"Nothing," Mark said, looking me straight in the eye. "Absolutely nothing." As I started to protest, he clarified. "I'm not saying that you can't talk to her or visit her."

"I should hope not," I said.

"But she can't be upset," Mark continued. "She's going to be on bed rest a lot of the time, just to be safe. I don't want you to drop in and brainstorm with her about the thrift shop break-in, or Pat Mathews' death, Carol. Or anything related to them. Do you promise?"

I was offended. I tried not to be, but I was. "I would never, *ever*, do anything to upset my daughter," I said in a hurt voice. "And I'm surprised that you would dare to suggest that I would."

Mark flushed. "I'm sorry to offend you, Carol. I'm just trying to do what's best for my wife. And fortunately, Lori Todesco is taking over Pat Mathews' funeral, so that's another item you don't have to concern yourself with. But no date's been set for that, yet."

I decided to let Mark off the hook for now. After all, he only wanted what was best for Jenny, as did we all. And he was calling the shots, for now. Instead, I focused on something else he'd said, other than his implied criticism of his mother-in-law.

"Why?" I asked. "Why is there still no date for Pat's funeral? After all, there's finally someone willing to take responsibility for it. What's the hold-up? Is there something you're hiding?"

"Nothing you need to concern yourself with," Mark snapped.

"Well, isn't it thoughtful of you, the way you're arranging my life for me?" I said with a phony smile. "Let's not forget that Pat Mathews fell on me when she collapsed. Her death is personal to me. I'm involved, whether you want me to be or not."

My sarcastic comment had the desired effect. "This is not to go any further than this room," Mark warned. "And if I hear anyone..." he fixed me with a hard stare and repeated, "anyone at all discussing this publicly, I'll know who the source is. And it could cost me my job."

"I swear, neither of us will say a word," I said, looking at Jim, who nodded.

"We think Pat Mathews was poisoned. It could be murder. The final toxicology panels haven't come back yet. And, until they do, we're not releasing the body."

"I knew it!" I said. "I knew there was something fishy about her death. What can I do to help you?"

"Didn't you hear what I said, Carol?" Mark asked. "You are to do nothing. Absolutely nothing."

"But, Mark, you know how good I am at finding things out. I've helped you before. Why can't I help you this time, too?"

Mark's face darkened. "I don't need your help, Carol. Leave this one alone."

"As a matter of fact," I said, choosing my words carefully for maximum effect, "it just so happens that I ran across some information that might be helpful to you. But I guess I won't bother you with it. You obviously don't need it."

"Carol, please," Mark said. "Don't be like this. You know I've always been grateful for your help in the past. And Jenny and I both love you very much."

"Well, you sure have an odd way of showing it," I said. And I stormed out of the kitchen.

I know. I know! You don't have to tell me. I overreacted. I was ridiculous. And I just may have ruined my chances of lifetime babysitting privileges. But Mark made me so mad, I just couldn't control myself. I sat down on the bed and allowed myself the luxury of a good cry.

This is the way you always behave. You stick your nose in everybody's business and try to manage everybody's lives. Especially your two children, who aren't children any more. You need to start living your own life instead of interfering in everyone else's. No wonder you haven't heard back from Mike yet. Concentrate on your own life for a change.

I heard Jim and Mark talking in the kitchen. Mark was full of apologies for the way he'd mishandled the situation. Good! Then

I heard Jim say, "I find it's best to leave her alone until she comes to her senses when she gets like this, Mark. It may take a while, but she'll come around. In the meantime, why don't you go off to work and I'll take the dogs for a walk?" The next sound I heard was the kitchen door closing. Then silence.

My nearest and dearest had decided to leave me alone to...how did Jim put it...come to my senses? It seemed like everybody was against me. And criticizing me.

I stood up and caught a glimpse of myself in the bedroom mirror. I looked horrible. And not just first-thing-in-the-morning-bedhead horrible. I looked *horrible*. Who was that old woman staring back at me? I looked again and gasped. Was that a line of white hair marching across my scalp? Oh, no. That was simply not allowed.

It was time to have a "Just for Me" day. And I knew where I had to start. I picked up my cell phone, called Deanna at my hair salon, and threw myself on her mercy.

Chapter 37

Life is more beautiful when you find the right hairdresser.

"I haven't seen you for almost three months," Deanna said, stepping away from my embrace and giving me a cool look. "It's not like you to wait so long between hair appointments. I figured you were either sick or found another stylist."

"Oh, no, Deanna," I said. "I would never let anyone else touch my hair. No one can style it as well as you do."

"The last part's true," Deanna said, choosing a lock of my hair and examining it closely. "No one does as good a job on your hair as I do. But you've obviously had someone else cut your hair since you saw me last. Someone who had no idea what she was doing. Your hair looks terrible."

Ouch. Hell hath no fury like a spurned hair stylist. I needed to make amends, and quickly. "We were in Florida and I desperately needed a haircut, because we stayed longer than we'd originally intended. And I couldn't fly home just to have my hair styled. Jim wouldn't have stood for that. After all, we were on our second honeymoon. Sort of. It didn't work out as well as we'd hoped, unfortunately, but I was desperate and I went to a walk-in beauty shop near our hotel and asked for a trim. I waited to come see you when we came home because I hoped the cut would grow out enough so you wouldn't know what I'd done. Please don't be mad at me. I'm under some extra stress right now and I really need you."

I paused to catch my breath. Groveling is not my strong suit, but Deanna did owe me a huge favor, since I'm the one who'd cleared her of being a murder suspect a while ago. Not that I'd ever remind her of that just to get her to style my hair, understand. I was glad to help her out, because I am a good friend. And that's what good friends do for one another. Without expecting anything in return. Unless absolutely necessary.

Deanna burst out laughing. "I'm just having fun with you, Carol," she said. "I'm not really mad at you. And besides, I have to admit that, putting aside the horrible haircut, which I can and will fix, you look terrific. Have you lost some weight? I hope it's not stress-related. You have to eat."

"Good heavens, I haven't lost that much weight," I protested, slipping into the smock that Deanna held for me. "I joined Tummy Trimmers, that new weight loss program. And mostly, I've been sticking to it."

"I know about Tummy Trimmers," Deanna said, mixing the miracle elixir she uses to restore my hair to its natural blonde color. "The Lorias are in here a lot."

"The Lorias?" I repeated. "Who are they?"

"Lori Todesco and her sister," Deanna said. "You must know them if you're going to Tummy Trimmers."

"I certainly know Lori," I said, sitting up straight in the chair and trying not to move while Deanna applied the color mixture. "But I didn't know she had a sister."

"The sister's name is Gloria," Deanna said. "They don't look anything alike, so I'm not surprised you didn't realize they were related."

"The only Gloria I know is a new volunteer at Sally's Closet," I said. "Her last name is Watkins, though, not Todesco. Is that who you mean?"

"I have no idea if Gloria does any volunteer work," Deanna said. "When the Lorias come in here, all they talk about is Tummy Trimmers and what a miracle weight-loss program it is. I finally had to ask them to stop using my hair salon to recruit new members. Some of my regular clients were starting to complain. But obviously Tummy Trimmers works, if you're any example." Deanna paused, then said, "Earth to Carol. Are you with me?"

"What?" I said. "Sorry, I was zoning out a little bit. I'm still trying to process the fact that the two of them are sisters. And I just found out that Lori's son works for Tummy Trimmers, too."

"It's a real family business," Deanna said. Then she caught the look on my face. "Why? Is that a bad thing?"

I started to shake my head but Deanna stopped me. "Hold still unless you want some of this glop to get on your face."

"No, it's not necessarily a bad thing," I said slowly. "But for some reason, it's a secret that they're all related. I can't figure out why. But..." I paused. My imagination was kicking into warp speed. "But, you may have finally given me information that ties together two of the things that have been worrying me. There was a break-in at the thrift shop recently, in case you hadn't heard about that," I said. "And a woman who called herself Pat Mathews collapsed at Tummy Trimmers and died. Unfortunately, she collapsed on me. And then, there's the mystery of the money." My voice trailed off. I had a feeling I was getting closer to the answers, but I wasn't quite there yet.

"Gloria was at the Tummy Trimmers class where Pat collapsed," I said. "I think they were sitting near each other during the meditation." I searched my memory bank, and this time, was able to come up with something valuable, although it could also be just a coincidence. "And Gloria volunteers at the thrift shop a lot, so she could be the person who's been hiding the money in the clothing donations."

"You've completely lost me, Carol," Deanna said. "Why in the world would Gloria hide money in a donation to the thrift shop? Why didn't she just make a donation and get a tax receipt, like anybody else?"

"Because I don't think the money was really a donation," I said, as my mind continued to race. "It could have been blackmail money. I overheard Lori admit that she and Pat knew each other a long time ago. What if Pat knew something incriminating about her or her sister and threatened to tell unless they gave her money? The Lorias paid her off for a while, using the thrift shop to hide the money, but Pat got too greedy, and they decided she had to die."

Deanna plopped down in the chair next to me. "It's a darn good thing that nobody else is in the salon right now. They would've called the police and had you arrested."

I held up my hand. "Please, bear with me, Deanna. You're perfect to bounce all my crazy ideas off of, because you have absolutely no idea what this is all about." I held up my right hand.

"Lori Todesco came to Fairport a few months ago to launch Tummy Trimmers, her supposedly new weight-loss program. Around the same time, Jenny and I began seeing a woman who turned out to be Pat Mathews while we were walking on the beach. Oh, Jenny's pregnant, by the way. I forgot to tell you that."

"Jenny's pregnant?" Deanna squealed. "That's fabulous! How could you forget to tell me such wonderful news? When is she due?"

"The end of the summer," I said. "And she's okay. She just has to take things easy until the baby comes. But to continue with my story, Jenny and I finally met Pat at the official Tummy Trimmers opening and we joined the weight-loss program. Around the same time, Sister Rose's niece, Destiny, was hired by Tummy Trimmers and Gloria started to volunteer at the thrift shop. Next, Jenny found a lot of money in the pocket of a dress I was buying for her at the thrift shop. Sister Rose said she had no idea how it had gotten there. Then, Pat collapsed and died."

"Did she die during an exercise class?" Deanna asked. "Maybe she had a bad heart or something."

"No, she died after a meditation exercise." I squeezed my eyes shut, trying to recreate an exact picture of what happened that awful morning.

"My meditation mat!" I said, as the memory floated to the surface of my mind. "I remember it was sticky. I bet something spilled on it when Pat collapsed." I jumped up. "I have to get home right away and find my mat. I'm sure there's something still on it, because I never washed it off. I'm so excited! I can take the mat to Mark and have him test it for poison." And I'll try not to gloat when he admits that, once again, I have solved his case for him.

Deanna pushed me down in the chair. "You're not going anywhere looking like that, Carol. Let me finish your hair and then you can go do whatever crazy thing you're babbling about now." She shook her head. "If you think this was murder, you better have some more conclusive proof before you go to the police or they'll just brush you off. So far, this sounds like a complete fabrication based on a few wild ideas that may or may not be related."

At my stricken look Deanna added, "I'm not saying you're wrong, Carol. I certainly know from personal experience that a lot of your so-called wild ideas are right on target. I'm just saying that you need proof. Let me finish your hair, and then get out there and find it."

I don't usually take advice from anyone. After all, who knows how to live my life better than I do? But Deanna and I are so simpatico that her words resonated with me more than, say, Jim's would have if he'd told me the exact same thing.

As Deanna prepared to blast me with the dryer, my cell phone rang. I was torn. On the one hand, I wanted to answer it. But I knew Deanna was rushing to get me finished and out of there. Of course, Deanna read my mind. "I'll clean up the salon before the next client comes in. Just don't take too long." She reached in my purse and handed me the phone.

I was thrilled to hear my son's voice on the other end of the line. My grumpy son. "For Pete's sake, Mom, I thought I'd hear back from you by now. I busted my butt to do what you wanted, and then, nada."

"Sweetie, I'm so sorry. I had no idea you texted the pictures back."

"I promised I'd help you, Mom," Mike said. "But by the time I got around to doing your bidding, it was late and I figured emailing them was better, so I wouldn't wake you or Dad up. I sent them last night." He sighed. "I forgive you, Mom. Aging those people in the beach photographs turned out to be a lot more complicated than I thought. But I found something interesting about the Mustang key, and I couldn't wait to tell you."

"That was very thoughtful of you," I said, feeling guilty that I'd thought, even briefly, that he'd let me down. "I never thought to check my email this morning. It'd be great if you'd text me the finished pictures now. And what about the car key?"

My phone started to ping. One text. Two texts. Three texts. Four texts.

"Don't try to open them now, Mom," Mike said. "You're no techie, and you could disconnect us by mistake."

Ignoring my son's comment, because he was absolutely right, I said, "Okay, I'll peek at them later. But my curiosity is killing me."

Mike laughed. "Let me tell you what I found out about the car key. Remember, you sent me two pictures of it. The key is definitely to a vintage Mustang. That was the easy part. But the back of the key had a date scratched on it, and it took me some time to alter the photo so I could read it. But it was worth it. The date was August 29, 1967. Does that mean anything to you?"

"Nope. Should it?"

"Maybe not. But I bet Dad might remember. Anyway, when I Googled the date, I found out there was a terrible car crash that day, and two people died. From what I could gather, there was a drag race at a local beach. If I was a betting man, or prone to jumping to conclusions like someone near and dear to me, I'd say that two of the people in these pictures were the accident victims. And here's where it gets really interesting. All the people that are shown in these pictures were part of the cast of that old television show, *New England Rock and Roll Dance Party*."

I paused, then said, "So, just to be clear, what you're suggesting is that the key belongs to the car that was in that accident, is that right?"

"Yes. I hope this is enough information for you, because I don't have any more time to look into this, Mom. Keep in touch, kiss Dad and Jenny for me, and stay out of trouble. Oh, and be sure to let me know when I'm an uncle, okay?" The next thing I heard was the dial tone.

Deanna tapped me on the shoulder, startling me. "I have exactly five minutes to finish you up before my next client arrives, Carol." And she turned on the dryer full force, thereby bringing my thought process to a complete halt. But, at least, my hair would look good, even if my brain was still a mess.

Chapter 38

Truth may be stranger than fiction, but it's not nearly as much fun.

Jenny and Mike hated doing puzzles when they were kids. There always seemed to be at least one piece missing, which would lead to frustration, which would lead to an argument, which would lead to one or both of them declaring that doing the puzzle together was a stupid idea, and blaming me for suggesting it in the first place. In my current frame of mind, I sympathized with them. This whole thing was stupid, and who ever said it was up to me to solve this puzzle, anyway? Just me, that's who. I was having major second thoughts about my so-called brilliant theory. Mike had done his best, but the photos of the group on the beach, which I hoped would prove that at least Lori was one of the teenagers pictured, were inconclusive. And the television show's connection to the fatal car crash was a tragic twist of fate that proved nothing. Bye, bye brilliant theory.

Even my horoscope was against me today. It read, "Once again, the moon is in your sign, at odds with another planet. You're too impulsive and trigger-happy. Just calm down and don't overreact, because you could make an error in judgment." Sheesh, the whole universe was criticizing me.

"I give up," I said aloud. "I really, truly, give up. And I don't want Mark to be mad at me. It's just a coincidence that Gloria Watkins was near Pat when she collapsed on me, and that she happens to be Lori

Todesco's sister. And that she wanted to do some volunteer work and ended up at the thrift shop. Three coincidences put together do not make them facts. Or proof of anything sinister." Fortunately, I was sitting all by myself in my car, idling at a red light, when I said it. And the windows were up, so nobody gave me a suspicious look.

Since I am a good citizen of Fairport, I always try to point the police in the right direction, if I can. All of a sudden, I knew what I had to do. "I'm going home and find the meditation mat. Maybe that's the real proof. Then I'll take the mat and the pictures to Mark at the police station. But first, I'll forward Mike's e-mails to Mark with a brief explanation of my theory, even though he'll probably think it's crazy."

By this time, I realized the driver in the car behind me was blasting its horn, and the traffic light had turned green. I gave him/her a fluttering wave, using all my fingers, and turned into a nearby parking lot. I sent my email and my possibly brilliant assumption. Then I reached around to the back seat for the box of Pat's pictures. Of course, I couldn't find them.

"Blast," I muttered. "Why are you so disorganized?" I got out of the car, taking a brief moment to admire my newly blonde locks in the side view mirror, yanked open the back door, and rooted around on the floor. I finally found the box, plus some dog biscuits, a pair of yoga pants and a sweatshirt that had been back there for who knows how long, and...something rolled up underneath my clothes. Can you guess? Oh, come on, don't spoil my fun. Guess! Okay, I'll tell you. It was my meditation mat! Thank goodness I rarely clean out my car. I put my mat and the box of pictures on the front seat so they'd be easy to find.

It was time to head to the Fairport Police Station and dump my "evidence" on my son-in-law's desk and let him decide whether it contained anything useful. At least, that was my plan. Until a car pulled up beside me in the parking lot and I heard a female voice say, "Carol, I thought that was you. It's Gloria, from the thrift shop. Do you have time for a quick cup of coffee now? I really need some advice about handling Sister Rose, and you know her so well. I don't know what to do."

I didn't want to be rude, and a coffee date had been my idea in the first place. But sipping coffee and making idle chit-chat with a possible (in my mind) murderer wasn't on my top ten list of things to do.

I thought fast. Maybe I could do something to force her hand. There were all those coincidences, and they all seemed to point directly at her. But, to be fair, everyone is innocent until proven guilty, and, as even my horoscope reminded me, I am way too impulsive for my own good. Oh, what the hell. In a split second, I made a decision.

"I can't go for coffee now, Gloria," I said. "Later this week would work better for me." And I waved a photo from the box in her direction. "I have to deliver these for a friend."

"You've had the photos all along," she screeched, jumping out of her car and trying to yank open my door, which was locked. "Give them to me. They're mine."

"I don't think so, Gloria," I said. I floored the car's accelerator and sped off, praying that she would follow me. Which, of course, she did. At times she was so close behind me that I worried she'd smash into my rear bumper. We continued our car chase, faster and faster, until we were pulled over by a Fairport policeman for speeding. I put up a real fight, and Gloria and I were arrested and taken to the police station. Which was, of course, exactly what I wanted all along.

Am I good or what?

Chapter 39

*As long as we do it all exactly as I planned
it, I can be totally flexible.*

I don't mean to brag, but thanks (mostly) to me and my
incredibly clever sleuthing ability, peace reigned once more in
our little corner of the universe. Because my crazy theory did turn
out to be 100 percent correct. Yay me!

There was only one thing wrong. Everybody was mad at me. At
least, it seemed that way.

Topping the list—no big surprise—was my son-in-law, who
freaked out when he was informed that I'd been brought into the
Fairport Police Station on a charge of resisting arrest. Which wasn't
true at all. I was resisting *not* being arrested. But since nobody
had ever heard of that before, I was charged with resisting arrest,
instead. (My charge was dismissed, in case you were wondering.)

I suspected that Gloria, and maybe Lori, would be charged
with a lot more than resisting arrest once there was a thorough
investigation about that long-ago car accident. I had done everything
I could to point the police in the right direction, including the
clever way I had lured Gloria to the police station in the first place.
And did anyone thank me for that? No, of course not.

Moving on.

Nancy was mad at me because she missed all the fun. She'd
always wanted to be in a car being chased by the police. And, just
between you and me, I'm surprised that with the way she drives,

it hasn't already happened. She did give the cell phone pictures she'd taken of Pat's collapse to Mark, for which she was profusely thanked. And she hasn't stopped bragging about how she "cracked the case" for the police. Humph.

Claire was mad at me because I asked her to research the car key and then found out all about it through Mike, so she felt I'd wasted her time and Larry's. Trust me, I'm not worried about that. She's always mad at me for something these days, but she doesn't stay mad for long.

Mary Alice and Jim (and maybe Lucy and Ethel, too) were mad at me for risking my personal safety. Which was totally understandable. I promised to never, ever, speed again. That promise, at least, I'll keep.

Sister Rose wasn't really mad at me compared to some of the other people in my life. She was relieved that Destiny wasn't responsible for the thrift shop break-in. Gloria finally confessed that she'd done it, desperate to find the cash and the incriminating photos and car key. Pat had promised to hide her "evidence" at the thrift shop in exchange for the cash, which, of course, she never did. No wonder Gloria trashed the thrift shop. And Gloria wore Destiny's jacket to throw suspicion onto her.

I didn't remain in Sister Rose's good graces for very long, though. Destiny and Liam eloped, and guess who was blamed for encouraging them? What can I say? I'm a sucker for young love.

Jenny wasn't mad at me, thank goodness. But she was mad at Mark for insisting I not involve her in my sleuthing, which made Mark even madder at me.

I hope you're following all this. I know, it's confusing.

Jenny finally persuaded Mark to tell me the basic details of the case by reminding him that, without my help (a.k.a. interference), the mystery of Pat Mathews' death never would have been solved. As I had suspected but couldn't prove, it all stemmed back to the old dance party television show and the car accident. Lori was the driver of the Mustang in the fatal crash, and the only survivor. Since she was underage, she never should have been driving in the first place. The television show producers hushed everything up—she was their star and they couldn't afford to lose her. Pat Murray (whom I knew as Pat Mathews) was also part of the dance party cast and was on the beach the day of the accident. According to Gloria, Pat had made a few threats "to tell all" over the years, but she and

Lori didn't take her seriously. Then Lori started Tummy Trimmers, and Pat saw a chance to make some real money.

I was right when I figured out that Gloria was the go-between for her sister and hid the blackmail payoffs in select donations at the thrift shop, which then Pat would come in and buy. But when Pat's money demands increased, Gloria decided to help out her sister and send Pat to that big dance party reunion in the sky, so she poisoned Pat with a Tummy Trimmers smoothie. I couldn't find out how she did it, although I sure tried. I guess I'll have to wait for the trial. Gloria insisted that Lori knew nothing about her plans, but I'm not so sure about that.

If you have any more questions, don't ask me. It was like pulling teeth to find out this much, and I'm not taking any more chances on making my son-in-law angry. No kidding, for the next six months I've decided to be absolutely angelic. And after that, well, all bets are off.

One more thing—my white Lilly Pulitzer jeans. Remember them? I finally found a pair on eBay in a size 10 and ordered them in time to wear for the Fairport Fourth of July parade. And they were too big! So I guess I have to gain back a few pounds so they'll fit. Yippee! Cheeseburgers and French fries, here I come! (For a little while, anyway.)

I saved the really important news for last. It's a boy! Jenny had the baby this morning and mommy and baby are doing great. Mark and I are now letting bygones be bygones, as the old saying goes. There's nothing like a brand new life to put things into proper perspective. The baby's name is Carlton James, and they're going to call him C.J. Do you get it? The middle name is for Jim, of course. But the first name is a feminine version of—Carol!

Holding my first grandchild in my arms less than an hour after he was born was the most profound feeling I've ever experienced. Jim leaned over, gave us both a kiss, and said, "This is the best day of my life. Let me take a picture of you. I want to remember every detail."

"I'll do it," the maternity nurse said. "That way, you can all be in it."

I reached down to return C.J. to Jenny's arms but she said, "You hold him, Mom. There'll be loads of other times for Mark and me." And she gave her husband, who was looking like he was in shell shock, a loving glance.

"If you're sure," I said, beaming at the camera, the world's most perfect baby nestled in my arms. Jim had just put his arm around me when there was a loud disturbance at the door. "Let me in!" a woman screamed. "You let me in right now!"

"This is for immediate family only," the maternity nurse said, opening the door a crack and putting herself between the woman and the rest of us. "If you don't leave at once, I'll call security and have you removed by force."

"Step aside and give me my baby," the woman said, not taking no for an answer and pushing her way into the room.

"Come to Glamma, precious," she cooed, holding out her arms.

Huh? How dare she insinuate herself between me and my grandchild. I was sure she was some deranged person that are in the tabloids people read while they're waiting in the supermarket checkout line.

Then Mark said in a shaky voice, "Mom? Is that you?"

Mom? This deranged woman was Mark's mother? How dare she show up now, after being the invisible woman for a bazillion years.

OMG. Did this mean that C.J. would have two grandmothers? That I'd have to share him? No way. No way! I immediately started to hatch a plan as I handed over the baby. First, I would…. Or, maybe…. Wait. I'm not going to tell you about that.

At least, not yet.

Dieting Doesn't Have to Be Murder!

According to a recent survey, the number one New Year's resolution most people make is to lose weight. And by some amazing coincidence, the most commonly broken New Year's resolution is to lose weight. In fact, the average time most people spend trying to lose weight is less than two months.

Here are some Tips and Tricks from Carol Andrews on how to motivate yourself so you'll start losing weight.

Set your expectations low in the beginning. Be realistic about your goals, so you'll succeed. Don't bite off more than you can chew—in every way!

In doing her Internet research, Carol found an article in the *Journal of Consumer Research* (noted in *AARP Magazine*) which concluded that eating off a blue plate will make food appear unappetizing, so you'll be likely to eat less. Since she didn't want to buy a whole new set of tableware, she settled for the blue sunglasses instead.

She also discovered that, according to the Delboeuf Illusion theory, people whose food choice contrasts with their plate tend to eat less because they are more aware of how much is actually on the plate. And the same article says that keeping the heat lower in winter and air conditioning warmer in summer makes the body work harder to burn calories. Since Jim insists on keeping the temperature in the Andrews house low in the winter and higher in the summer, to save money, he's definitely a fan of this idea. Jim also found an article in a 2013 issue of *U.S. News and World Report* which said that, according to data compiled by Marketdata Enterprises, a firm which specializes in trafficking niche industries, Americans spend more than $60 billion annually to lose pounds. This includes everything from gym memberships and joining weight loss programs to drinking diet sodas. He was shocked.

Carol warns that there are many dangerous diets on the Internet these days. If a diet sounds too good to be true, it probably is. The best way to start is with the advice of a medical professional.

Recipes from the Andrews Household (with the help of some friends)

Thanks to the Centerville Library on Cape Cod, which hosted a recipe contest for this book, here's a low-fat smoothie to help you get started in the right direction. (Of course, in the book, the villain added one extra ingredient!)

Cape Cod Cranberry-Almond Smoothie

1 cup almond milk
1 banana
1 cup fresh kale
½ cup fresh cranberries
1 Tablespoon honey
Handful of slivered almonds

1.) Mix almond milk, banana, kale, cranberries and honey in a blender.
2.) Top with a smattering of slivered almonds. Enjoy!

Recipe provided by Pat Steacy, Centerville MA

Thanks to the other finalists in the library recipe contest: Louise Murphy, Barbara O'Neill, Ellen Clarke, Kim Cormier, and Anita Bennett. You're all winners!

One of the most important things to practice when trying to lose weight is portion control. Here's a variation of the Weight Watchers recipe Jim Andrews found on the Internet which Carol made in Chapter 35. This meatloaf is cooked in a muffin pan, yielding smaller, individual portions rather than one large loaf. Instant portion control!

Turkey Meatloaf Muffins

Cooking spray
2 lbs uncooked ground turkey breast
4 tsp fresh thyme

½ tsp table salt
½ tsp black pepper
2 Tbsp olive oil
2 Tbsp regular butter
1 cup uncooked onions, finely chopped
3 cloves garlic, finely chopped
12 oz. mushrooms, finely chopped
1 tsp soy sauce
½ cup fresh parsley
½ cup white wine
Canned fat-free gravy

1.) Pre-heat oven to 350. Fill 12 muffin pan holes with liners. Coat large mixing bowl with cooking spray.

2.) Place ground turkey breast in prepared bowl; season with salt and pepper; mix well and set aside. Place butter and oil in large frying pan and cook over medium high heat until butter melts. Add onion and sauté about 5 minutes. Add garlic and cook for an additional 2 minutes. Add mushrooms and sauté 3-5 minutes. Add soy sauce and white wine; cook until mixture thickens, about 5-10 minutes. Add parsley and cook 1-2 more minutes. Add mushroom mixture to turkey and mix thoroughly.

3.) Drop by heaping tablespoons into prepared muffin tins until each tin is 2/3-¾ full. Bake muffins until center seems firm to the touch and turkey is completely cooked through, about 22-27 minutes. These muffins can be made ahead and warmed up in the microwave. Yum!

About the Author

Susan Santangelo pens the best-selling *Baby Boomer* mysteries, a series of humorous cozies which follow the adventures of a typical boomer couple as they navigate their way along life's rocky highway toward their twilight years. She is a member of Sisters in Crime, International Thriller Writers, and the Cape Cod Writers Center, and also reviews mysteries for *Suspense Magazine*. Susan divides her time between the Gulf coast of Florida and Cape Cod, and shares her life with her husband Joe and two very spoiled English cocker spaniels, Boomer and Lilly. Boomer also serves as the model for the books' covers, and Lilly is pictured on the back covers.

You can contact Susan at ssantangelo@aol.com or find her on Facebook and Twitter. She'd love to hear from you.

Made in the USA
Middletown, DE
19 August 2023

37002336R00126